ANOTHER MAN'S GROUND

ALSO BY CLAIRE BOOTH

The Branson Beauty

ANOTHER MAN'S GROUND

CLAIRE BOOTH

Minotaur Books
New York

ANOTHER MAN'S GROUND. Copyright © 2017 by Claire Booth. All rights reserved. Printed in the United States of America. For information, address St. Martin's Press, 175 Fifth Avenue, New York, N.Y. 10010.

www.minotaurbooks.com

Designed by Omar Chapa

The Library of Congress Cataloging-in-Publication Data is available upon request.

ISBN 978-1-250-08441-5 (hardcover)
ISBN 978-1-250-08442-2 (ebook)

Our books may be purchased in bulk for promotional, educational, or business use. Please contact your local bookseller or the Macmillan Corporate and Premium Sales Department at 1-800-221-7945, extension 5442, or by email at MacmillanSpecialMarkets@macmillan.com.

First Edition: July 2017

10 9 8 7 6 5 4 3 2 1

31088100983103

For Carolyn
and
Meredith

ANOTHER MAN'S GROUND

CHAPTER

1

The dispatch call said there was stripping going on in the woods, and the property owner was not happy about it.

So now Hank stood at the base of a fairly tall tree that was, well, naked.

"Do you see that? Do you? All of the bark, gone. And those are just the first ones." Vern Miles waved his rifle in the air to emphasize his grievance and headed deeper into the woods. "More. Here, and here. Over there. Every single one I've got. Stripped."

Hank turned in a circle and took in what looked to be a perfectly normal patch of Branson County forest. Birds chirped from the trees. Flowers poked through the earth, and the foliage was the bright young green of early summer. Sunlight pierced the high canopy and dappled the ground. Peaceful and pretty. Except for the mutilated trees. They stuck out like the stripped things they were.

The bark had been cut away from the trees up to a height of at least eight feet. He slid his hand along the soft inner wood, tracing the deep, haphazard gouges left behind. Whoever had done this had not been careful.

"That's seventeen . . . wait, no. Eighteen . . . no . . . nineteen trees, Sheriff. And I haven't even been over my whole property yet. This is my main grove, though. I'd have never even thought this could happen. It's just terrible. Terrible."

Vern took off his battered Kansas City Chiefs ball cap and rubbed at his bald head. He must have been spending a lot of time out here recently, and enjoying it, Hank thought. His sunburned face was just starting to turn to tan, except for the laugh lines around his eyes. Pulled taut now by his frown, they ran like pale streaks up to his temples. Vern slapped his hat back on his head and cradled his.22 in the crook of his elbow.

"So, you're going to put out an APB, right?"

For a barknapper? Hank tried not to smile.

"Vern, I gotta be honest. You don't strike me as much of a tree hugger. Why are you so wound up? This is sad and all, but they're just trees. You want to explain to me why this is more than just simple vandalism?"

Vern leaned his gun against the nearest tree and looked around. He wandered through his denuded grove for a minute before coming back. He slapped a curl of bark in Hank's hand and splashed it with water from his canteen, turning it into a slimy goo.

"Uh, Vern, what the hell is this?"

"It's what they took. From my slippery elms. It's the inside bark stuff. Medicinal. It gets processed and then sold in those frou-frou drugstores."

Hank looked at the stuff oozing through his fingers, which was apparently a cash crop.

"How much are we talking?" he asked.

Vern scratched his head. "Well, when I do it proper, I strip sections off the branches of each tree. That doesn't kill the tree. This"—he waved at his woods—"this all has to be at least three grand. And they took so much, it'll kill the trees."

Well, now. That upped the ante.

That amount could make it a felony, and an interesting one at that. Hank smacked his hands together and turned back toward Vern's truck, which was parked on the muddy track that ran along the east end of the stand of trees. The department's Crown Victoria hadn't been able to make it that far into the woods, so it was still parked up at the Miles homestead.

"C'mon. I've got to get the evidence bag out of my car. We'll have to tag and catalog all of this. And"—he looked down at his slimy palm—"I'm going to need to wash my hands. This stuff's gross."

They ended up finding twenty-four stripped trees, including two that Vern hadn't even realized existed. That's what you get when you inherit thirty acres from your crazy old man, who didn't bother to pass on any information about the land before kicking the bucket last fall, he grumbled as he helped Hank mark each elm with red flags. Hank half-listened as he snapped photos and jotted notes. And mostly breathed in the sweet fresh air. He was enjoying himself immensely. He hadn't been out of the office for what seemed like months. And when he did get out from behind his desk, it was for budget meetings, or staff reports, or all that other organizational crap that he hadn't realized came with the top job.

But this, well, this was excellent. A nice little crime to investigate, but with no violence, no trauma. Sure, Vern was bent out of shape, but it was more of a financial upset than an emotional one. Hank marked the last tree and turned toward Vern, who was now muttering something about a work crew.

"Should we check the other side of the creek?" he asked.

"Oh, no," Vern said. "That's not mine. The creek is the property line. That's Kinney's land."

Hank nodded. He'd have to get this Kinney guy to take a look then. He doubted the tree barkers had been stopped by the easily waded creek. And the woods on the other side looked identical to where he was standing. In fact—

He raised the camera to his eye and zoomed in on a tree about a hundred yards away. It was hard to see, but the trunk looked pale and smooth when the shifting sunlight hit it directly. All right. Mr. Kinney was next.

"How long has he lived there?" Hank asked.

Vern laughed. "Longer than we have. Four, five generations, maybe more. Old Mr. Kinney is still alive, though. Probably happier than a clam that he's outlasted my dad. They never did get on."

Growing up, they were under strict instructions not to cross the creek, Vern said. But they had the run of their own property.

"I hunted these woods all my childhood. Camped in them, played cowboys-and-Indians in them," he said as he retrieved his rifle from its place against an unmolested hickory tree. "Then I went off to college in Springfield and got a decent job there. Never thought much about this place. Now I own it. And I got to figure out what to do with it. The property taxes are going to kill me if I can't figure out some way to make an income off it."

The two men started walking back to the truck.

"The slippery elm was great. It brought in a little, but dependably. And it was one of those . . . those sustainable crops they're always talking about now. Keeps on going if you do it right." He sighed. "Now I'm back to square one, I guess."

Kinney's land might have been right next door, but it took two miles and several winding roads to get to the entrance to the property. Hank pulled the Crown Vic up to the driveway, which was blocked by a chain-link gate padlocked to a tree. Which did not appear to be a slippery elm.

He sighed and got out of the car. He hated this. Houses so far off the road that you couldn't see them, and most of them behind locked gates. No landlines so you could call and have someone meet you to let you in. He moved his sheriff's badge from his belt to a more prominent place on his shirt pocket, double-checked his gun, and climbed over the gate.

The satellite map had shown the house about three hundred yards in from the road. He strode up the gravel driveway, half expecting someone to pop out of the trees with a twelve-gauge pointed at him. But he made it to the front porch without incident and rapped on the door.

The house was old and had obviously been added on to in various stages. One room jutted out from the right side, and he could see a long, low addition out the back to the left. The brown paint was peeling and the roof was old, but the windows were clean, and the porch railing showed signs of recent repair. He knocked again.

Heavy footfalls approached the door, and it slowly swung open. A rail of a man stood there. Thin, tall, hard, and probably preserved with creosote. His eyes were deep-set and almost black. His skin was dark with sun damage and tobacco use, and the lines etched in his face were deep and currently bent in a frown. He stared at Hank's face and then deliberately lowered his gaze to the badge on his chest.

"What brings you onto my property, Deputy?"

Hank didn't bother to correct him.

"I'm investigating a theft, and I think you might also be a victim."

The man raised an eyebrow split in half by a scar.

"Really? I was not aware I'd had anything stolen."

"That's not surprising, sir. It's probably out at the edges of your property," Hank said. "It's trees. A certain kind of tree, actually."

The eyebrow climbed higher.

"And why the hell would someone steal my certain-kind-of trees?"

Hank explained about the bark stripping. The man's expression did not change.

"I will look into it. Thank you for the information." He started to swing the door shut.

Hank held up his hand. "Sir, wait. Your neighbor's tree bark was stolen this way. I'm fairly certain I saw trees of yours with the same damage. I need to get out there and take a look."

"My neighbor? Who—ah, Miles. Those assholes. Never could take care of their land." He let out a laugh that sounded like a dry cough.

"I need to know if you've seen or heard anything, and I need to see your trees," Hank said.

Kinney, who had seemed plenty sturdy before, squared himself in the doorway and became even more solid.

"I have not seen or heard anything. Thank you for your concern, but even if someone did take bark off of one of my trees, I will not wish to press charges. So your business here is done, Deputy. Good day."

Hank drew himself up and looked him in the eye.

"I don't want to have to get a search warrant, sir. I'm simply asking that you let me walk through your woods."

Another cough-laugh was cut off by the door closing in Hank's face. Well then, he'd just go find a judge. And he'd bring back more than a warrant. He'd seen the stock of a shotgun poking out from behind the door, within easy reach as they stood there and talked. He had no desire to see the business end of it without backup.

"Sheila, can you draw me up search warrant paperwork? Up in the northwestern part of the county. Rockbottom Road, off N Highway, owner name of Kinney."

Sheila, who had been about to write on the big whiteboard filled with deputy scheduling, stopped with her arm in midair. She turned around to stare at her boss, the Magic Marker still dangling from her upraised fingers.

"Who? Who did you just say?"

"Kinney. Jasper. I want to get it signed and get back out there fast. I don't know what he's up to, but he wouldn't let me in his woods to look at his trees. Don't want to give him time to hide anything."

Sheila finally lowered the marker. She slowly capped it, patted at her already immaculate black hair, and sat down at her chief deputy desk.

"Are you nuts?"

"What?"

"Are. You. Nuts. Jasper Kinney?"

"What? What's the problem? You act like I asked you to draw up a warrant for Jesus."

That broke her stunned slowness. She guffawed.

"Oh, honey, he ain't no Jesus. He's just one of those people you don't touch. You're never going to get a judge in this county to give you a warrant to search the Kinney place."

"Why the hell not?"

Sheila pursed her lips, then stood and walked across the room to Hank's office. She stood at the door and waited for him to follow. He let out an exasperated sigh and followed her. She was taking the fun out of this.

She closed the door behind them.

"Jasper Kinney is the Kinney family. The Kinney family is about as old as they come. They've been in this area forever. They've got roots that go everywhere in that part of the county. And I mean everywhere." She emphasized the last word.

"What does that mean? They've got people in their pocket?"

She shook her head.

"There's no need. That implies there's some kind of payoff, or bribes, or the like. That's not it. You just don't cross the Kinneys. Folks' granddaddies didn't cross them, folks' daddies didn't cross them, folks today don't cross them."

Hank leaned up against his desk. "So because of nothing but historic reputation, this guy is considered untouchable?"

Sheila shook her head again. "No. They're not untouchable. Jason—Jasper's youngest son—is up at Jefferson City Correctional. He killed his wife. That was hard to ignore. But even during all that—which was about ten years ago—I don't think anybody ever searched that property. Gibbons was sheriff then and he even went and let Jasper know that he was arresting his son. Like a courtesy call."

This was unbelievable. Hank slumped against the desk. All he wanted to do was look at some stripped trees. And now he was being told he couldn't, which was never something that set well with him.

"I agree," Sheila said.

"What?" He shook himself out of his sulk.

"It is bullshit. But it's something you're going to have to think about very carefully. Do you *really* need to get onto that property right now? Can it wait? Can you solve whatever crime you're looking at without getting involved with the Kinneys?"

What on earth was she getting at?

"What else is going on in your world right now?"

He groaned.

"That's right. The election is next month." The look on her face said the rest. *Tread carefully, ignorant newcomer.*

Great. His nice little felony theft had turned political in the space of an hour. He sat down at his desk and stared at the empty blotter as Sheila left to return to her whiteboard. He didn't like politics, and he sure didn't like limiting an investigation for that reason. So he wouldn't. He'd hold back on Jasper Kinney for now, but he'd get to the man soon. Even if it was just to charge someone with trespassing on his property. Just to prove to Kinney—to everyone—that it was the law that called the shots in this county.

CHAPTER

2

The law spent the afternoon calling herbal medicine companies. The company that bought Miles's harvests confirmed that they hadn't received any slippery elm from him since a small batch the month before. The other four Hank contacted maintained that they hadn't gotten any slippery elm shipments from anyone that weren't completely accounted for and legally obtained. Considering how easy it seemed to be to just walk out and strip somebody else's trees, Hank doubted that.

He called Miles's company back, this time at the executive number he'd found buried deep in the Web site.

"Old Mountain Natural Herbs, Cathy speaking. How may I help you live healthfully?"

Hank introduced himself and started in on an explanation for his call. Cheerful Cathy interrupted him.

"Oh, yes. We've heard that you spoke with our receiving department. Did they not give you everything you need?"

"Yes, they did, although I'm going to need to see those records."

Offended silence came down the phone line. Hank suspected

that even though this was one of the bigger herbal companies, they were still small enough to find police calls and record demands unsettling. They weren't a large corporation with a whole unit devoted to legal affairs, thank God. Those places were a nightmare.

"It's only for the file," he said soothingly. "It was a fairly big theft, and we want to make sure that when we find who did it, the prosecutor has all the information he needs to send the guy to jail."

"Oh. Well, then, I suppose. But you're going to have to speak with Mr. Miller first. And he's, ah . . . he's not here at the moment."

Cheerful Cathy was a rookie.

"Now, Cathy," he said. "I know that's not true. I appreciate you doing your job, but this is a police investigation. And I need to speak to Mr. Miller immediately. I know Old Mountain wants to be helpful, right?"

There was a moment of silence, then a reluctant yes, and Cathy put him on hold. Hank spent the time clicking through the Old Mountain Web site, which had a whole lot of pictures of plants that looked identical to him but apparently did entirely different—and miraculous—things to people who ingested them.

Miller finally picked up. Hank could feel his nervousness through the phone line.

"So you've been in business for fifteen years? And you started the company after you discovered that the feverfew plant"—he peered at his computer screen and a picture of what looked to him like ordinary daisies—"helped your daughter's migraine headaches?"

"Yes. That's right—wait, how did you know that?"

"It's right there on your Web site, sir."

Miller let out a strained laugh. "Of course. Yes. I'm sorry. It's just that we go to great lengths to make sure that all of our herbs are properly sourced. For just this reason. We don't want anything to do with the black market. Heaven forbid. We follow all the proper procedures."

"And what, exactly, are those procedures?" Hank asked.

That turned out to be something Miller was comfortable with. To the tune of a twenty-minute discourse on the purity and verification of herbal medicines. Complete with scientific names. Hank ignored those.

Old Mountain inspected every grow site before signing a contract with the owner. Its employees showed landowners exactly how to harvest the herbs. Once collected, they were picked up by company drivers and brought to the company facility in Indianapolis. There, they were tested for purity and to make sure they were indeed organic. Some people tried to cut corners and started using chemical fertilizers. Or even, heaven forbid, sprays. They certainly couldn't have that, now could they? After testing in the lab, the herbs were transformed into whatever was necessary—powders, syrups—all in their high-tech facility. In fact, that marvel of herbal formulation was taking place right down the hall from him as they spoke. Hank stopped him there.

"Has Vern Miles's slippery elm ever tested badly?" he asked.

He heard papers rustling.

"I pulled his whole file," Miller said. "No, all of his quality control tests have been fine. He's only sold us four batches. Started last spring. Spring and early summer are the best collection times for *Ulmus rubra*. The sap is flowing heavily and the inner bark is at its best, and is easiest to remove. He seemed keen on sustainability, so he wasn't harvesting in the off-season. We were expecting good things from him this year."

"Did you find him, or did he find you?"

More paper flipping. "Let's see . . . he found us. Contacted us last April. We sent Lee down to certify the place. The report says he's planning to add different crops, see what else he can grow.

But the elms were already there, obviously, and ready to go, so he started with those right away."

"Do you know why he chose your company instead of one of the others?"

"Huh. No idea. Our sterling reputation, maybe?"

The guy certainly wasn't nervous anymore, Hank thought as Miller chuckled at his own humor. Get people talking about their passions, and they loosened up. Happened every time. And relaxed people didn't think as much about what they were saying.

"So you must have herb growers all over," Hank said. "How many states do you cover? What herbs do they grow?"

Miller gave him a list. All over the Midwest. Kentucky was especially good for slippery elm, but Missouri was rapidly gaining ground. The state also had a good inventory of sassafras trees. The bark and root were used for fever reduction and as an anti-inflammatory. There also was a good supply in the state of bone-set plant, a slender plant with spiky white flower clusters that helped with colds and flu.

And then there were the root plants, ginseng and goldenseal, which southern Missouri forest was so good at growing. Powdered-goldenseal-root tea was used for digestive problems or colds. And ginseng root, of course, was so good for so many things—fighting disease, increasing stamina, reducing the effects of stress—and the wild stuff was extraordinarily valuable. Missouri had some great patches, and looser laws than some other states. Harvesting on private land was allowed. It just took forever for it to grow.

"All of those darn root plants take years to mature," Miller said. "It's really too bad Miles didn't have some in his forest. He's got the perfect terrain for growing them. We searched the whole darn property—they're just little leafy things—but didn't find ginseng at all. We're going to get him started growing some, but then we can't market it as 'wild' and the—"

Hank interrupted. The line between relaxed interviewee and

time waster had been crossed. He steered the conversation back on track.

Old Mountain had ten inspectors, Miller explained. Each had a geographic region. The aforementioned Lee Sells was assigned to Missouri for all initial evaluations and subsequent spot checks.

"When was the last check on Miles?"

Flip, flip. "Last summer. Since there was no harvesting in the fall or winter, Lee didn't check in. He'd already inspected the trees, when we contracted with Miles. He was scheduled to go back in two weeks for a spot check during the harvest season."

"So who else besides Lee, or the other inspectors, knows where the owners' plants are?"

"Oh, we know where all of our growers are."

"No," Hank said, "I mean, does it say in your files exactly where every stand of trees is?"

"Oh, goodness no. Some of these groves are miles from anywhere. That would be impossible to write down."

"You could use GPS coordinates."

Silence. Hank doodled a tree on his notepad. He'd drawn half the branches by the time Miller spoke.

"That would be technically possible, yes. But that is proprietary information. It needs to be known by the fewest number of people possible. Our growers sign nondisclosure contracts. Our inspectors sign those and noncompete contracts. We take that *very* seriously."

So who knew exactly where Miles's stand of slippery elm was located?

"On our end, Lee. That's it. Even I don't know. And on the other end, Miles. And whoever he's told. Which is hopefully nobody."

"What about your company drivers? They have to know where to pick it up, right?"

Miller let out a sigh that made clear Hank was not getting the gravity of the matter.

"They only know in general terms. The grower has to be able to deliver the harvest to a centralized spot. We contract with drivers who truck several delivery points at a time up to us here in Indianapolis."

"Wait. Contract with? Not employ directly?"

"Well, no. That would be impractical. It's usually truck drivers who are at a seasonal low point. So they drive for us at certain times of the year but not others. We couldn't keep them all on permanent payroll."

"Who's picked up deliveries from Miles?"

There was more paper shuffling. "Lloyd Taylor. The four deliveries last spring and also the one so far this year." His voice had tightened again. The worry was back. "You don't think . . ."

"I don't think anything at this point, Mr. Miller," Hank said. "But I'm going to need Lloyd Taylor's contact information and the names of any other of your growers that he picks up deliveries for."

Hank wrote down the information, gave Miller his fax and email so he could send both paper and electronic copies of Miles's paperwork, and wished the Old Mountain man a nice day. Then he punched up Lloyd's driver's license information on his computer.

Fantastic.

He was one of *those* Taylors.

The kid came out of the Easy Come & Go convenience store carrying two bags full of merchandise Hank assumed he must have paid for, because no one came running out after him. He was skinnier than his DL photo, which showed an already thin nineteen-year-old wearing a carefully buttoned Oxford shirt and studious-looking glasses. The shirt had, as Hank suspected, covered

Lloyd's tats, which he could now see snaking across the portion of his chest visible under the wife beater he was wearing. One half-done tat was even in color, which was surprising. Most Taylor ink was strictly the standard black. Wonder where he got the money for that, Hank thought as he started his borrowed Ford and slipped out into traffic behind Lloyd's battered pickup. He stayed well back. The ratty camper shell on the back looked like it could come loose at any moment.

They drove out Highway 160 toward the Stone County line and then turned north. Traffic thinned out until they were the only two cars on the road. Good thing he'd borrowed Sam's Bronco—his Crown Vic would have tipped Lloyd off immediately. The whole family could smell a cop a mile away. At least that's what they bragged at the local bars.

They continued for another ten minutes, until they came to the Stout Oak Road turnoff. Then a mile west and Lloyd turned onto the Taylor property. Hank hadn't been out here since Sam gave him a driving tour of the county's hot spots when he became sheriff, nine months ago. His deputy had stopped right outside the gate.

"Now this here is the Taylors'," Sam had said. They had stared at the half-cleared acreage, and Hank felt his skin crawl. "Yeah," Sam said. "That's the normal reaction. You know, for a normal person. For a Taylor . . . well . . ."

Trees were haphazardly chopped down. Stumps of varying heights dotted patches of otherwise barren dirt. One pine looked like it had fallen victim to an ATV, which was still stuck on the snapped trunk and looked like it had been for a while. Piles of trash were everywhere. Hank counted at least three rusted-out car frames, plus a large van whose engine block lay five feet away.

There was a dilapidated mobile home farther back where the trees hadn't been cut. "And that," said Sam, who had been following Hank's gaze as it came to a thick stand of trees and brush that looked like it might be camouflaging a small structure, "is what I figure has to be the meth lab. Back in there. But we've never had probable cause to search. And it's never exploded, which is a bummer. That would make things nice and easy."

Even without an explosion, you'd need a hazmat suit to enter that property, Hank had thought as he and Sam pulled away. Now he drove past at normal speed as Lloyd turned in. He had some asking around to do before he let Lloyd know he was interested.

The third tattoo parlor Hank visited was the most upscale.

"That dude? Oh, yeah, he's been here. Didn't look like that, though."

Hank nodded, took back Taylor's driver's license photo, and asked what he had looked like. He focused on the parlor man's eyes. Everything else was covered with tattoos.

The man continued wiping his hands on a cloth. "Sorry. We mix all of our own inks here. Everything's custom. I was just doing a batch. Need to wash up. Come on back."

Hank followed him past a massage table and two padded chairs with large armrests and into a small break room with a table, refrigerator, and brand-new Keurig.

"Is this going to take long? I was just going to make some coffee. Do you want any?"

"I do have quite a few questions," Hank said, eyeing the Keurig.

The man popped in a coffee pod as he introduced himself. Dan Larkson and his wife had opened up Custom Body Art of the Ozarks three years ago. They'd chosen Branson because she was also a makeup artist, and that work was easy to find with all the shows on the Strip. They'd been ready for some blowback. Everybody knew Branson was a really conservative Christian community. But they'd been welcomed right off. The other strip mall tenants brought them a "business-warming" basket, and they'd even been invited to join the Chamber of Commerce.

"I was dead wrong," Larkson said. "This place is great."

He handed Hank a cup of coffee.

"Plus, I got to be honest," he said, and pointed to the photo Hank had laid on the break room table. "I think it helps that we don't cater to, well, to people like that."

"Tell me about him," Hank said.

Larkson settled his dazzling array of tattoos back in his chair and sipped at his gourmet coffee. It was an incongruous sight. Incongruous for Hank at least. It was obviously completely normal for Larkson. Maybe I need to loosen up, Hank thought.

"Lloyd was real determined. Wanted lots of color. But nothing anywhere that could be seen with proper clothes on. No face, no neck. A real Brian Setzer."

Hank grinned. He was familiar with the Stray Cats singer's advice about never getting a tattoo where a judge could see it.

After a consultation on artwork and prices, they'd decided on a full sleeve on his right arm. It would take multiple visits. Especially since Lloyd couldn't pay for it all at once. The kind of intricate artwork and color he wanted ran at least twenty-five hundred bucks.

"How does that compare with the standard tats he already has?"

"It doesn't. Not even on the same planet. Those . . . those were, um, poor quality, shall we say? Some were definitely prison-inspired. Slightly higher-quality ink than what they can do in prison, I think, but still. And a couple of them looked like they'd been done by some drunk guy on a dark night."

"That's probably not far off," Hank said. "When is his next appointment?"

Larkson rattled off a date and time without a pause.

"You know your calendar pretty well."

Larkson laughed. "No way, man. Only him. I don't schedule anybody near when he comes in. He is not the kind of clientele I want people knowing about. I wouldn't have said yes to him in the first place if he hadn't paid half of it in cash right then. Plus, artistically, it's a pretty cool challenge. Trying to make the *Mona Lisa* out of mud, you know?"

Hank did. A professional challenge could indeed be fun. He stood up and Larkson walked him to the front of the shop. They shook hands, Hank's chapped and scratched from that morning's trek through woods and Larkson's green and blue with some kind of ocean wave action. Hank pushed on the door handle and then paused. He turned back around and pulled out a business card.

"Go ahead and keep this. If Lloyd shows up any time before his appointment, call me. Or . . . if anything else comes up, let me know. I'm always available."

That last part was new for him. And difficult. But he'd better get used to it, he thought as he headed across the parking lot to Sam's Bronco. He just hoped Larkson was registered to vote.

CHAPTER

3

"So we'll just meet at the restaurant up in Springfield tomorrow? I should be done with my shift by then."

Maggie set the lasagna in the middle of the table and sat down. Hank groaned.

"You forgot, didn't you?" she said.

He groaned again. "Yes. And now I can't. I've got a theft investigation going."

She slapped the serving spoon into the cheese with more force than necessary.

"We have rescheduled this thing twice already. We are not putting it off again. She's not going to want to work for you if you keep this up." She scooped lasagna onto his plate, again with a little more force than necessary.

"I'd want to work for you, Daddy."

"Thank you, Maribel," Hank said, ladling green beans onto his daughter's plate.

"Yes," Maggie said, "but Darcy Blakely is not a five-year-old you can bribe with extra dessert. She's a highly sought-after campaign manager who you need to help get you elected. 'Cause we don't know sh— . . . we don't know anything about running a campaign."

Hank sighed as he turned to the opposite side and dished vegetables into his son's bowl. Benny made a face and pushed it as far away from his booster seat as possible. Hank pushed it back and turned to his wife.

"I know, honey. I just . . . this is just such . . . a leap. I'm not a politician."

"No kidding." She laughed. She reached across the table and took his hand. "Think about it. Wouldn't it be easier if you just had someone telling you what you need to do? That way you don't have to figure it all out on your own. You can pay more attention to police work."

She had a point. She usually did. He kissed her hand and held it, a little more tightly than necessary.

Darcy Blakely sat across from him and adjusted glasses that looked like they came out of a magazine ad. Pressed, plastic, and expensive. Like her.

"Now," she said, straightening the notepad on the table between them, "we need to go over a few things. The first thing is you. I need to know all about you—your background, your beliefs, etcetera. That way, we can tailor the campaign toward your strengths. And downplay anything we need to."

She gave him a bright and cheery smile and poised her pen over the paper. Hank tried to smile back, but he was pretty sure it came out as a grimace. He wished Maggie were there. There'd been a heart attack and a motorcycle accident right before she was scheduled to get off work, so she'd called him to say she'd be late. She was much better at this sort of thing. He had no idea what to say. He grilled a mean tri-tip and told excellent knock-knock jokes? He doubted that was what Darcy wanted.

She let out a little exhalation of disappointment. "We'll have

to work on getting you more comfortable talking about yourself. Let's try it this way: How long have you lived in Branson?"

"About nine months."

"And you were appointed sheriff by the County Commission?"

"Yeah. Darrell Gibbons was elected to the state senate. I'd
just applied for a job as a deputy, but the commission appointed
me to fill his vacancy."

"Oh," she said. "We're certainly not going to mention that
you didn't intend to apply for the sheriff job. Don't tell people
that part."

"Uh, okay." He was beginning to feel like a suspect—artfully
omitting certain details when questioned.

Darcy blazed right ahead. "And why did you move here?"

"My mother-in-law died—Marian McCleary, she was the
high school principal. We moved down so we could be closer and
help out my father-in-law," he said. "And it's a good place for the
kids."

Darcy beamed. "Excellent. Just perfect. Family. Devotion.
That'll play well with women. And your wife's family has been
here a long time?"

"Yeah. Three generations, I think."

"Um. That's not all that long for around here. Oh, well. We'll
make do. Where were you before you moved to Branson?"

"Kansas City. I was with the police department there."

"Doing what?"

"I was with the gang section of the street narcotics unit.
Before that, I spent nine years in patrol."

"Any commendations? Awards?"

He'd gotten a Meritorious Service Award a few years back
for working with the mothers in a neighborhood to get a grant
that turned a weedy, drug-dealer infested lot into a park. Darcy
nodded enthusiastically and jotted in her notebook.

"And where were you before Kansas City?"

"I was at Mizzou. I went from there to KCPD."

She nodded. "State degree. Good. And when in that time period did you get married?"

Hank's smile was genuine this time. "Ten years ago."

"And where did you meet?"

"At school."

"Oh, so you met at Mizzou?"

Hank nodded. On the Quad, at twilight, when she ran into him with her bike. But he wasn't going to share that with Darcy.

"And her name is—?"

"Maggie McCleary. She's head of the emergency department over at Branson Valley Hospital."

Darcy's brows furrowed. "McCleary? Do you mean she doesn't use your last name?"

"Nope."

Her eyebrows sank farther down behind her designer glasses. Hank was starting to enjoy himself.

"That's . . . not ideal. Is there any way she would let us refer to her as 'Mrs. Worth' during the campaign?"

"Well, you'd have to ask her that. You might also want to ask her if she'd like to be addressed as 'Dr. Worth,' since that's what she is."

Maggie normally didn't give a damn whether people outside the hospital addressed her as "doctor" or not. But pair taking away her name with taking away her hard-earned title, and she might have a problem. Hank decided Darcy could test that water by herself.

"A doctor? Oh, my. That's impressive. Always good stature in the community. Does she do volunteer work—like with the homeless or anything?"

Hank could see her designing the photo op in her head right then. No point getting her hopes up.

"Ah . . . she works," he said. "A lot. And we have two small kids. So her time is pretty much spoken for."

The photo op dissolved, but this lady was nothing if not resilient. She brightened.

"The children. Let's talk about them. Names and ages, please." Her pen hovered.

"Whoa," he said. "No way. They do not need to be involved in this."

This time, there was no brightening.

"Oh, yes, they do. Family is of utmost importance in this area of the state. Showing that you are a caring father tells the electorate that you would make a good sheriff. Sheriff is a very paternal type of position—protecting and serving and all that—and having cute little kids will go a long way toward making it look like you are the right man for the job."

Hank raked his hands through his hair as he tried to think of something to say that wasn't rude.

"My children are very young and can't in any way decide for themselves whether they'd like to be a part of my campaign or not. So I am going to decide for them. No."

She pressed her lips together in a frown for a split second before the happy face came back. "Well, you just talk it over a little bit with your wife, and then we'll all discuss it later. I'm sure it will all work out fine."

This woman just glossed over everything that didn't suit her. Hank didn't know how much of her he could take. He ran his hand through his hair again.

"Oh, goodness, stop that. It makes your hair stick up. Ruins the whole image."

He glared at her.

"No one is going to take you seriously if you look like a scarecrow," she snapped. She sat back and gave him The Eye. It was the same look he got from Maggie whenever they were ready to go out and she didn't like the shirt he was wearing. He braced himself.

"That's it." She snapped her fingers. "A cowboy hat. That's exactly it. Law. Order. Manliness. Perfect."

Hank burst out laughing. He couldn't help himself. He would look like an idiot in a cowboy hat.

The Eye hardened into a full-on glare. Damn, maybe he'd really pissed her off. He calmed down and apologized.

"I'm sorry," he said. "I didn't expect that. I thought we were going to talk about my campaign, not my wardrobe."

She sniffed and carefully laid her pen on top of her notepad.

"Your campaign is your wardrobe. It is everything about you. It all comes back to you. What people think of you. And even more so, how people *feel* about you. Whether they feel that you are a good person, and a competent cop. Your appearance plays a large part in that. If a candidate went around in a dirty under-shirt and ripped jeans, would you vote for him? Or if he walked around in a bow tie and a pocket protector, would you think he was well-qualified to be the top officer in the county? No, you wouldn't. You would think he was a nerd who couldn't defend himself, let alone defend all of his constituents. It doesn't matter if that's not true, because if you feel that it's true, you're not going to vote for him. Are you?"

He had to admit that she was right. So he did. Then he apologized again. Then they agreed that he would wear jeans and button-down shirts while campaigning at informal events, and a suit and tie if it was at an event with businessmen or the Rotary. And he would try on a cowboy hat in the presence of both her and his wife, and they would have the final say on whether it would be included in his "outfit."

Darcy made several indecipherable notations on her pad and then started tapping on her phone. Hank took the opportunity to breathe deeply for a moment. How badly did he really want to be sheriff? Badly enough to subject himself to this? He stared out the restaurant window and thought about the alternatives.

The only other person running in the election was Gerald Tucker, a longtime deputy with the department. It was safe to say that he and that Good Ol' Boy did not have a good working relationship. If Tucker became his boss, he would not hire Hank back on as a deputy. That was a definite. And there were no openings at any of the city police departments like Branson or Forsyth. He'd have to go out of the county to find a job. And that kind of defeated the purpose of moving to a small town in order to spend more time with his family.

Plus, that small town would become unbearable to live in. Hank was positive the GOB was in Henry Gallagher's pocket, and giving that crook control of local law enforcement would be a disaster. Gallagher was Branson County's most prominent businessman and, in Hank's opinion, a man who endorsed arson, insurance fraud, and probably extortion. Naturally, Gallagher had endorsed Tucker as well. Hank firmly believed Tucker had set fire to Gallagher's paddle-wheel showboat in February so that Gallagher could try to collect the insurance money, but so far he'd been unable to prove it. Hank did not want to think about what Tucker would be able to do for Gallagher if he ran the department.

"—you were younger?"

Hank refocused on Darcy, who had started talking again. She sighed and started over.

"Your past. Did you have any run-ins with the law when you were younger?"

"Uh, no."

"Nothing that could come out and cause embarrassment? Or a scandal?"

He thought back to the St. Patrick's Day incident in the dorms his sophomore year. They'd never been able to prove who'd done it.

"Nope."

"Good. Now, you're from Columbia, right?"

"No." He shook his head. "I went to Columbia to go to Mizzou. I'm from California."

She stared at him like he'd just grown a third eye. Horror, with a little bit of incredulity and a smattering of fascinated revulsion. "Oh, no," she breathed. "Like, you were born and raised there?"

"Yep."

She sputtered.

"The whole time . . . not just because your father got transferred out there from some nice Midwestern town?"

"Nope. No Midwestern ties at all."

"Then why on earth did you pick the University of Missouri?"

He shrugged. "I was thinking about journalism, and it has the best school in the country. Then I got there, and figured out I didn't want to do that. So I majored in psychology."

"But why did you stay here? Why—" She cut herself off when she realized what she'd said.

He grinned at her.

"Why did I decide to stay in Missouri instead of going back to beautiful California?"

"That . . . that wasn't what I meant."

He waited a moment, feeling on slightly more even footing with her.

"Because Maggie was in medical school at Mizzou," he finally said. And there had been no way in hell that she would have transferred med schools. And no way in hell he would have left her. So he'd found a job as close as he could. "So I got the job in Kansas City. That's why."

She nodded and took a deep breath. "Okay. We're going to just try to gloss over all that. Maybe no one will ask where you're from. An outsider is one thing, but California . . ." She shook her head. Hank was pretty sure she was regretting not asking for a bigger retainer.

"We'll just let them assume you're from Kansas City. Hopefully no one will dig into it."

Hank couldn't imagine who would care enough to dig into it. Then he thought about Tucker. And Gallagher. Maybe Darcy was right to be worried.

CHAPTER

4

Surveillance on Lloyd Taylor had not been fruitful. In a week and a half, the kid had done nothing. Hank was very disappointed. He had at least expected some stupid stunts like the one that left the ATV in the tree. Or maybe a DWI, or a bar fight. But Lloyd was keeping his nose clean. Which in itself was suspicious. No one in that family ever kept their noses, or anything else, clean.

He, however, would have to be spotless. His college roommate had called him that morning and said that someone from Tucker's campaign had been poking around, asking questions about their days at Mizzou. Jerry had assured Hank that he hadn't said anything, especially about the drunken hikes through Rock Bridge Park in the middle of the night. Or the time they'd accidentally set fire to that Dumpster, or the one St. Patrick's—

"Okay, Jer. I get it. Just keep your mouth shut, all right?"

"Hey, I got your back, man," Jerry said. "I told him you were just a regular student and that I couldn't remember the names of anyone else that he should talk to about you." He paused. "But this guy sounded like he knew what he was doing. He tracked down my cell, which isn't listed anywhere. And he had more names—people from the dorms and from your psych classes. More than I would expect a normal campaign worker to have been able to find out. He could be a professional."

Hank put down the surveillance reports on Lloyd Taylor and leaned back in his desk chair. He hated having his attention tugged in unrelated directions, but he couldn't stop thinking about Jerry's phone call. He raked his hand through his hair and looked down at his desk blotter, where he'd scrawled the name Jerry'd given him. Carl Kondakor. Mr. Kondakor was not registered in the Missouri Private Investigators license database. Nor was he in the phone book. Nor did he pop up on Google.

Hank stared at the ceiling for few minutes, then grabbed his cell. He quickly found a phone number online and dialed.

"Wikson and Clancy, attorneys-at-law," said a smooth female voice.

"Mr. Kondakor, please," said Hank.

"I'm afraid he is not in the office today. Would you like his voice mail?"

Hank declined and hung up the phone. It appeared that Henry Gallagher's St. Louis law firm employed an off-the-books PI. He was nowhere on the firm's Web site, but he was definitely on the job. Hank wondered who he'd track down next.

On the way down the station hallway, Hank caught a glimpse of his reflection in a window. He looked like he'd just flown a kite in a lightning storm. His hair stuck out in a dozen different directions. He thought about sending a selfie to Darcy. But no. He was the new, improved, electable Hank. So he took the less-fun route instead, and headed up Main Street toward Shadowrock Drive for a haircut.

Two blocks down was Stan's Barber Shop. The bell over the door tinkled as Hank walked in and was immediately hit with the smell of Brylcreem and cigarette smoke. Stan hollered from the back that he'd be out in a second. Hank wandered around, looking at the posters of cars and sports stars that spanned several decades and papered every inch of wall space. Except for the top right corner of the shop, which held a thirty-two-inch flat-screen TV. It was a concession Stan said he'd made a few years ago. It was the only way to get the younger guys into the shop.

Hank folded himself into one of the chrome-and-vinyl waiting chairs and reached toward the little table in the center, only to come up empty.

"What, no magazines anymore?"

Stan bustled out from the back room and shook his head. "Eh. I finally said screw it. Nobody reads 'em. They all just watch the TV. Had to get satellite, too. People gotten all snobby about their sports. They expect every baseball game, not just the Cards anymore." He shrugged. "Have to roll with the times, I guess."

Hank moved to the barber chair and settled in as Stan slid his sleek, daggerlike scissors out of their leather sheath. "Lemme guess, you want it so it doesn't stick up like that."

Hank grinned at them both in the mirror. "Exactly. I've been told this isn't acceptable for a man running for election."

Stan chuckled. "Lots of things not acceptable for folks running for election, but they do 'em anyway."

Hank didn't nod in agreement—Stan was already at work on his hair. He studied the older man in the mirror as he worked. He must be more than seventy. Skin not too lined from a life indoors, but shoulders rounded forward from who knew how many decades of bending toward people's hair. Stan's own was his best advertisement. Blazing white and criminally full, it rose in a wave from his forehead and ended in an immaculate line at his collar. Hank knew he would not be as lucky, as Stan trimmed delicately around his own emerging bald spot.

"How long you lived here, Stan?"

"All my life. My daddy, too. Course the town isn't where it used to be."

Hank's confused stare reflected back in the mirror. Stan chuckled.

"We moved it—you didn't know that? I was 'bout four years old, but I remember it clear as day. The feds built the dam down at Bull Shoals and in 1950, we all had to up and move away from the river 'fore it became a lake. Daddy'd tell the story of everybody voting on it, and the verdict was to move up the bluff instead of just throwin' in the towel and abandoning the town." He grinned. "We're a stubborn bunch out here."

And now Bull Shoals Lake stretched from here all the way down into Arkansas. Hank tried to imagine the kind of determination it would take to move a whole town. And how that quality could often calcify into obstinacy.

"Were there families who . . . who held more sway than others?" he asked. "Who kind of ran things?"

"What, like the Wild West?" Stan laughed. "No, I'm kidding you. There sure were some families that folks listened to. Because they'd always been prominent."

"Listened to out of respect, or out of fear?"

Stan's scissors stilled. "Well, now. That's an interesting question. I don't know that, back in the day, you could distinguish between the two." He stood for a moment and gazed at the ceiling. "Now, though, it's not really an issue. There aren't many such families anymore."

He resumed his work, but more slowly this time, obviously pondering the topic.

"Ties have dissolved," Stan said. "Old families move out or die off. And the pool's diluted, too. Lots of new folks moving in. They've got no ties at all—they're not beholden to anyone. The ones who had power and influence back when there were just a few hard-knock villages, they don't anymore."

"Nobody?" Hank asked. "Nobody has that kind of sway anymore?"

Stan gave him a sharp eye in the mirror.

"You getting at someone particular, Hank?"

"You tell me. Am I?"

Stan gave in to a full belly laugh this time.

"I'd hate to be 'cross the interrogation table from you," he said. "Leading me right into a trap, you are."

Hank just gave him a sheepish grin in the mirror. Stan sighed.

"Yes, there are the Kinneys. And to a lesser degree, the Miles clan. But the Kinneys are the ones. They've always been the ones in that part of the county. They own an awful lot of land. They always have an awful lot of sons. And they always been the ones in charge."

"How? How are they in charge? Do they terrorize people? Come scare them in the middle of the night?"

"No, nothing like that."

"Then how?" Hank said. "They don't own the business district. Or the bank. Or anything like that."

Stan bent down toward the back of Hank's head and concentrated on his hairline for a good long while. Finally, he stood and looked Hank straight in the eye through the mirror.

"They own people's minds. I guess you could say it that way. I don't know how else to explain it. It's better to just move around with caution and respect when it comes to them. Then nothing happens and everyone goes about their merry way."

"What happens if you don't—move with caution and respect?"

Stan shrugged and smiled. "I don't have any idea. No one's ever done it, in my lifetime. Wait—I take that back, sort of. My daddy would tell me stories about them and the Miles clan. They've bickered for years. Used to be more of a thing, but not so much now. Vernie went off to Springfield. The youngest kid—

Charlie, I think—he died young. And the little girl married some out-of-towner. So their pull isn't so strong anymore."

He pulled the towel off with a flourish and smoothed Hank's shoulders with a brush, just for good measure. Then he looked Hank in the eye again.

"But the Kinneys, their pull is still . . ." He trailed off. "I think you're a good sheriff, Hank. I'd like to see you stay in the job." He nodded at their reflections to emphasize his point.

Hank stood and pulled a twenty out of his wallet.

"I'll get you change."

"No," Hank said. "Keep it. And Stan—thanks."

"I thought we were headed out to the Taylor place."

Sam sounded disappointed.

"Oh, we will be." Hank smiled. But not right then. He still had a tail on Lloyd Taylor, so that kid wasn't going anywhere he didn't know about. Right now, he wanted to take another look at Vern's stripped trees. And this time, he was prepared. They were heading down Deer Spring Road in Sam's Bronco, which could manage the rutted track through the Mileses' land. And Hank had a pair of high-powered binoculars in his lap. Those also were Sam's, pulled out of his hunting gear in the back.

Hank didn't want to depend on Vern's pickup to get to the grove of trees, and he did want to get as close to the Kinney property line as possible.

"I'm going to get reimbursed for the gas, right?"

"Yeah, course. And if you get your uniform dirty, I'll even pay for the dry cleaning."

Sam rolled his eyes.

"Turn here."

The Bronco rattled up to the Miles place, a traditional farmhouse with a wraparound porch and a second floor with dormer windows. It had seen better days—several shutters hung off their window frames by only one hinge, the porch sagged at the corners, and the chimney perched on the left side of the roof looked less than secure.

No one answered the door. Hank frowned and turned around on the porch. Sam stood at the bottom of the steps, looking out at the view. The farmhouse sat on a hill, and Miles land rolled out behind it in a riot of undulating greenery. It was stunningly beautiful.

Sam yawned and shrugged. Local boy, Hank thought with a shake of his head. He was heading down the steps when the chain saws started up.

They both turned toward the sound, which was coming from the same direction Vern had taken Hank in two weeks before. Sam grinned, and they climbed into the Bronco and took off down the dirt track toward the noise.

The SUV's already stiff ride became positively bone-jarring as they got deeper into the woods. The track was more torn up than it had been, and the going was slow. Sam was having a ball, downshifting and revving the engine. Hank wasn't. Finally, his thirty-eight-year-old back couldn't take any more.

"I'll get out and walk," he said. Sam laughed and pulled away with a spine-crunching lurch.

Hank started to follow the track as it headed right, but then stopped as he heard a tree come crashing down to his left. The track must curve around before turning back toward the slippery elms, he thought as he changed direction and struck out through the vegetation, which, despite snagging on his jeans and windbreaker, was a whole lot easier to walk through than the dirt track had been to drive on.

Five minutes later, he entered a clearing that had not been there fourteen days earlier. It was filled with Vern's truck, a wood chipper, several large cans of gas, and numerous thirty-three-gallon black garbage bags overflowing with bark strips.

The slippery elms that had stood naked now no longer stood at all. They lay scattered around like giant discarded toothpicks. Behind a stand of pines, he heard a yell and then another one came crashing down. Good grief. Was Vern going to cut the whole damn place down? He cupped his hands around his mouth and yelled over the sound of several chain saws.

Vern gave a start and then put down the ax he was holding and trotted over to where Hank stood at the edge of all the activity.

"What are you doing, Vern?"

Vern took off his baseball cap and mopped a very sweaty brow.

"Whew. Sure warmed up out here today. Sorry you came all the way back here. You shoulda called first. I would have met you up at the house."

"Yeah . . ." Hank said. "Sure . . . anyway, what's going on? You're cutting them all down?"

"Well, yeah. They were going to die anyway, after that much stripping. So I figured I'd cut 'em and strip the whole tree. At least make *some* money off them."

"That's an interest—"

"Why don't you come on back up to the house. I can get you a glass of sweet tea." Vern started to steer him toward the pickup. Which was still attached to the wood chipper. Which was currently in use. Hank pointed to the man feeding a barkless elm limb into the machine.

"Oh, shit—er, goodness. Yes. Well, maybe we can walk." Vern tried to turn Hank back the way he'd come. Hank, not inclined to do so, stayed put. He was about to start speaking again when the Bronco roared into the clearing in a cloud of exhaust and dust.

Everyone turned to stare as Sam's SUV shuddered to a stop, and he climbed out. He had hitched up his gun belt and taken one step toward Hank when the man at the wood chipper let out a cry. Like a bird in mortal danger, he kept calling even as he dropped the tree limb and took off into the woods. His flock followed. Every man ran—in whatever direction he could. All of them yelling and stumbling and wide-eyed with fear as they took flight.

Sam froze. Vern groaned. And Hank laughed. And laughed. And laughed.

"*Adiós, mis amigos.*"

CHAPTER
5

Sam, resplendent in his deputy uniform, spun around in confusion, looking in the dozen different directions the men had fled.

"What the hell?"

Hank ignored him and turned to Vern.

"Well, Mr. Miles, did you find yourself some cheap labor?"

Vern groaned again. Then he stuttered some, and dug the toe of his boot in the dirt, and scratched his jaw. Hank was looking forward to hearing the story he came up with.

Sam walked over and turned off the wood chipper. Silence dropped down on the little clearing instantly. Hank waited patiently. He knew the verbose Vern would feel obligated to fill it if it lasted long enough.

Finally, Vern stopped toeing the dirt and took a deep breath. He opened his mouth, and a terrified shriek split the quiet.

All three men whipped around toward the sound, which came from the direction of the creek. It ended as suddenly as it began. Hank and Sam took several steps toward it. Vern took several in the other direction.

Then it started again, less surprised but more urgent. This time, it was recognizable as a man screaming for help in Spanish. Hank and Sam took off at a dead run. They splashed through the creek and scrambled up the short but steep bank on the other side. The shrieks grew louder as they made their way deeper into the woods. Then Sam, whose youthful agility and speed had him about ten yards ahead of Hank, suddenly sank into the earth.

His huge feet disappeared and the rest of him started to follow. He threw himself back toward solid ground, but his forward momentum continued to carry him down and away. Hank dove.

As if he were sliding into home plate, Hank skidded forward on his belly with his arms stretched out in front of him. He grabbed Sam's wrist and stopped his deputy's fall. He held on tightly as he crawled backward, dragging the thankfully skinny deputy with him.

They collapsed against each other as they reached solid ground. All Hank could hear was the sound of their raspy breathing. Wait—the screamer.

"¿Oye? ¿Dónde estás?" Hank called out.

"Sirs? Sirs, I am here. Please . . ." The voice broke off in a sob. It came from just beyond and well below where Sam had started to sink into the ground.

The two men looked at each other. Sam had regained his normal breathing. Hank was still fighting for his. Between gasps, he told Sam they would circle around together, testing where the sink began to see how close they could get to the poor bastard in the ground.

"We'll be together, so that way, if you go in again, I can pull you out," he said.

Sam took a look at his boss's more substantial frame and sighed. They both knew he'd be the easier one to pull back from the edge. As they began to move to the right of the sink, Hank could hear his thoughts clear as day. *Maybe if you laid off the Pecan Delights, asshole, you'd be able to do more than stand back in the safe zone.*

They slowly made their way around, Hank calling reassuringly in Spanish to the man, who had fallen silent except for the occasional sob. The hole, now that they weren't running full tilt, was clearly visible as a tear in the ground, about five feet wide and fifteen feet long. The laborer had clearly gone in on the long left side. Freshly mangled earth slid down the hole from that direction. They had approached from the southern tip of the gap, and torn it even longer with Sam's rescue.

Sam grabbed a fallen tree branch and poked at the ground before risking each step. They kept three or four yards from the hole. Anything closer and the branch sank quickly into the earth. They weren't close enough to see down into the narrow opening.

They had made it about forty-five degrees around what they figured was the circumference of the hole when Sam's stick hit rock. He walked rapidly another quarter of the way around the gap before the branch began sinking into the earth again.

"Okay," Sam said. "This part is solid. I think it goes all the way to the edge, kinda like a cliff."

He returned to where Hank was standing. They both crept forward, Sam's stick rapping a safe passage against the Ozark limestone. When they got within a few feet, they both knelt and crawled the rest of the way. The ground was solid under them until their fingers curled around the lip of the cliff. Relatively sure their perch was secure, they looked over the edge.

The stench sent them back again. Sam reeled backward and vomited. Hank sank back on his knees and bowed his head, like he was praying. Which he was. *Please, God, let it be an animal . . .*

But he knew it wasn't. The smell of decay and rot had that overlay of putrid fruitiness that meant only one thing. He took a deep breath of the clean air at the top and leaned over again.

The *inmigrante* stood at the narrow bottom of a twenty-foot-deep fissure, in the middle of a decomposing human chest cavity.

He was covered with gore and flies. He must have landed directly on the corpse, breaking through the weakened skin and releasing built-up gases and bodily fluids. Hank rolled away from the edge and gasped for air.

"What is . . . oh, God. Is that what I think it is?" Sam's voice was thin and rough. He was still balanced on his haunches.

"Yeah." Hank's voice sounded almost as bad.

"Por favor . . ."

"Oh, man, we gotta get that guy out of there." Sam rose unsteadily to his feet.

It was a potential crime scene. They needed to get the techs out here and some kind of hoist so they could get the guy up without damaging any more evidence. Hank hesitated. Sam glared at him.

"Dude, everything's already screwed up," he said loudly, pointing to the opposite side of the gap, where the *inmigrante's* fall had sent a large cascade of dirt into the fissure. "Nothing's going to be able to be preserved anyway."

Hank raised an eyebrow. His deputy rarely yelled, and he'd never before called his boss "dude." But he was, as usual, right on the money.

"Okay," Hank said. "You're right." He looked around. "Where's your branch?"

Sam grabbed it and they quickly decided it was not long enough to reach down to the *inmigrante*. They fanned out through the woods, looking for a better one while carefully placing each step they took. Neither one wanted the forest floor to open up beneath them. Finally, Hank found a sturdy tree limb and dragged it back to the hole. He yelled directions in Spanish, and the *inmigrante* got as close to the rock-wall side of the fissure as possible.

They lowered the tree limb and the man stretched as high as he could, which was still twelve inches too short. Hank sighed and waved Sam away. He stretched out on his stomach and leaned out over the edge, extending the branch's reach. The man swayed and grabbed. And missed. Hank's shoulders were starting to ache. He stretched farther and the man tried again.

Hank felt more than saw him succeed, as the man's weight made his own body slide even farther over the edge. He started to inch back, grunting and swearing. As soon as he'd gotten far enough back, Sam grabbed on to the limb as well, and together they pulled the man out of hell.

With him came globs of putrid gore and a cloud of flies. He crawled away from the hole on hands and knees until he got to a large hickory tree, where he collapsed with dry heaves. Hank hauled himself away from the gap as well, and tried to force his shoulders back into their normal position. Sam walked a short distance away and battled his own stomach again. For a while, the only sounds were the feasting flies and the wretched breathing of the small huddled form under the tree. They approached the *inmigrante*, who was mumbling what sounded like the Lord's Prayer.

Hank pulled his windbreaker up so it covered his nose and knelt down next to the man, who was small and wiry and probably in his late teens. He spoke calmly, and the rapid praying began to slow. Eventually, the kid raised his head and looked at them. He nodded at Hank.

"What'd you say?" asked Sam, who did not speak Spanish.

"I told him that we're going to take him to town, but we're not going to arrest him. And I said that right now, you're going to walk him down to the creek so he can wash off as much of that . . . grossness . . . as he can."

Sam nodded. The teen looked at him apprehensively and tensed as he stood. Hank shot a look at Sam.

"Oh, um, yeah. Hello. Um. *Hola*." He pasted a smile on his face and gestured encouragingly in the direction of the creek. The kid didn't move. Sam pointed again and got the same result. Then he put his hand on his holstered gun. That did it. The kid jumped slightly and then darted off, followed by his swarm of flies and one annoyed, queasy deputy.

Hank moved just as quickly in the opposite direction, heading deeper into the woods and away from the hole. Once he was beyond the reach of the flies and the smell, which had by now traveled up and out of the fissure into the surrounding air, he called in the incident. Human remains—unknown cause of death, unknown place of death, unknown gender.

"Well, what *do* you know?" asked Sheila.

"I know I'm going to need both Alice and Kurt. They've got respirators with their evidence-collection gear, right? And also some winches and pulleys to get down in the hole. Oh, and Sheila—I also know I'm going to need a search warrant. Name of Kinney. We've crossed the creek."

Sheila burst out laughing. "Well, there's no question about it now. Even if they didn't have anything to do with it, we got to have access to the property." She paused for breath. "Leave it to you to get your way anyhow. You are something."

Hank smiled, but he couldn't maintain it for long. He hung up and looked back toward the corpse hole. Then he turned in the opposite direction. It would be a bit before all those emergency personnel got this far out in the county. He might as well take advantage of the downtime. He headed deeper into the woods.

CHAPTER
6

He'd stopped at seventy-five. There were even more stripped slippery elms than that. Certainly enough to have caught the attention of their owner, even if he never ventured too far out onto his acreage.

So why did Jasper Kinney not care? He seemed like the type of man who wouldn't take kindly to trespassing, let alone thievery. Which meant that either he was stripping the trees himself and there was no crime, or he needed to hide something on his land more than he needed to report a theft. Hank knew which possibility he'd bet on.

Kinney could easily have been hiding that rotting corpse. And even with it dumped in such a well-concealed spot, it still would have been risky to allow the law on his property to look at some stupid trees.

But now . . . Hank smiled. A wonderful, fortuitous accident would open up a section of the forbidden Kinney real estate to him. He couldn't wait to see the look on the old man's face. It wouldn't be long. Sheila had picked him up in a marked patrol car and slapped a signed search warrant in his hand. They took the winding roads from the Miles property to the Kinney driveway looking like a parade. Hank was done with polite. He had three cruisers following Sheila's car, each holding two deputies. Let that old pillar of creosote think about pulling a shotgun on him now.

The cars drove up to the gate. Hank left two deputies with the vehicles, and the rest of them scaled the barrier and trudged up the lane. They fanned out behind Hank and stood at ease as he walked to the door with Sheila right behind him. They'd just reached the porch steps when Deputy Pimental gave a short whistle. They turned to see Kinney coming around the side of the house. He dropped the tip of the shovel he was carrying into the ground and casually leaned on the handle.

"You got a lot of people with you this time," he said.

Hank changed direction and walked toward the old man. "Yes, I do. I also have a search warrant. We need to search your property."

Creosote reached into his shirt pocket for a pack of Marlboros, smacked the package, and pulled one out. He slowly extracted a lighter from the pocket of his jeans and lit the cigarette, never taking his eyes from Hank's face.

Hank forced himself to look as relaxed as Kinney did. He hooked his thumbs on his belt and calmly waited. Kinney blew streams of smoke out his nostrils, and said, "A judge in this county granted you a warrant to look at my trees? Well, well."

Hank shook his head. "No. That is not why we're here. Deputy Turley—"

He moved to the side, and Sheila stepped forward with the paperwork. She held it out. Kinney stared at her and then turned back to Hank.

"So if it isn't my trees, what does bring you and your boys here?"

"A body has been discovered on your land. We need access to investigate."

Creosote's scarred eyebrow lifted. He blew more smoke and said nothing. Hank had to admit he was impressed.

"Do you know anything about it?"

"No."

He could feel Sheila tensing next to him, but she kept perfectly still, the hand holding the warrant now down by her side.

"When was the last time you were out along the creek that borders the Miles property?" he asked.

Kinney shrugged. The average person would have asked if that was where the body was found, or if it had been identified. Kinney was clearly not an average person.

"We need to know the easiest way out to that section of your land. You'll need to take us."

Kinney took another drag. "No."

"Excuse me?"

"You must know where it is, since you say you got a warrant and all. Get out there yourself."

Interesting. That was certainly one way to play this, but definitely not what Hank had expected.

Hank turned to Sheila. "Deputy Turley, please serve the warrant."

Sheila stepped toward Kinney, who did not acknowledge her. She got as close as she could without touching him, rolled up the warrant, and stuck it in the shirt pocket that didn't hold the cigarettes. As she backed away, Hank wondered how they would find their way to the scene from this direction without making fools of themselves. His eyes fell on Bill Ramsdell, an earnest middle-aged deputy who had three sons and had just asked for time off to attend the Boy Scout Jamboree.

Hank strode over to Ramsdell's squad car like he'd planned this all along.

"Bill, please tell me you've done the orienteering badge," he said in a low voice.

"Uh. Yeah. We finished it in the fall. It was a doozy. We—"

Hank cut him off. "Can you find this site? We have to get into it from this direction. Can you do that? Cell and GPS is sketchy out here."

Ramsdell pulled up the left sleeve of his uniform and stuck out his wrist. A shiny new Casio watch sparkled in the sunlight.

"Compass, altitude, everything," Ramsdell said with an eager grin. "Got it for Christmas." He paused. "You're sure, though? You want to take this on? Take him on?" He made the faintest of nods toward Kinney, who still hadn't moved.

"There's a dead body out there," Hank said. What was it with these people? "We are well within our purview as local law enforcement."

"Okay, then." Ramsdell shook his head. "Traipsing around on Kinney land. I never would've thought I'd see the day. Unbelievable. Wait until I tell my folks."

Hank sighed and walked back to Sheila's squad car, where she appeared to be casually leaning against the hood. He knew better. Her jaw was clenched tight and she had reached up to pat at her immaculate hair, which she did only when she was either flustered or pissed off. He strolled around her and then stopped and turned as if he'd forgotten to say something. His position blocked her from Kinney's view.

"You don't have to stay," he said in the same low voice he'd used with Ramsdell. "If he's making you uncomfortable—"

Sheila suppressed a snort. "No. He is not making me uncomfortable. He's making me reinforce my stereotypes. Backwoods racist asshole. I bet he's never even had a black person on his property before." She grinned. "So I'm going to stay right here."

"Oh," Hank said, "I figured it was because you're a woman."

Sheila gave him a you're-an-idiot look. "Nah. If that was it, he'd have leered at me, or stared at places lower than my eye level. When they don't look at you at all, it's your skin, not your tits."

Hank looked at her flawless complexion, the color of a good medium-roast coffee, and the brown eyes that crackled with intelligence behind her glasses.

"Okay, then," he said. "Go take command of the orienteering party." He jerked a thumb toward Ramsdell, who was enthusiastically waving his watch in the air and pointing his fellow deputies into the woods behind the Kinney house. "When you find the most direct route, radio me and I'll bring in Kurt and Alice."

She straightened and gave him a grin. "With pleasure."

He watched as half of his deputies headed into the forest. Then he sent one back to the road with orders to cut the chain on the gate so the forensic team could get in. He then made himself comfortable leaning in the same spot Sheila had occupied and started an in-depth conversation with Pimental about the Cardinals and the Royals and which team was more likely to make the playoffs this year.

Kinney watched silently for a few moments and then deliberately walked across the front of the house, still carrying the shovel, and went inside. The door shut behind him without a sound.

Hank waited about a minute and then sent Pimental around the back of the house. The last thing he wanted was Kinney coming out a back door without him knowing. Twenty minutes later, the evidence van came down the lane and bounced to a stop behind the fanned-out patrol cars. Alice Randall, barely visible behind the wheel, shut the engine off and hopped out. She stood about five feet two and, as always, was dressed in a button-down shirt, black cargo pants, and sturdy work boots. She reached back into the van, pulled out a wide-brimmed sun hat, and slapped it over her short, steel gray crew cut.

"So," she said as Hank approached, "we got a decomp?"

"That's putting it mildly," Hank said. "Did you bring respirators?"

"Kurt did."

At that, the van lurched and Kurt Gatz, clad in similar boots and pants but a bright blue T-shirt, climbed out of the passenger door. He wasn't much taller than Alice, but was probably three times her weight. He hustled his considerable bulk toward the back of the vehicle, calling out that he'd be ready as soon as he unpacked his cameras. Hank still hadn't figured out how he managed to haul all of that equipment and his extra pounds around crime scenes so nimbly.

The radio crackled. They'd gotten to the hole. And from the sounds of gagging in the background, the smell hadn't dissipated much.

"It's not a bad route, but no vehicle access," Sheila said. "Should be fairly quick on foot. We had to backtrack twice, which was why it took a while." Hank could hear someone making a crack about Ramsdell's watch.

"Just follow the crime-scene tape tied to the trees," Sheila continued.

Hank told her to send someone across the creek to help Sam with the *inmigrante* and Vern Miles. He wanted them both back at the station for interviews, and Sam couldn't drive them out of there alone in his Bronco—he'd need a partner. Then he and Kurt and Alice set off into the woods.

The body had been there at least a week. They'd lowered Alice down into the narrow fissure (the choice between her and Kurt had been an easy one) and she'd done the photographing and somehow managed to get what was left of the body into a body bag. They'd used the pulleys to haul it topside and then she'd gone to work collecting the maggots and other lovelies that had set up shop around the remains. Everyone was staying well clear of the edge when she let out a shout.

"What? You okay?" Hank peered over . Alice sat back on her haunches and grinned up at him.

"Sometimes," she said, "sifting through bucketloads of dirt actually pays off." She held up something so small Hank couldn't make it out. "Buckshot. Covered with deceased-person goop. And there's more of it down here."

Well, damn. That changed things. They'd have to wait for the autopsy to be sure, but he could certainly start operating as if this were a homicide. He stood up and smacked his hands together.

"Kurt, find the metal detector, please. Alice needs to bag up some buckshot."

He hollered down a big "thank you" as everyone settled in for a longer wait. Finally what was left of the remains was on its way to the medical examiner in Springfield. The maggots were on their way to a forensic entomologist at the University of Missouri in Columbia. And his deputies, several of whom had the same nauseated reaction as Sam, had gratefully departed the scene.

They would have to come back for final cleanup and cataloging, but otherwise were done.

"You're not going yet, I hope," Sheila said.

"Hell, no," Hank said. "There's a lot of woods we haven't seen. And if that body somehow turns out to be an accidental death, we won't have as strong of grounds to come back."

Sheila shook her head. "Even if the guy was accidentally shot, whoever did it didn't report it. And that's a crime, too. Plus, who'd be traipsing around uninvited on Kinney land? Nobody, that's who."

Hank sighed theatrically. "Such a dark view of humanity you have. Wanna bet on it?"

Sheila shot him a look. "No, 'cause you know it wasn't accidental as well as I do. Now let's get going before we lose the small light we got left."

Before they headed deeper into the Kinney property, away from the house and away from the creek bordering Miles's land, Hank found them both long, strong branches to test the ground with as they walked.

"Thanks," Sheila said. "I don't want to end up looking like you."

Hank glanced down at his filthy clothes. He had dirt and leaves smeared all the way down his front, and he was pretty sure he had a bit of corpse on him somewhere. He could smell it, but hadn't been able to find it.

They walked for what seemed like miles and saw nothing but trees, gullies, rock outcroppings, and the occasional clearing. Almost every slippery elm they saw had been stripped, some of them long enough ago that they were starting to die. Otherwise, there was nothing out of the ordinary.

So disappointing.

They used Ramsdell's watch, which Hank had borrowed, to find their way back to the Kinney house. Pimental greeted them as they emerged from the woods and said there had been no activity in back of the house. They all three walked around to the front. Hoch, the deputy Hank had stationed there, had the same report. Almost.

As Sheila turned away to walk to the squad car, Hoch pointed quietly at the house. A Confederate flag had been hung in the front window. Hank scowled and instinctively started toward the house.

"Stop."

Both he and Hoch froze. Sheila hadn't turned, but as usual, seemed to have eyes in the back of her head. She continued toward the car.

"It isn't illegal," she said, never looking back. "No point banging on his door. It's what he wants. Besides"—she swung open the patrol-car door—"we'll be back."

CHAPTER
7

Hank slid a fresh bottle of water across the table. The *inmigrante* huddled under a blanket opposite him, dry now but still cold from his emergency bath in the creek. He didn't seem to be able to stop shaking. His hand trembled as he unscrewed the bottle top, and his Adam's apple slid up and down his skinny neck as he took a swallow. *Pájaro.* Poor bird.

"You are not under arrest," Hank said in Spanish. The bird blinked at him. "You are safe. No one is going to hurt you."

More blinking. Hank wondered if he was in shock.

"Can you talk to me? I need to know how you came to be chopping down the trees."

The bird took another unsteady drink. A smear of dried mud ran from his ear down to his chin. Hank fought the parental urge to wipe it away. He sat back in his chair. Time to take a different tack.

"How old are you?"

"*Dieciséis.*" Sixteen. A minor. Hank wondered what he'd gone through to get this far north. "What's your name?"

The *pájaro* shook his head violently. Hank sighed. There was a rap on the interview room door and Sam stuck his head in. He muttered about searching through Hank's desk and handed him two granola bars and a Pecan Delight. The bird chose the candy. When he was finished, Hank started again. This time, he answered. Slowly, in fits and starts, his story emerged.

His name was Javier. He had come over the border from Nuevo Laredo three months before. He and a few others had made it up to Little Rock before they became separated. He was trying to get to his aunt in Chicago. A man in a big blue van had found him outside a Mexican restaurant in the downtown area and offered him a ride as far as St. Louis. But that was not what happened.

Instead, the man—Jorge—had taken him to a campsite where a dozen other men were living. He ordered them all into the van and drove three or four hours until they arrived at another camp, deep in the woods. The bird didn't know where it was, but he would recognize it if he saw it again. They lived in tents and used a trench latrine. Jorge's van was the only way out.

From there, Jorge would take them to different laborer jobs, dropping them off for the day and returning for them at nightfall. The gringo foremen would pay Jorge, who would put the cash in his pocket with a smile. He promised to pay them once he had gotten back his own money for the gas and the tents. The bird smiled ruefully. They all knew that was *mierda,* but they had no way out. All of the work sites were too far away from the towns. If they just walked off the job, they'd have nowhere to go.

And so they had ended up chopping down trees for the bald white man, way back in his property in the middle of nowhere. It was their second day there. He had been told to strip the bark off the cut trees, which he thought was incredibly stupid. Who wanted slimy bark? He thought it was gross, but he was the youngest, so he always got the worst jobs. The man had tossed him a knife and told him to get to work.

Then he—the bird pointed at Hank—had appeared. No one had known he was the police, but when the younger man in the uniform came, they all realized what was going on.

And so he ran.

Tears filled his eyes, and he began to shake again. Hank slid a granola bar across the table. The bird slipped it into his pocket. When's the last time this kid ate, Hank wondered. On the heels of that—what was he going to do with him? The jail would provide a roof, a shower, and a meal. But Hank hated to put him there. He'd have to book him, which would put him in the system. Plus, he had a feeling that a night in jail would shatter the fragile hold the bird still had on his nerves.

He stepped into the hallway and flagged down Sam.

"Take him to the locker room. There shouldn't be anyone in there right now. Have him take a hot shower. You have a change of clothes stashed in there?"

Sam gave an exasperated snort and pointed to his Garth Brooks World Tour 2014 T-shirt. "I did. I'm currently wearing them. Got my uniform a little dirty, remember?"

Hank looked down at his own filthy shirt and jeans. He couldn't even remember where he'd left his windbreaker.

"Okay, fine. Then give him mine. Hopefully that'll calm the kid down." And give Hank time to figure out what to do with him.

In the meantime, Vern the bald white man awaited. Hank walked down to the next interview room and opened the door. Vern jerked in his seat and then slumped back.

"I didn't realize—" He took a few quick breaths and started over. "I didn't know that they were illegals. I of course . . . I never would have hired them."

Hank didn't even bother to sit down. That would be taking this bozo too seriously. He leaned against the doorjamb.

"Oh, really? And where exactly did you hire these men?"

"Um . . ." He picked at a fingernail. "Off Highway 160 way out east. It, ah . . . I'd heard that there was someone there who had people willing to do day jobs."

"Oh, really?" Hank didn't try to keep the contempt out of his voice. "So you thought that some guy on the side of the road who was offering up a bunch of half-starved men who don't speak English—that was legit?"

"Well," Vern said, pulling his face into an almost-pout, "when you put it that way . . . I guess not. But I'm really sorry. I'm not going to be arrested, am I?"

Now Hank sat down. "Tell me everything."

Twenty minutes later, Hank emerged from the interview room. He now knew that Jorge was a big guy, about six-two and muscular, with shaggy black hair and a mustache. Vern had heard about him from some guys on a street corner near the Home Depot in Branson. They'd said there was a man who could deliver cheap labor to out-of-the-way work sites. He'd hooked up with Jorge in that spot off Highway 160. The van was an old blue Ford with Arkansas plates and no windows in the back. Jorge had shown him ten men sitting inside and then followed him to the slippery elm grove. He'd unloaded the men and left.

The arrangement was that Jorge would return at sundown to pick up the crew and get paid—six hundred bucks cash. That happened seamlessly, and Vern requested a second day to finish up the tree cutting. Jorge had dropped the men off at eight that morning. At no point had he mentioned his full name, where he was from, or where the crew was staying. The deal was another six hundred at the end of the second day, but, well, that had been cut short. Obviously.

Sheila met him in the hallway with a sheet of paper.

"Get him to sign this. It's not lawyered—I just made it up right now—but it gives us permission to go onto any part of his property at any time during this investigation. His consent to search would mean we wouldn't have to get a warrant. I figured since you've got him over a barrel on the illegals . . ."

Hank grinned. "Sometimes, I think I love you."

"Don't get smart." She shoved the paper at him.

Vern was more than happy to give up a signature instead of his freedom. Hank sent him home with a stern admonition to call immediately if any of his tree workers showed up at the farmhouse. So far, none of them had been found. Except the *pájaro*.

He stuffed everything into a thirteen-gallon trash bag, cinched it tight, and left it on the garage floor. He was pretty sure his right sock was the worst of it, but he certainly wasn't going to do a sniff test to confirm it. He quietly slipped through the mudroom and into the kitchen. It was almost midnight. He knew Maggie was still at the hospital. Everyone else would be asleep, the kids in their rooms and Dunc downstairs in his basement en suite.

Or not.

"What the hell?"

His father-in-law stood next to the kitchen island, half illuminated by the small bulb over the stove, which was all they left on at night. At that moment, it was bright as a spotlight.

"You're in your underwear, boy."

Hank glared at him.

"Shouldn't you be in bed?"

"I sure wish I was. Woulda missed your little show here." Dunc put the canister of Metamucil he was holding down on the counter. "Is this how you always come in after we're asleep?"

"No." It came out louder than Hank had intended, and they both jumped. He lowered his voice. "No, it is not. Since you're wondering, I got dirt, and mud, and decomposing corpse on my clothes today. They stunk. So they're in the trash. You're welcome for not bringing the smell into the house."

Duncan started stirring his powder into a glass of water.

"Well, when you put it that way, I suppose I am grateful to see you in your skivvies then." He eyed Hank. "I got to say, you're no spring chicken anymore."

Hank snorted. "Says the man up in the middle of the night for a fiber laxative."

Dunc let out a bark of a laugh. "True enough. But just you wait, boyo, because—"

The door to the mudroom clicked shut. Maggie stood there. She looked at her husband in his tighty-whities, then turned toward her father, who toasted her with his bright orange drink. She rolled her eyes.

"I'm going to bed."

CHAPTER

8

Sam and Sheila huddled together at the computer monitor on her desk, pointing and arguing. They apparently had differing opinions regarding which areas needed to be searched, and the satellite photos weren't helping any.

"We're going to need to look at this stretch of creek that's upstream from Kinney and Miles," Sam said, jabbing at the screen.

"What about over here?" Sheila pointed at a different section of the screen. "Screw it. Let's just do them both. That way the whole area's covered."

Sam nodded. "So we're looking for, what—the illegals, and also evidence relating to the death and possible murder of the John Doe. We're going to—"

Sheila chuckled. "Honey, I got a feeling we aren't looking for the illegals."

"Why not? They've got to be in those woods somewhere."

"Not necessarily," said Hank.

They swung toward the open doorway, where he was leaning against the jamb.

"You haven't seen a real disappearing act until you've seen

someone who knows it's the only way he'll get to stay in this country," he said. "They're long gone. They've caught rides somehow, or hiked the miles overland into town, or if they have the skills, they're hunkered down somewhere in the woods where we'll never find them."

Sam looked skeptical.

"Plus," Hank continued, "our job as local law enforcement is to investigate a suspicious death. Not to chase a bunch of immigrants around the woods."

Sheila shot Sam an I-told-you-so look. He retaliated by leaving her to finish the search warrant paperwork by herself. Hank smiled as she glared at Sam's retreating back. Then he explained how he wanted the paperwork worded—very broadly, so they'd have authority to look for anything in that stretch of forest that might possibly perhaps be evidence that could maybe somehow pertain to the body in the crevice. Sheila scowled at him.

"That's a lot easier for you to say than for me to do," she said. "You can't use the word 'maybe' in a search warrant application."

"True," he said. "But I have full faith in you to figure it out."

More scowling, and some muttering about stupid stripped trees. Hank suppressed a grin. No point getting her more riled up. He turned to leave.

"You going to check on the Mexican kid?" she asked. "You better make sure he gets a good breakfast in that holding cell."

Hank shook his head. "Nah, he's not in holding. He's staying somewhere. Safe and warm and not a jail. He'll be fine there for a few days."

Sheila nodded and then did a double take. "Dear God. You didn't take him home with you, did you? With the kids there? Maggie'll kill you."

Hank burst out laughing. "What, now you think I'm an idiot? Of course not. I know Maggie would kill me—justifiably—if I brought a stranger home in the middle of the night." He stood up.

"But there are places that specialize in lost travelers. He's doing fine."

Hank set down his coffee cup and smiled at the man across from him. Tony always made a great brew. He was a broad-chested man with thick dark hair cut close to his head who at the moment was dressed in a pair of gray sweatpants and a plain black T-shirt. Hank never got used to seeing him without his collar.

"As you can see, he is much improved," Tony said. The *pájaro* was in the next room, curled up in a blanket on the couch and listening to a Latin-music radio station while he ate a bowl of soup.

"Thank you for taking him in, especially so late at night."

"It is my pleasure. He is welcome here for as long as he wants."

"About that," Hank said, "I need you to make sure he doesn't leave. He's a witness, and I can't have him disappearing back into the underground."

"I am not a prison, Hank."

"I know, I know. But he didn't do anything wrong, and I'd hate to have to put him in a real prison just to keep him from running."

Tony smiled. "You are starting to sound like a politician, my friend." He continued as Hank groaned. "How is that going, by the way?"

Hank slouched in his chair and swigged his coffee.

"You know, the religious vote in this part of the state can be very important," Tony said. He looked shrewdly at Hank. "It might help for you to be seen at church."

Hank looked sheepish for a second, then countered with his own sly grin. "Who's the politician now, Padre?"

Tony wagged his finger at him. "Oh, no. If I were a politician, I'd tell you to go to a Baptist church. Much bigger, many more votes."

Hank laughed so hard he had to set down his coffee mug. "That's the best joke I've heard in a long time."

"Oh, no," Tony said again. "I mean it. You need to think seriously. At least go to your father-in-law's Presbyterian church once in a while. Go everywhere. I'd rather have you go to Protestant churches and get elected, than come just here and not be," he said. "I have to live in this county, too."

Hank stared at him in surprise.

"Hey," Tony said, "it's the age of practicalities. Who am I to judge?"

Hank grinned. "What about my immortal soul?"

Tony looked over at the teen, who was now delightedly playing with the priest's cat. "I'll have a word with the boss. I think you'll be okay."

There were three increasingly annoyed voice mails from Darcy on his phone. He sighed and hit the call-back button.

"Where have you been?"

"Fighting crime." He really just couldn't help himself.

She gave an exasperated snort. "You are supposed to be at PFI here in Springfield with your wife to look at cowboy hats. I am currently standing in the hat department. By. My. Self."

Oops. He really needed to start looking at his calendar every morning. At least Maggie had forgotten, too.

"Oh, and look, here's your lovely wife now."

Great.

He heard Darcy greet Maggie, and then a muffled conversation ensued that Hank prayed did not involve them deciding to pick a hat without him. He waited for Darcy to get back on the line, and his gaze landed on the *Daily What's-It* newspaper box on the sidewalk down the street from the church.

"So," Darcy said, "we've decided—"

"I thought you'd be interested to know," Hank interrupted, "that I was doing an interview. A media interview."

There was a pause on the other end of the line. "Really?" she finally said. "What—"

"So I apologize," Hank interrupted again. "I didn't mean to stand you up, but I thought it was really important to be quoted and I didn't want to put him off, because you've said that it's important to be accessible, and he's got a deadline, and—"

Darcy gave that delighted little trill he was coming to recognize meant he'd done something right. "Well, that is just wonderful. Superb. Was it the *Post-Dispatch*? The *Star*? I'm so pleased. You *have* been listening. I'll need to log this in the media-coverage folder. Of course we can reschedule the hat shopping. You have prioritized well, Hank."

Hank rolled his eyes and then quickly got off the phone before Darcy realized he hadn't told her anything solid about the interview. Then he immediately started scrolling through his contacts for the kid at the *Daily What's-It*. It took him a minute to remember that he never called from his cell phone in case the kid had caller ID at the local newspaper office. Cardinal cop rule: never give out your cell number. But dire circumstances warranted dire actions. He bought a copy of the paper, dug through it to find the newsroom phone number, and dialed.

"*Branson Daily Herald,* this is Jadhur."

Hank identified himself in entirely too jolly a manner, silently cursed himself for it, and then forced himself to take a deep breath. He was helped out by Jadhur, who was clearly stunned to get an unsolicited call from the sheriff.

"Um, how are you, uh, Sheriff? It's, uh, nice to hear . . . um, can I help you?"

He should have spent two minutes planning what he wanted

to talk about before he called, Hank thought. It was going to have to be the only thing that had happened lately.

"I wanted to clear up a few things about that emergency call yesterday out in the northwest section of the county. While we did need a large number of personnel, no deputies were injured. We did recover one unidentified deceased person."

He heard Jadhur typing away on the other end of the line. Then silence. Jadhur's brain was now working as fast as his.

"I appreciate that," Jadhur said. "I would have hated to get that incorrect. So . . . how about we go over a few more details? Just so, you know, I get everything right."

Hank consoled himself. Jadhur certainly would have found out about the body during one of his regular calls to the pathologist to check on recent local deaths. He wasn't really leaking anything. Plus, wasn't it a leak only if you weren't supposed to give out the information? He was the sheriff. He could give out any information he wanted. He didn't need anyone's permission. Therefore, no leak. And no way Darcy would find out that the interview had happened in not exactly the order he'd told her it had.

So he confirmed that a body had been found in an isolated stretch of woods in the northwestern part of the county by a member of a work crew. He left out the undocumented Mexicans, the slippery elms, and especially Jasper Kinney. This was supposed to benefit him, not stir up sentiment against him. Good grief, maybe Darcy was getting through to him after all.

CHAPTER
9

The good Dr. Whittaker was taking his sweet time. It had been two days, with no word yet on a cause of death. And certainly no ID.

Hank straightened his tie and made sure he'd pinned the badge on firmly. Instead of searching for evidence in the woods with his deputies, he was going to a Rotary Club luncheon. Dry chicken, limp salad, too many handshakes, not enough sincerity.

"Don't forget your speech." Maggie turned him away from the mirror and gave him a kiss. "You're going to do fine." She re-straightened his tie. "Is your speech in your pocket?"

"Yes." It came out as a growl, not a word.

She grinned. "Don't be a baby. This is part of the deal. It's called campaigning. It's only for two hours. Even you can be charming and sociable for that long."

Doubtful.

She gave him that raised-eyebrow look that meant she knew exactly what he was thinking, then turned him around and steered him toward the front door.

"Let's go, Sheriff. You can sulk later."

• • •

Maggie worked the room like she was running for Congress. Of course, she knew everybody already—she'd even gone to school with half these people's kids. But as he stood near the windows clutching a Diet Pepsi, he had to admit that wasn't the only reason. She was warm and funny and kind and brilliant, and beautiful in her light green spring dress with her long brown hair down around her shoulders.

And he was a moron. Hiding in the corner behind a glass of soda, when all he had to do was follow her. He pushed off from the wall and joined her as she talked to an old man in a blue cardigan that had to have been knitted by the woman across the room with a scarf the same color draped over her shoulders.

"Hello," he wheezed. "Margaret here was just telling me that you have many years of experience from up in Kansas City."

"Yes, sir," Hank said. "I was a member of the police department before we moved down here to Branson."

"I'd imagine our little town is a bit boring for you." He paused to wheeze again. "All that exciting, big-city crime up there."

"Oh, no, sir. Not at all. Community policing has always been my passion. I feel it's much better for me to get to know the people I serve. After all, we're neighbors."

Out of the corner of his eye, he caught Darcy listening as she adjusted a flower centerpiece at a nearby table. She shot him a delighted glance before heading off to check the seating arrangements. Maggie, on the other hand, gaped at him. He'd kind of surprised himself, too, to be honest.

Finally, Wheezer tottered over to his scarved companion. Hank hoped the old guy wouldn't die before the election. He turned around and stumbled into—

"Oh, hey, Lovinia."

A short, slightly plump woman with gray hair and bright purple glasses stood in front of him.

"Sheriff," she said with a smile. "How are you holding up? I don't imagine campaigning is really your thing, is it?"

"Not really. I'd much rather be seeing you out at a crime scene." He stopped. "That wasn't what I . . . I didn't mean . . ."

Lovinia burst out laughing. "I know what you meant. And me, too. I'd much rather be out at something exciting than about to listen to some boring campaign speeches." She winked at him. "Of course, there hasn't been anything good lately. Unless that body out in the woods up north of Branson turned into something . . . ?"

She trailed off and raised an inquiring eyebrow. He grinned.

"I half expected to see you out there," he said.

She sighed. "I tried. There was no way in that wasn't clearly trespassing and that didn't require a mile hike through the wilderness. In my younger days, sure, but now, not quite as doable." She gave him a jaunty grin and started to move away.

"Wait." Hank stopped her. He wanted to show Maggie that he knew at least one person in the room after she'd introduced him to so many.

"Maggie, this is Lovinia Smithson. She lives just west of Branson. Lovinia, my wife, Maggie."

"How do you do?" Lovinia extended her hand. "I'm the old lady who listens to the police scanner and shows up at crime scenes. Your husband is gracious enough not to tell me to get lost."

Maggie laughed and asked how Lovinia was enjoying her retirement in Branson.

"Pretty well. I'm much happier now that winter's over, and I can get out hiking in the beautiful weather," she said. "And I tutor over at the Branson Hills After-School Program. That's a lot of fun."

"Oh, were you a teacher?" Maggie said.

Lovinia laughed. "Good Lord, no. I couldn't handle a whole class of them. One or two at a time is all I can do."

"Two at a time is all we can handle, too," Maggie said, nodding at Hank. "And even then, we feel outnumbered."

Lovinia laughed, that big, infectious chuckle that had lightened Hank's heart at so many crime scenes.

"I wouldn't know about being outnumbered at home," she said. "I never had kids. All for the best, though. Walter and I had a great time, just by ourselves."

Maggie offered condolences on Walter's passing. Hank was amazed she remembered. He'd only mentioned once long ago that Lovinia's husband had died about a year earlier—shortly before he'd become sheriff. But then, Maggie'd always had a mind for that kind of stuff.

"How are you getting on, out there in the house by yourself?" Maggie asked. "If you ever need a hand with anything, please just let us know. We'd be happy to help."

"Oh, I'm just fine," Lovinia said. "I spent my life around a whole lot of people, so the peace and quiet is kind of nice at this point ."

She shifted her gaze back to Hank.

"Now, you two'd better get back to drumming up votes," she said. "You've already got mine, so don't waste any more time on me."

She sailed off toward the bar and Maggie turned him toward a couple in their sixties whose daughter had been one of Maggie's grade school friends. Hank was in the middle of an unexpected hug from the woman when he saw Gerald Tucker enter the room.

"Well, haven't you done well, Maggie dear," the woman said. "So tall and . . . rugged-looking." She gave Hank a charitable smile. "My Lauren, of course, married a lawyer. They're up in . . ."

Hank nodded automatically at the conversation as he positioned himself to watch Tucker chat people up on the other side of the room. GOB appeared to have bought some new clothes. Hank was damn sure he hadn't owned such a nicely tailored wool suit before he became Gallagher's personal pet.

Insubordinate asshole.

It took an elbow in the ribs from Maggie for him to realize he was scowling. He slapped on a smile and followed her around several tables, steering well clear of Edrick Fizzel in the process. Of course the Branson County commissioners would be here. He thought he saw the other two standing over by the windows. And he certainly knew Fizzel, whose ruddy face had gotten much too close to his own during several arguments about the Mandy Bryson case in February.

They slowly made their way around the room, avoiding any contact with Fizzel or Tucker. It worked fine until Hank, in an effort to get around a woman headed straight for the Good Ol' Boy, turned and came face-to-face with Henry Gallagher.

"Well, hello, Worth." Gallagher had never—not once—addressed him as Sheriff. And they sure as hell weren't on a first-name basis.

"Gallagher." He didn't move. Let Branson's Leading Businessman be the one to walk away.

Branson's Leading Businessman obviously thought the same thing. He stayed put as well, nonchalantly sipping on his iced tea. The crowd bustled around them. Hank took a swig of his now-warm soda and studied the glass. He could see Darcy gesturing at him over from near the podium. He ignored her. Gallagher flicked nonexistent lint off his shirt cuff and stirred his tea. Hank tried not to fidget.

And then, like an angel of mercy—or a boxing referee—a short, compact man with a clipped mustache and a tailored navy suit stepped in between them.

"Gentlemen. Wonderful. It's time to begin. If you'd come up

to the head table, Sheriff, we'll get you seated. And Henry, if you'd go ahead with your welcoming remarks while lunch is being served, that would be great."

What the——?

The referee stood aside so Gallagher could move between the tables. As he passed Hank, a reptilian smile flashed across his thin face. "I can win an election, Worth. Can you?"

Hank followed the referee to his reserved seat next to Maggie at the left of the podium. Tucker sat on the right. And Gallagher took his place behind the microphone.

"Good afternoon, ladies and gentlemen. Welcome to the Branson Valley Rotary Club monthly luncheon. I am Henry Gallagher, and I am quite honored to be your newly elected president."

Hank stifled a groan as the audience applauded.

"Today, we are pleased to have with us the two candidates for sheriff of Branson County. Gerald Tucker"—Gallagher waved toward him—"is a lifelong county resident and has been with the sheriff's department for twenty-one years. Hank Worth," he said with no accompanying wave, "was appointed to the sheriff's position nine months ago when our beloved Darrell Gibbons was elected to the state senate. Both gentlemen will share with you their views of law enforcement and what they each plan to do for our beautiful Ozark county if elected.

"But before we get to that, I wanted to highlight some of the activities and initiatives that Rotary has planned for the coming year . . ."

People dug into their lunches as Gallagher droned on. The clinking of glass and silverware muffled the buzz of Hank's cell phone. He discreetly pulled it out of his pocket and laid it on his thigh. He made a show of arranging his napkin on his lap as he read the text from Sheila.

At John Doe site in the woods. CSU just found another one.

He pretended to drop his napkin and texted her back as he bent to retrieve it.

Another what?

He straightened and waited for her response.

Body. It's a kid.

CHAPTER
10

Hank threw his napkin on the table and pushed back his chair. Maggie looked at him, startled. He leaned toward her so that Darcy, seated on Maggie's left, could hear him as well.

"There's been a development in a case," he whispered. "I have to go."

Maggie looked aghast. Darcy looked livid.

"You're about to give a speech," Maggie said, a bit unnecessarily.

Darcy scooted back her own chair and leaned behind Maggie for cover, gesturing for Hank to do the same. He stayed put. He didn't want to be any closer to Darcy than he had to be at the moment.

"You are not going anywhere," she hissed. "This is one of the most important appearances of the campaign."

What terms would Darcy understand? He reluctantly leaned behind Maggie's chair. "There is another dead person," he spat out. "Possibly a murdered person. I have to get out there."

"You can wait one goddamn hour. If you don't, you'll ruin

your chances. Your already slim chances. And I'll . . . I'll quit," she said.

"So you're telling me that because I'm doing my job, you're going to bail like a total—"

"You. Are. Staying. Put."

Both Hank and Darcy froze. Maggie was still facing the audience, but her whisper came through loud and clear to the two people hiding behind her. Darcy shot him a large dose of smug before she straightened and resumed eating her lunch as if nothing had happened. Hank slowly hitched his chair back up to the table and stared out into the crowd. He did not look at his wife.

She leaned over and handed him his napkin. Then she whispered in his ear.

"This is our future. Our family's. We all need you to win this election. I know you want to go racing off. I know you want to be anywhere else but here. But this is it. So suck it up."

Suck it up. It was a skill he had never acquired, and she knew it. He smoothed his napkin over his lap and contemplated making a break for it. He could be out that door behind the drink station before anybody noticed him missing. Yeah, and while he was at it, maybe he should take a bunch of the silverware, too. He sighed. He hated feeling trapped. He hated not being personally in charge of an important crime scene. He hated campaigning. He hated wearing a suit and tie. He hated the chicken entrée in front of him (rubbery, just as predicted). He hated speeches, both giving and sitting through. He hated—no, he didn't. But he did avoid looking at her. Especially when she squeezed his knee during the coin toss to see who would speak first.

He won. Fantastic.

He stepped up to the podium and looked out at the audience.

Then at his notes. Then back to the crowd. Someone a few tables
to the right cleared his throat. If only he were out in the woods
with a dead body. Then, from the very back table, he saw a mass of
gray curls and a lively wave.

So he took a deep breath and began. He talked about his
plans to increase community policing and decrease deputy response times. He talked about why his newcomer status made
for a fresh perspective. He even told the joke Darcy had inserted
midway through the speech. No one laughed. He was perversely
pleased.

Finally, it was over. Or he was done. Whichever. He sat down
to a decent amount of polite applause. Maggie squeezed his knee
again. Then the referee introduced Tucker. The insolent GOB,
who had been sitting next to Gallagher, picked up a sheaf of notes
and his phone and took the two steps to the podium.

"Ladies and gentlemen, I can't thank you enough for the
opportunity to speak to you all today." More polite applause. Hank
tried not to roll his eyes.

"I had planned to speak to you about the future of your
Branson County Sheriff's Department," he said, holding up his
notes. "But"—he stopped and raised his phone—"something
much more urgent has come to my attention. The body of a
child—a poor, defenseless child—has been found deep in the
woods north of here. I apologize to you all, but I must go."

The crowd erupted. Gasps and mutters and even a little shriek
from a lady in the middle of the room. Then they rose and formed
an aisle through the sea of tables for Tucker to walk through on
his way to the door. Some even slapped him on the back.

And Hank sat there. Frozen until the door closed on the sight
of Tucker striding off into the sunlight, going to bring justice to
a murdered child. Then he rose and turned, not to his left, but to
his right and the referee. He didn't even try to spin it.

"I need to go, too," he said.

And then he fled out the door behind the drink station.

How had that fat bastard known? Who tipped him off? He rounded the corner of the community center and jogged across the grass toward his car. Then he smelled smoke. He slowed to a walk, but not before Tucker saw him and let out a loud chuckle.

"In a hurry, Worth?"

Hank desperately wanted to ram that cigarette up his nose. Instead, he muttered "electable, electable" to himself and turned away. Then Tucker laughed again. And "electable" went out the window.

"You're not even assigned to the investigation," Hank snapped as he whipped around and came back toward his deputy. "You had no reason to leave."

Tucker smiled, the kind that tugged up only one side of his lips and managed to convey condescension and smugness all at the same time. He must have been taking lessons from Gallagher.

"I know that. But *they* don't know that. So who's the one that cares about justice now? The guy that was willing to sacrifice a campaign appearance to go catch a murderer? Or the guy that was more interested in sticking around and blow-jobbing a bunch of businessmen for their votes?"

Hank stopped himself just before he grabbed Tucker by his nice, new lapels. He gently reached in and straightened the asshole's silk tie instead.

"Nice outfit," he said. "Did Daddy take you shopping?"

He left the community center less of a candidate than he had been going in, with a vow to never listen to anyone's orders ever again.

CHAPTER

11

"What the hell took you so long?"

Sheila stood near the solid side of the fissure, snapping her surgical gloves impatiently.

"Don't. Ask."

The look on his face must have reinforced the anger in his voice, because she took a step back and dropped the reprimand.

"Alice was down there, just cleaning up, making sure there weren't any plastic evidence bags or tape or anything that could cause a bird to choke, or whatever." Sheila did not roll her eyes, although her tone implied that she wanted to. "Anyway, she shifted some of the dirt. It was covered with a layer of soil that had been undisturbed for quite a while, and also some of the surface dirt that slid into the crack when the illegal fell in."

"It" lay in the bottom of the fissure in an almost-fetal curl. Delicate, cream-colored bones just emerging from the Ozark loam. Alice knelt on the bottom with a camel hair brush in one hand and a small metal pick in the other.

"I'm so sorry. I broke the fibula. I stepped on it. I had no idea," she said, not looking up at Hank perched on the edge of the gap.

He stared down at his crime-scene tech and felt the vise around his chest loosen. This was what was real. The emotional well-being of his employees. And the death of a child. Probably out here all alone in the woods. The anger and the frustration and the Rotary all faded away, and the fragile bones seemed to glow in the low light of the narrow rift in the rock.

"It's okay, Alice," he said. "Everything's all right. If it hadn't been for you, we wouldn't have found it at all. Now we have. And we can start to figure out what happened."

She nodded slowly and resettled herself on the small patch of ground where she was wedged between the wall and the skeleton.

"Where's Kurt?"

"Went back to the van for more gear," Sheila said. "And Bill Ramsdell went back to the station for floodlights, 'cause we're going to be here a hell of a long time, and some tarps, 'cause the forecast says it might rain."

Wonderful.

At least they hadn't yet taken down the pulley-and-rope contraptions they'd used to get the first body out of the hole. He was starting to make sure they were still solidly braced when the sound of sniffling drifted up from below.

"How long has she been down there?" he asked Sheila.

She stopped jotting on her clipboard and thought. "I think they got out here about twelve hundred hours. They called it in at"—she consulted the clipboard—"twelve thirty-six. Then I notified you at twelve thirty-nine."

And it was now 2:45. Too long for someone who just expected a quick stop so she could do something nice for the birds. He stuck his head over the side.

"Alice, why don't you come on up here for a bit? Take a break."

She nodded without looking up at him, then stood and sat herself in the rope sling hanging next to her. She stayed silent as Hank hoisted her to the surface. He dug around in her gear bag until he found the bottle of water he knew she always carried. He pressed it into her hands and led her away from the ravine and over to a hickory tree. He sat her down and left her whispering the Hail Mary to herself.

They heard Kurt long before they saw him. Although, in fairness, it wasn't just him crashing through the woods. Bill Ramsdell was with him, and between them they seemed to have brought the entire contents of the crime-scene van.

"Here . . . you . . . go," Kurt puffed as he dropped the gear bags and then himself on the ground about twenty feet from the hole. He dug a handkerchief out of his pocket and sponged off his face. "Man. That's some hike."

Ramsdell, who hadn't even broken a sweat, set down his load and set to work stringing up more crime-scene tape. Hank began to help Kurt unpack the rest of the gear. Everyone worked quietly for a while, until Sheila couldn't take it anymore.

"How long are we going to wait?" She nodded in Alice's direction.

"You are a hard heart, you know that?"

She sighed. "I'm not. Really. I just see the rain clouds coming."

She pointed toward the west. "For all we know, that hole fills with water when it rains. We need to at least get down there and get some more pictures taken."

A gathering storm. He'd have to make Alice go back down there. God, he hated this job. Why, why was he fighting for it? He headed over to the hickory tree, pausing to let her finish.

". . . now and at the hour of our death. Amen." She looked up and met his gaze for the first time that day. "Hi."

He squatted down in front of her. "Hi. How you doing?"

"I'm better now." She unclasped her hands. "I think."

"It's okay, you know. To get upset. Especially about a child."

She shook her head and her hands came together again, probably without her even realizing it.

"No, it's not okay. We are all God's creatures."

"Yes . . ." Hank said, confused. "That's why there's nothing wrong with it upsetting you."

She ducked his gaze.

"But I wasn't that upset about the other one. You know why? Because I figured that one's got to be some junkie meth-head who got killed during a drug deal or something."

All of this made perfect sense to Hank. He nodded and reached out a hand to help her up, but instead of taking it, she gestured toward the crevice.

"But this one isn't like the other one." She paused. "I don't know anything at all about either one of them, but I think this one is worth more than that one. This person is worth more than the first one."

Oh.

"And that's wrong," she said. "We're all God's creatures. I should've been just as upset about the first one."

Behind him, Hank could feel the storm clouds rolling in and hear Sheila snapping her gloves. He ignored them both.

"No, you should not have been. Any decent human being would be more upset about a child. And that skeleton is—was— obviously a child, who obviously should not be out here in the middle of the woods."

"But we are all created equal."

"Well, yes . . ." He thought for a moment. "And there you

go. *Created* equal. That means at the beginning. How you choose to live from then on does have an effect on your worth, don't you think?"

She stared at him with a furrowed brow.

"Say you sat and didn't do anything at all," he said. "Didn't contribute to society, weren't nice to little old ladies, didn't . . . didn't *do* anything. You'd be worth less than someone who worked hard, volunteered their time, who took care of their kids, who contributed to the world in some way. Right? Your decisions and choices as you go through life can maybe have an effect on your worth."

She stared at him with the same look that Maribel gave him when he insisted that early bedtimes were good for her.

"So some CEO is worth more than me? Because he does more, because he affects more people? What about the—"

Crap. He had made himself a sinkhole before the rain even got here.

"No, no. That's . . . I didn't mean that. I just meant that— hell, Alice, I don't know." He raked his hand through his hair. "I see what you're saying, and you're right. Everybody is somebody's child. And deserves respect. But do you see what I mean? You're human. You're going to be upset. And sometimes, you can't control when that happens and when it doesn't. It doesn't make you a bad person."

"It doesn't make me a good Christian."

A raindrop landed on his cheek.

"Did you do your best work with the first body?"

"Of course."

"You didn't shortcut anything?"

"No." Now she was getting offended.

"Do you plan to do a good job with this one?"

She spat out an affirmative.

"Okay," he said. "So you're going to treat them both the same. That counts for something, doesn't it?"

She thought on that one. Hank said his own prayer as she sat there. Then she pressed her lips together and got to her feet. Thank God.

The rain fell slow and fat, landing with individual splats on the tenting they had rigged over the excavation to keep Alice and Little Doe dry. She had crouched into a ball and wedged against the rock wall to give herself as much access as possible. Kurt sat like a teetering boulder on the edge, plotting the scene below onto graph paper and calling nonsensical encouragements to his partner.

Hank felt horrible that he'd had to send her back down there, but no one else was small enough. The longer he stood there, the worse the churning in his gut. He spun around and walked off into the woods.

The rain fell more softly there, pattering on leaves instead of smacking against waterproof tarp. He wandered farther in, among the scattered undergrowth of vines and bright green, shin-high flowering plants. Eventually they got so thick on the ground, he felt like he was wading through a sea of broad leaves and delicate little purple blossoms. He finally took shelter under another hickory tree. He stared at the sky and then at the ground. Neither made anything more clear. He leaned against the rough bark of the tree, but it did not seem to ease the weight on his shoulders. The only thing that did when he felt this way was a plan. What next?

He started a list.

Pull all unsolved cases involving missing or runaway children.

Get a hold of a forensic anthropologist—maybe at
Missouri State or Mizzou? That weird Whittaker in
Springfield doesn't know a damn thing about old
bones.
Make sure Alice gets some time off after this.
Fire Darcy.

He stopped. That one had popped into his head unbidden.
But yes, he would do that. Good grief, was his campaign in trouble.
He had no idea how to salvage it, but it was quite clear that woman
didn't, either. He'd be lucky now to just lose the election and not
be run out of town by an angry crowd with pitchforks.

He mopped his increasingly wet face with his tie and looked
up, but he couldn't tell whether the rain was tapering off or getting worse. He moved away from the tree's canopy to get a better
look at the clouds.

His neck started to hurt, and as he brought his gaze back
down, levelheadedness returned. What the hell was he doing? He
was avoiding his real problems, that's what he was doing. Divin-
ing patterns in trees instead of investigating a murder. Or facing
angry voters. He gave himself a mental shake and stomped off
back to the crime scene.

He didn't call it until after eight o'clock, when every last ray of
sun had retreated behind the western hills. Then they hauled
Alice up, and fell silent as Kurt walked her out of the woods, his
arm around her middle as she wobbled away on cramped and
unsteady legs.

Hank walked over to Bill Ramsdell, who had just finished
putting up his tent.

"You sure about this?"

"Oh, yeah," Bill said. "A night in the woods is no biggie.

It'll give me a chance to test this new tent out before the Jamboree. Plus, I can use the overtime."

Hank tried not to think about how much that would take out of his budget. Guard duty was expensive. Guard duty—he stopped Ramsdell as the deputy started to walk away.

"Just so we're clear on everything, Bill. You're not to leave this scene until you are personally relieved by either me or Deputy Turley. No matter what time it is, or anything else. Got it?"

Ramsdell cocked an eyebrow. "That's what guard duty is, boss. You don't leave."

Hank smiled at his properly trained deputy and walked away. It was the first time he'd appreciated getting looked at like he was an idiot.

CHAPTER
12

He hoped Maggie was in bed. Or had been called into the hospital. He hoped she was somewhere—anywhere—they would be unable to have a conversation right now.

The kitchen table was not one of those places.

"Hi."

She sat there in the dim glow of the light over the stove, wearing pajamas and her old blue robe with the spit-up stains on the shoulder and the belt chewed on one end by the dog.

He went over to the pantry and rooted around for the bread and peanut butter. The rubber chicken had been an awfully long time ago. He made himself a sandwich and poured a glass of milk. She didn't move. He took a long drink and a big bite and then finally met her eyes.

"I'm sorry."

He took another bite.

"I'll say it again. I'm sorry," she said.

He took another big bite.

"I'm really tired. I'm going to go to bed."

She stood. Right in front of the doorway. She shoved her

hands in the robe's pockets and said, "You're not going to go to sleep. I know you. You're going to toss and turn and fume. We might as well talk about it now."

"Talk about what? The state of my campaign? The effect that today will have on it? I'd rather not. I'm going to have nightmares as it is."

She stiffened her spine in that way she did when she was about to do battle. He did not want to do this tonight. He was tired and worried and embarrassed and resentful and he just wanted to finish his damn sandwich.

And he hated that she knew all of that just by looking at him. Her spine softened and she stepped forward.

"Honey, it's going to be okay." Like she was soothing Benny after a scraped knee. "I know it doesn't look so good right now, but it will be all right. There's still a way to go before the election. You can do it."

He couldn't stop the look that crawled onto his face.

"Oh, yeah. Just like that. Easy. Well, it's not easy. You can't just put a Band-Aid on it, Doc. That's not how it works. . . . This . . . this is not an easy thing for me. I'm not the one who knows everybody. I'm not the cute local girl who came back home. I'm the outsider. Now, after today, I'm also the politician asshole who doesn't care about dead kids."

"No. No. You're not. We can fix that. We talked about it, and—"

"We? Who's 'we'? You and Darcy? Well, she's fired."

Maggie jerked back as if she'd been slapped.

"What? No—you can't do that. Especially now. She's going to be the one to help with this."

"Well, unless she can suddenly rewind time and make it so neither one of you says a word at that lunch, then no, she can't help."

Pain flashed across Maggie's face, but Hank didn't stop.

"What does she do for me? Make me wear a tie. Make me get a haircut. Screw up today, that's for sure."

"If that's your beef, then you need to fire me. I'm the one who told you to stay put today. And I'm the one who would have made you do all those other things. You need to, to get elected. They were all commonsense changes on the surface, not about who you are." She took a breath. "Well . . . except today. That was just a cluster. And I'll say it again. I'm. Sorry."

He took a big bite of peanut butter and bread and chomped away while he continued to glare at her. Reasonableness hadn't worked, so she went back to the Band-Aid approach.

"What about the speech?" she said. "That went over really well. And the campaign signs? Those look great, and they're going up all over. We couldn't have done that by ourselves, either. Darcy's getting volunteers to put them up. People are volunteering for you." She stopped and her blue eyes bored into him. "You didn't even know that, did you?"

He did not.

And from the look on her face, he should have. She turned and marched, straight-backed, out of the kitchen and down the hallway. The door to their bedroom closed with the kind of definite click that meant he would not be following her through it. He stared at his befuddled reflection in the microwave door. How the hell had this suddenly become about *his* failings? *He* was the one who had been wronged. He was the one with the right to be angry. He stuffed the rest of his sandwich in his mouth and stomped off to find a spare pillow for the couch.

He knew he should. But Lord, he didn't want to. The smell of must and age rose from the gash in the earth in ever greater intensity as more bones were disturbed. The air was sticky and still up here, and he knew it was worse down below. Alice's shirt was drenched, as was the old terry-cloth headband she wore to keep the sweat out of her eyes. He didn't know if it was working. She hadn't looked up in more than an hour. But the bones kept coming. One at a time, in separate paper bags, sent up in the bright orange five-gallon bucket swinging from the pulley line.

And the space between the rock wall and the skeleton had slowly grown bigger. Big enough for someone who was not Alice. He knelt at the edge and rolled a rock between his palms. His neck already had a crick in it from sleeping on the couch last night. The hiking boots he had on were really too bulky to allow for easy footing in the small space. He wasn't as fast at evidence collection as she was. He didn't really like bugs.

And he was an ass. An ass full of excuses. He stood and called for Alice to come topside. Ramsdell replaced the bucket with the sling contraption, lowered it, and hoisted her up once she settled herself for the ride. Then he turned white when he realized what Hank intended to do.

"You're going down there?"

Hank would have appreciated him at least attempting to hide his dismay.

"Kurt can help you lower me," he said. "It'll be fine."

"I guess . . ."

Except that his excuse-heavy ass wouldn't fit in the sling. After some debate that was entertaining to everyone but him, they all decided that he should stand on it and they would lower him that way.

"Lucky thing you're wearing those sturdy boots," Kurt said. "They'll support your feet on the way down."

Yeah. Lucky him.

He swung like a drunken pendulum all the way to the bottom and ignored the applause as he plunked gracelessly down in the soft soil. He braced himself on the rock wall while wrestling his feet from the sling. Ramsdell pulled it back up, and the voices above faded as everyone moved away from the edge. Now it was just him. And Little Doe.

The child was on his right side, with his face against the rock and his back to the dirt slope. Hank had no basis for using "he," but the poor kid had to be called something. There was a very slim chance they might get lucky and know the gender after forensic anthropologists analyzed the pelvis. It was the last bone Alice had excavated—Hank now knelt in the space where it and the legs had been. He settled himself a little more and took a better look around.

Most of the dirt and detritus was fresh and must have come down with either the fleeing *pájaro* or the initial corpse. That soil was getting lifted out by the bucketful. Then came the harder earth, packed down by who-knew-how-many years of weather and gravity. It was a wonder Alice had even seen the bones in the first place. Only the tips of two ribs had protruded from the ground. Now enough had been cleared away to see that those were the only two that had stayed intact. The rest were a mess, broken and jumbled together in the space that once held a heart.

Hank lowered his head. Kids were so tough. The loss was inversely proportional to their size. And he had no problem admitting it. Kids' lives were worth more. Worth more grief, worth more effort. He'd never say that in a court of law, of course, but in a fissure twenty feet below ground level with nothing but a skeleton for company, well, how could you not be honest with yourself?

He shook himself out of his rumination and started to work on the rib fragments, tiny and fragile as the bones of a sparrow. Little Doe had been a small one. No older than eight or nine, he was sure of that, even without a forensic analysis. Did he like to run through the woods? Had he fallen? Man, he hoped not. Stuck here for days, starving to death, probably injured, crying for help that never came.

He was going to be as big a mess as Alice if he kept this up. He started reciting the Cardinals roster, and by the time he got to the bullpen, his headache had faded and his breathing was back to normal. He made it through the entire National League and had just finished listing the American League's designated hitters when his back muscles seized up.

He tottered to his feet with a groan.

"I know. You got to do that more often—stand up, I mean. Otherwise, it'll kill you."

A glowing bristle brush was addressing him from above. He blinked away the vertigo and saw Alice peering over the edge, her face in shadow and her spiky gray hair backlit by the sun.

"What time is it?" he asked.

"Time for you to quit," she said. "It's getting towards sundown, and your light down there is going to go right quick. We can start again tomorrow and trade off shifts." She stopped and her tone changed. "Uh, that is, if you want to. I didn't mean to be giving you orders . . ."

Hank actually laughed, which he didn't think would have been possible down in this godforsaken crack. "Alice, now that I know *exactly* what you've gone through for the past two days, I'd say you've earned the right to order everyone around. Including me. Just, please, no applause as I get lifted out of here."

He thought he saw a grin flash across her shadowed face before she disappeared from his sight. It was the first smile he'd seen from her since she'd started on the rotting John Doe four days ago. His back felt a little bit better as Bill and Kurt lifted him to the surface.

He awoke to a two-year-old belly flopping off the arm of the couch and onto his stomach. Not the best way to start a day, unless you were Benny.

"Daddy, Daddy, Daddy. Up. Up. Up." Each word was punctuated by laughter and a bounce that did no favors to Hank's gut. He groaned and grabbed his son just as Guapo scrabbled on board and dug his paws into the parts Benny wasn't sitting on.

He dumped them both on the floor and sat up with another groan. Benny popped up and trotted off to the kitchen. Guapo decided he was content where he was and started licking Hank's toes. Well, Hank thought as he stared down at his muttstrosity of a pet, the day can't get worse than this.

This second night on the couch had been an accident. He'd been waiting for Maggie to get home from the swing shift at the hospital and must have fallen asleep. She obviously hadn't woken him up. He sighed.

"I'm more in the doghouse than you are," he said to Guapo, who responded with a belch and a liberal licking of his own underparts. Hank removed his toes from the dog's reach.

"Has he gone out yet?" Dunc stood in the kitchen doorway with a cup of coffee in one hand and Benny's sippy cup in the other.

Hank shook his head. The two men stared at each other. Guapo started to whine.

"You're the one who brought him home from the pound," Hank said.

Dunc scowled at him, then whistled for Guapo. "No walk yet, you varmint. Go out back."

They disappeared into the kitchen as Maribel and Maggie came down the hallway from the bedrooms. One of them gave him a hug and skipped off to breakfast. The other crossed her arms and sighed.

"Good morning," Hank said brightly. Then his voice returned to normal. "Look, I didn't mean to sleep out here again. I was waiting up for you and . . ."

She sat down next to him. "I know. Your case reports were

spread all over. I stacked them over there. Didn't want you to roll over on them."

"Thanks."

They sat there, side by side, for a bit, Hank staring at the floor and Maggie at the ceiling. Finally, Maggie began to speak. Hank laid his hand on her leg.

"No. I should go first. I should have known that people were volunteering for me. I should have been up on that. I wasn't. I should have been paying attention to Darcy. But you have to admit, when I did listen to her, it didn't work out so well."

Maggie gritted her teeth. "Yes, and I've apologized for that. And she will, too."

"Then why hasn't she?"

"I guess that's my fault, too," Maggie said. "I told her to give you a few days."

He grunted. "And that gives you more time to try to convince me not to fire her."

Her jaw was still clenched. "Yeah, Mr. Cynical, that was just what I was thinking. You know me—playing every angle."

"That . . . that's not what I meant." He raked his hand through his hair. "I don't know what I mean. I don't know what I'm going to do. This election is . . . is . . . I just want to do my job."

Maggie put her hand over his. "Maybe," she said carefully, "it might be good to think of it—of the campaigning—as part of your job. Not as something separate. Not as something that's keeping you from your job." He started to speak, and she raised her hand to stop him. "I know, I know. It *is* keeping you from the bodies in the woods. I get that. But I mean psychologically. If you accept that campaigning is a part of this job—and you need to do it to be good at your job—that might make it easier."

She dropped her hand back onto his. He looked at it and sighed. It was his "I'm tired and I want this conversation to be over" sigh. She, as usual, ignored it.

"Well, how about this?" she said. "You meld the two together. That might get you to the right place mentally."

"What the hell does that mean?"

"You put this away, just for a day." She waved toward the stack of missing-children reports on the coffee table. "That poor kid's been down there for years. One more day isn't going to hurt that case any. You put that aside, and you get going on who tipped off Tucker."

Hank, for the first time during the conversation, looked at his wife full-on.

"Somebody is working against you," she said. "You need to know who it is. Use those investigative talents of yours and figure it out."

He glared at her. "What do you think I've been doing?"

"Not that. Have you gone through duty logs? Have you narrowed down exactly who knew and when? Have you charted out all of the possibilities?"

"You're the one who makes charts," he snapped.

"Yes," she said, so calmly that it made him even more irritated, "and you're the one who doesn't confront things when they have the potential to be upsetting."

"What are you talking—I investigate murders, for chrissakes. What's more upsetting than that?"

She put her other hand over his. "That stuff isn't personally upsetting. Not like finding out someone you trust is sabotaging your campaign against Tucker."

He tried to take his hand away, but she wouldn't let him. He wanted to protest, but he couldn't think of anything to say that would undercut her argument. Instead he started to pout, which she took as a win, releasing his hand and kissing him on the cheek before going in to breakfast. Damn woman.

CHAPTER

13

"I was starting to think you thought it was me."

Sheila settled into the seat in front of his desk and took a sip from her fresh cup of coffee. As part of their well-established tradition, she had not brought him one.

"What? Why on earth would you think that? You're the only one I'm sure didn't do it."

She gave him a small, resigned smile. He cringed.

"That's not what I meant," he said. "I . . . I just . . . I trust you. That's all I meant."

Her smile didn't change. "I know. You trust me, because I'm the only one with less options than you if you lose. You at least could find another job in southern Missouri."

He wanted to argue, to say it wasn't true and she wouldn't be stuck here on permanent graveyard shift at the jail if Tucker won. But she would, and they both knew it. And Hank, not for the first time, wondered what it was really like, being the first African American deputy in the county. And one of the first female deputies as well.

She sure as hell wasn't going to tell him, though. Instead, she sat there and sipped her coffee and waited for him to speak. He wished he knew what to say.

"I . . . you . . . you have been invaluable to me since my first day at this job. I think we make a good team and I . . . I hope you feel the same way." He stopped. Anything else he could say would probably come out the wrong way again.

But Sheila wasn't going to take pity on him. She sat there calmly, holding her chipped Branson Mountain 2011 Fun Days mug with both hands, and didn't say a word.

"So . . . um . . . would you mind—only if you want to—could you help me with the time line for contacts when Little Doe was found? If you don't want to, that's okay. It's totally up to you." He was doing his best not to look desperate, but had a feeling he wasn't succeeding.

She looked out the window—his office had one, hers didn't—and then back at him. Then she pulled a piece of paper out of her shirt pocket and slowly unfolded it.

"I got a call from Alice at twelve thirty-six P.M. She had tried yours, but you didn't pick up," she said, reading from her notes. "She and Kurt were the only two out there when she found the skeleton."

Hank let out a slow sigh of relief.

"I immediately called Sam—via cell, not the radio—and told him to get out there. Then I texted you." She looked up. "Since I knew you were at the luncheon. That was twelve thirty-nine P.M. I then called Bill Ramsdell, again on mobile, and told him to bring back out the rest of the pulley equipment and tarp awnings that we'd used for the first John Doe. Then I left for the scene. That was one oh-two P.M."

When she arrived at Kinney's house, she saw that Sam's cruiser was already there, parked next to the crime scene unit van. The Confederate-flag curtain twitched and fell back into place as she'd walked by the house, so she'd known he was aware of the increasing police presence.

"So—me, Sam, Bill, Alice, and Kurt. And probably Kinney."

Hank raised an eyebrow. "How do you figure?"

"I swear I was being followed through the woods to the crime scene. Never could see anybody, but you know that feeling that you're being watched." She shrugged. "To be honest, though, I probably would have done the same if it was my property. The law finally says they're about done and then comes back again in full force? Anybody'd wonder why."

Hank thought that was awfully charitable of her, considering the man they were talking about.

"And that's it. From me, anyway. I've got no idea about the others." She neatly refolded her paper and put it back in her pocket.

"Do you think any of them would have done it? Any of them closer to Tucker than they let on?"

She gave him another small smile, this one full of forbearance.

"I meant exactly what I said. I don't have any idea where other people's loyalties are. People don't tell me what they're thinking. It might be because I'm considered to be so close to you"—she paused and the smile turned to wry resignation—"or it might not."

Hank nodded and said thank you. As the office door clicked shut behind her, he swore at himself for even bringing the whole thing up. Her job in this department was hard enough without him piling his own political needs onto it. And he'd just done exactly that. What an ass.

Vern the Verbose wanted to know if he could finish clearing his trees. The slippery elm harvest wouldn't be worth selling if he didn't get the bark out of those plastic bags and properly dried pretty darn soon, and seeing as the whole area was still roped off

with crime-scene tape, he wasn't going to start doing that without permission, because he'd seen the light and had no intention of breaking, or bending, or even slightly nudging, the law
again.

Hank stopped him there. Man, could that guy talk. He was
about to agree that Vern could start up again when he stopped
himself. It wouldn't hurt to take another look around the Miles
side of those woods first.

"Tell you what, Vern," he said into the phone, "I'll come out
and do a post-event inspection, and then you should be able to
finish the job—with properly employed labor, of course."

Five minutes of animated agreement later, Hank hung up and
decided he had enough time to grab a Reuben sandwich at the
Whipstitch Diner on his way out there. Who knew how long he'd
be stuck out in that part of the county? Maybe he'd order some
extra fries. Be prepared.

He pulled up to the yellow farmhouse to see a silver Audi SUV
parked in front. He got out, brushed salt off his shirt, and took
the porch steps up to the door. Vern opened it before he'd even
knocked.

"Hello, Sheriff. Thanks for coming out to do your inspection. I really appreciate it. Would like to get that elm taken care
of. You know. Got that property tax bill to pay. Plus, I could really
use my truck back."

Oh. Hank had forgotten that Vern's pickup was parked in the
middle of that clearing.

"So, what'd you do, borrow that?" He pointed at the Audi.

Vern snorted. "Not likely. That's my sister's. She's come
down. To help." He did not sound appreciative.

Hank hid a grin. Then realized that without Vern's truck,
they'd have to walk all the way to the clearing. The grin became
a sigh.

Vern made to step through the door but froze as a voice called from inside.

"Invite the man in, Vernie. We're not heathens."

Vern heaved his own sigh and held open the screen door for Hank. He walked through an entryway cluttered with muddy boots and two full gun racks, and into a sunny living room full of spindly furniture that Hank would wager had not been chosen by Vern.

A woman rose from the couch and came forward to shake his hand. And it was the damnedest thing. She looked exactly like Vern—but was attractive. He had no idea how genetics had managed it. She was the same height and had the same green eyes and roundish face. But where Vern's eyes seemed to pop out of his face like radioactive plutonium, hers refracted like emeralds. And the jawline that was starting to sag on Vern still held tight on his sister.

"How do you do? I'm Donna Kolpeck—Donna Miles Kolpeck. You're the sheriff?"

Hank introduced himself and sat in a wingback chair across from her as directed. There was already a pitcher of iced tea on the coffee table between them. Vern stood impatiently, shifting from foot to foot until he must have decided it was better to just give in. He sat heavily in a matching wingback and stared at his sister. As did Hank.

"I was hoping you would give us an update on your investigation, Sheriff," she said as she handed him a glass of tea. "Other than the unfortunate illegal-immigrant situation"—she glared at her brother—"there is no connection to our property, correct?"

"*My* property," Vern muttered out of the side of his mouth as Hank took a sip of tea. Amazing how that mouth and Donna's were the same, full bottom lip and turned up at the corners, and yet so different. Maybe Vern would look better with lipstick.

He pulled himself back to the conversation, where Donna was clearly waiting for a response. He cleared his throat.

"The investigation is ongoing," he said. "So, there is not much I can tell you about it at the moment. Except that I do need to inspect your clearing again before I release it back to you."

He looked at Vern as he said the last bit. No reason to get him muttering again. Vern seized the moment and rose to his feet. Hank took a final swig of his tea and stood as well. As did Donna.

"Then let's get to it," she said with a smile. Vern glared at her and stomped out of the room. Her smile widened, and she gave Hank a little shrug. He stepped back and gestured for her to go ahead of him. As she made her way toward the door, he looked around. While the coffee table and the sideboard shone, the crowded fireplace mantel and the clock busy ticking away in the corner were still covered with dust. And the olive green curtains, pulled back to let the golden Ozark sunshine in, had left tracks along the neglected pinewood floor. Vern apparently hadn't done much entertaining since moving into the family farmhouse. At least the kind that called for serving refreshments and finding a bottle of Pledge.

He took a last glance at the room and followed Donna into the entryway. Vern was wrestling a rifle out of the closest gun rack.

"You know, I don't really—" Hank stopped himself. He might not think a gun was necessary for their little hike, but Vern obviously did. He'd had one with him the first time they'd gone out to look at the elm trees. Hank couldn't make a stink about it now. That'd divulge more about Vern's status as a possible suspect than Hank was willing to say at this point. He'd just make sure that Vern stayed in front.

That didn't turn out to be a problem. Donna was in no hurry and strolled along farther and farther behind her brother, who had taken to muttering again. Hank kept with her easy pace.

"So, how often do you get down here?"

She thought for a minute. "Well, I was down when Dad died. I haven't been back since then, though. It's hard to find the time, with the kids and everything."

Hank asked how old they were. Teenagers, she said with a laugh. Fifteen and thirteen and in need of rides all over the St. Louis area for all of their various sports and activities. That, plus her interior-design business, kept her days full. And her husband was of little help. He ran a technology consulting firm, so he was just as busy.

They veered left, taking the same route Hank had walked the day he and Sam had discovered the undocumented immigrant crew. Donna kept up the conversation, chatting about the kids' Little League achievements and academic honors, her hands fluttering descriptively as she talked. She never once broke her stride on the uneven ground or shied away from a buzzing insect. For all of her citification, she was just as at home in these woods as her brother.

He asked if she'd played out here when she was a child. The question was met with another laugh as she easily sidestepped a tree root Hank hadn't even seen.

"Oh, yes. All day long in the summers. We just had to be back by dinnertime. Those were the days when parents didn't care where you were, as long as you didn't break a bone or someone else's window. Of course, we did both. Vernie broke both arms at different times. Falling out of trees, I think. I twisted a few ankles, but that was it. I was always the better one in the woods." She gave Hank a wicked grin. "And we did hit the kitchen window with a baseball once. I threw it, and Vernie should have caught it, so we both caught hell from Mama. She was standing at the sink and saw the whole thing, so there was no shifting blame on that one.

"When we could get some of the other neighbor kids, we'd

play cops and robbers. They always made me be the cop, which I hated." This time she actually stopped walking as she realized what she'd said. "Oh. I'm sorry. That was rather impolitic. But you're laughing. You're not offended?"

Hank shook his head. "Not at all. The robbers were always the more exciting ones. I never wanted to be the cop, either. Until I grew up and realized that their retirement plan is better." He shot her his own wicked grin, and they both laughed.

Vern glared back at them and kept walking. Donna, with the practiced skill of a little sister, ignored him and continued talking.

"We knew every inch of these thirty acres. We'd roam all over." She paused. "Up to the creek, that is. But then, you know that by now, don't you?"

Good. The conversation was going in exactly the direction he wanted. He shrugged nonchalantly.

"I know that's the property line. And I know that your daddy and Jasper Kinney didn't get along. I—"

Her laughter cut him off.

"Didn't get along? Sweet Jesus, that's an understatement. They hated each other. Hated. Always had. Their fathers hated each other, too. Multigenerational, I guess you could say."

She looked at Hank and answered the question he hadn't asked.

"Why?" She shrugged. "They were always going off about one encroaching on the other's property. There's a stretch upstream where the property line isn't so clearly delineated. A border war, I guess you could call it."

"So what was that like for you growing up?"

She thought for a minute. "Not much of anything, really. We couldn't cross the creek, and we weren't supposed to talk to any Kinney we happened to run into. But that's about it."

"Didn't you go to school with Jasper's boys?"

She nodded. The older two—Jeff and Jed—were around the same age. Jason was much younger. "What about his wife?"

"She was killed in a car crash, coming back from Springfield, back when Highway 65 was a two-lane death trap. Mama wanted to go to the service, but Daddy wouldn't let her. It was no wonder that no Kinney showed up for her funeral, or for Daddy's."

They had almost caught up with Vern, who had reached the edge of the clearing and whipped around toward them at her last comment. His rifle swung through the air. Hank tensed.

"They wouldn't have dared. Those bastards. Especially Jasper. Probably ecstatic that he outlived Daddy. Sitting over there"—he waved the gun in the direction of the creek—"laughing at us. I'll bet—"

Hank grabbed the rifle barrel with his right hand and gently patted Vern's shoulder with his left as he eased it away. "I'm just going to set this here, by this tree. Just for now." One last pat and the gun was safely out of Vern's grasp and leaning against a naked elm.

He opened his mouth to protest, but the sound came from his sister.

"Oh, my Lord," she gasped. "The trees. What have you done? Our poor trees."

Vern began to turn a worrying shade of purple. "*My* trees."

Donna didn't hear him as she ducked under the crime-scene tape and walked slowly into the clearing. Vern followed her, stiff-legged and straight-backed. Hank stayed by the rifle.

"How could you—"

"I'm not the one who stripped them. I'm just trying to salvage—"

The next ten minutes involved a lot of yelling, some pointed gesturing, and frequent use of the word "my." Hank used the time to tuck the rifle, the same old .22 Vern had carried before, behind a sizable hickory tree a short way down the path. He then walked the perimeter of the clearing, snapping photos of the machinery and piles of trees.

Finally, the siblings' hollering petered out. He had a feeling the argument was far from finished, though. Donna walked over and placed a careful hand on one of the few stripped elms left standing. Vern stomped up to his pickup, slumped against the tailgate, and shot his sister a dirty look.

"She's probably gonna hug it next." He sounded like a eight-year-old.

Hank leaned against the truck's rusty fender.

"Do you two usually not get along?"

Vern rubbed the stubble on his chin and took a deep breath, which helped return his coloring to its normal sunburned shade. "Nah. We're okay most of the time. There's never been something like this to divide us, though. She doesn't get it. I want to keep this land just as bad as she does. But to save it, I've got to make a business of it. Otherwise—"

Hank put up a hand as he started to gesticulate again.

"Oh. Yeah, sorry." Vern shoved his hands in his jean pockets and gave Hank a lopsided grin. "The two of us haven't argued like that in years. We used to go at it like two roosters in the ring, though. When we were little. But then . . ." He looked down at his boots. "Then my little brother got cancer. We didn't argue much anymore after he died." He shrugged. "And that's that, I suppose."

Hank helped him fill the bed of the pickup with the sweet-smelling bark and then gathered up his crime-scene tape. Donna stood scowling the whole time, and declined a ride back to the house. She'd rather walk. Hank, relieved that he wouldn't have to spend the trip sandwiched between the two combatants on the front seat, climbed in. He needed to get back to the office.

Halfway into the truck, Vern froze. Damn. He'd remembered his rifle. Hank sighed and got out of the truck. He retrieved it and nonchalantly stuck it in the bed with the bark. Vern grunted and got in the cab.

"I usually put it on the seat with me," he said. "Since you're sitting there, though . . . maybe I should put in a gun rack." He pondered the back window for a moment and then fired up the engine. Hank didn't tell him that he wouldn't have allowed the gun up front even if there had been a gun rack in the cab.

"Daddy left me quite a collection of them when he died. Course, you couldn't have too many guns, living so close to the Kinneys. That was his philosophy." He pulled out of the clearing on the opposite side from which they'd entered and onto the rutted track that led back to the farmhouse. He waved back toward the truck bed. "That one was a gift from him. Brought me out here on my twelfth birthday and gave it to me. It's a Remington 552 .22-caliber. He told me that I was never, ever, to come out here by the border unless I had it with me. And I never have."

CHAPTER
14

Hank was almost late for the appointment the next morning. He parked in back of the strip mall and entered through door number five. That let him into the break room, where the Keurig sat quietly on its shelf and the *Daily What's-It* lay open on the table. He skirted the table and walked down the short hallway, where he could wait without being seen from the shop. Dan Larkson had set one of the break room chairs there for him to use. Hank liked this guy more and more all the time.

Hank had originally planned to show up for Lloyd's tattoo appointment as part of the investigation into the bark theft. But now, that was the least of his priorities. He had a homicide that needed solving, and he had to wonder—did the brothers who likely stole from Kinney's land also commit murder there?

He didn't suspect the Taylor boys in the death of Little Doe. That skeleton was probably older than any of those yahoos. Plus, they didn't know yet how the child had died. But Rotten Doe— that could be a greedy accomplice, or a rival bark thief, or a—

The bell on the shop door chimed. He stopped theorizing

and started paying attention as something heavy thunked onto the counter.

"You paying in cash again?" Larkson asked.

"Yeah." And then the rustling of a grocery sack and a series of smaller thumps.

"Damn," Larkson said. "How much is that?"

"Fifteen hundred. I want as much of the sleeve, plus color on this other arm one, as you can do today. Now. Let's go."

There was a noise that sounded like Lloyd making to come around the counter toward a chair, but Larkson must have stopped him.

"Dude. Hold up. I thought you didn't have all the money. How'd, uh, how'd you manage it?"

Nice. Maybe. As long as he didn't go overboard, Hank thought. Don't press too much.

"I mean, I'm stoked to do the whole thing," Larkson continued as if he'd heard what Hank was thinking. "But, man. That's a lot of cash all in one place. It's pretty sweet."

Now they were moving away from the counter and toward one of the chairs. Lloyd snorted with laughter. "You bet your ass it's sweet. You're lucky I chose you. Otherwise some other tat dude'd be seein' all that money." He settled into the chair, his skin squeaking against the cushioning. Hank figured the odds were good he was wearing another wife beater.

Larkson started fiddling with his equipment, the metal instruments clinking against one another. "Yeah, the only other time I've seen a bunch of money like that in a sack was this bank robbery movie. Couple of summers ago. I don't remember the name of it. Had that guy in it that was in that old TV show . . ."

They spent five minutes nailing down the film title, while Hank shifted in his chair and hoped Larkson could bring the conversation back around to where Taylor had gotten his money.

After a brief detour into both of their hopes for another Fast and Furious street-car-racing movie, Larkson fired up his liner motor and steered things back in the right direction.

"You didn't do something as cool as that, did you?" he asked Lloyd. "Racing and stealing cars all over the world and hanging with beautiful women? Walk away with a bag of cash?"

Oh, the guy was good. Hank was tempted to offer him a job right then and there.

Lloyd snorted another laugh. "Nah. I'm just a delivery driver," he said in a tone that quite clearly implied the opposite. "I drive truckloads of plants. For people stupid enough to pay for them."

Hank leaned forward to try to hear Larkson better over the whine of the motor.

". . . parts of the country, plants can be a dangerous business. We're not in Colorado where it's legal, you know."

"Man, I don't do that. There's not as much money in that anymore. It's all in that herbal sh—"

The sound of the needle equipment stuttered suddenly. Larkson grunted. Hank rose quickly to his feet.

"What the hell are you up to, Tats? You seem too damn interested in my money." There was a smack and another grunt as Hank drew his gun and rounded the doorjamb.

Lloyd's right arm with its incomplete sleeve was still strapped to the chair. He was bringing his free left one back for another punch to the tattoo artist's face. Hank leveled his Glock just as Larkson raised his own weapon.

"I don't think so, asshole." And Larkson sank the motorized needle into Lloyd's shoulder.

He stepped away and picked up his hand towel as Hank walked forward, his gun still pointed at Lloyd.

"Did you get what you needed?" Larkson asked over the high-pitched screaming coming from the chair.

"It's definitely a start," Hank said. "And with what he just did to you, we can make him a guest of the Branson County Jail for a while, that's for sure." He looked at Larkson's face. "Sorry about your eye."

"Eh. I guess I wasn't as subtle as I thought I was being." He grinned.

So did Hank. "No, you did great. If this tattoo thing doesn't work out, let me know. I might have some detective work for you."

He holstered his gun and pointed at Lloyd, who was now crying and trying to get the needle out of his right shoulder while his arm was still strapped to the chair. "Will that come out?"

"Yeah," Larkson said. "I'll get it out of him. Mostly cuz I'm going to want my liner back.

"He can keep the needle."

Hank hated this place. Much more than he'd ever hated the morgue in Kansas City. And he couldn't figure out why. Maybe it was just unfamiliarity. This was only his second time here. He'd already made one wrong turn. He stopped at an intersection of hallways and sighed.

"That way." An elderly woman with a volunteer badge pinned to her crisp white button-down shirt pointed to the left as she passed him in the corridor.

"What?" he said.

"The morgue's that way." She smiled when she saw his puzzled stare. "Anybody with that horrible look on their face is looking for that place." She gave him a pat on the shoulder and a little shove. "Go on, then. It'll be okay."

He sighed again and trudged down the corridor until he found the correct set of doors.

"Sorry I'm late."

Dr. Whittaker chortled as he pranced around his desk to shake Hank's hand. "Don't worry about it. He's not going anywhere."

Hank appreciated a sense of humor as much as anybody in this business, but there was something about Michael Whittaker that just wasn't funny. He'd been the medical examiner in southern Missouri for decades, though, and Hank was stuck with him.

Whittaker whipped two surgical masks out of a box and a jar of VapoRub out of a drawer.

"You're going to need these for this guy. Whoowee. Very ripe."

Hank swiped a streak under his nose, strapped on the mask, and followed the roly-poly doctor through the main morgue area and into the exam room reserved for homicides and suspicious deaths. The doc slid open the cooler, and he stared down at the mess of a human being.

It was a male measured at five feet eleven inches and 184 pounds, give or take. There was no gray in a full head of hair, so he likely was not too old, Whittaker said. Otherwise, the identifying characteristics of the face were completely destroyed, by both the decomp and that illegal kid falling on it. Same went for the chest cavity, which now had snapped ribs and a bunch of mush where the organs were supposed to be.

"He must have fallen from a pretty good height to cause that kind of damage," Whittaker said. "Then it looks like he did a jig on the body, because everything is all torn up. No respect for evidence."

"Well," Hank said through gritted teeth, "he was actually trying to get off it. It was in a fairly confined space."

"Eh," Whittaker said. "Shoulda been more careful."

Hank tried to keep his voice neutral as he asked how long Rotten Doe had been dead. Whittaker flipped through his chart.

"Your techs measured the temperature at the bottom of the fissure at ten degrees cooler than the surface air. So assuming that's a constant deviation, it probably took the body about ten days to reach that state. Give or take a couple days."

Well, that narrowed it down. A not-old, not-fat male, five feet eleven, dead anywhere from one to three weeks. Whittaker snapped the file shut and informed Hank that he had several bodies ahead of Mr. Doe. He'd probably get to the full autopsy in a day or two. Hank spun on his heel and left the room before he added to the morgue's body count. The jerk could have told him that before he drove all the way up here to Springfield. He ripped off his mask, used it to wipe off the VapoRub, and stomped out to his car.

He pulled into his space at the office in Forsyth and saw Sam pacing the sidewalk. He pounced as soon as Hank got out of the car.

"You arrested him? Really?" he said, bouncing on the balls of his enormous feet. "Awesome. Do we have enough for a search warrant? For their land?" He bounced some more. "We could finally get back there, see what's in the darn woods. Oooh, meth bust, here I come—"

Hank held up a hand to slow his deputy down and to keep himself from laughing. "Hold on. Let's get him in front of a judge first. Hopefully we can get bail set high enough on the assault of the tattoo guy that he can't make it—seeing as I seized his bag of cash this morning. Then we'll focus on trying to get in to search the property. Have you figured out any of the other herbal businesses he drives for?"

No companies other than Old Mountain Natural Herbs had admitted to Sam that they used Taylor as a delivery driver. And all the companies he talked to were being very tight with their lists of local drivers and growers. Kept blathering on about security concerns, Sam said with an eye roll.

"You'd think they were mining gold instead of growing weeds," Sam growled. "I told them all that they had a day to rethink themselves into a more cooperative position, or I was calling a deputy attorney general friend of mine and asking for agricultural and environmental investigations into their business practices."

Hank looked at him in surprise. Sam wasn't usually that heavy-handed. "Nice. Good job. And I didn't know you knew somebody in the AG's office."

Sam rubbed at the back of his neck. "Well, no. Not exactly. I did meet some lady AG at a training class last year. I think she was in Medicaid fraud, though." He grinned at his boss. "But you always say, what they don't know . . ."

Hank burst out laughing. His eager Pup was coming along quite well. As a reward, he told him about Taylor getting stabbed by the tattoo artist. That had Sam bouncing again as he gleefully volunteered to check on the new inmate's medical care.

"Just don't 'accidentally' poke him in the shoulder while you're there," Hank said as Sam headed to the jail, and he turned toward his office.

Where Darcy Blakely sat waiting for him.

She stood as he entered and folded her hands in front of her. She looked as poised and put-together as usual, except for the tightening around her mouth that Hank had come to associate with his presence.

He stopped in the doorway.

"I am here to offer my resignation—well, first, I'm here to apologize. And then to offer my resignation," she said.

That was not what he'd expected. After getting pounded by Maggie for the past three days that he couldn't fire her, now here she was quitting.

He opened his mouth and then shut it because he couldn't think of anything to say. Instead, he walked around his desk and sat in his chair. She sank into the one opposite, straightened her pale pink skirt, and held his gaze steadily.

Great. He'd thought this would be a quick phone call, and

he'd end it with a feeling of relief. Now—not so much. He started to run his hand through his hair, but froze halfway. She smiled.

"Well, at least I've had some positive impact."

He lowered his hand. "Yes, you have. You have done a lot. And I thank you. I—" He stopped. He should think of it like a witness interview. He knew how to handle those.

"Can I ask you why you're resigning?"

"You haven't contacted me since the Rotary lunch. You obviously aren't interested in me trying to crisis-manage the situation. Someone else can perhaps better advise you about responding to the allegations. I will of course hand over all of the campaign volunteer lists and—"

"Wait—what? Allegations? What allegations?" He half rose out of his seat before catching himself and sitting back down. Darcy bit back a sigh, and her perfect posture slumped a little. Hank cringed.

"Do you not pay attention to anything? Really?" she asked. "You haven't heard about the radio interview? That Tucker did yesterday?"

Hank shook his head slowly. He thought about pointing out that he had two death investigations going on and they were certainly justifiable cause to have missed a campaign item. But he risked a look at Darcy and decided to keep his mouth shut.

She shoved her designer glasses back up her nose with untypical haste and leaned forward. "Tucker gave an interview with Dick Battenberg on the AM Christian station that broadcasts out of downtown. He called you a carpetbagger and a bad cop who cared more about campaigning than solving crimes—which I was expecting, honestly—but then he said you also screwed up the Mandy Bryson murder case, *and* were involved in criminal behavior when you were up at Mizzou. *And* that you're Mexican."

Hank blinked. That was about all he could do. They stared

at each other for what felt like several minutes. She looked as pissed off as he felt, at least.

"It's not true," he finally said. "None of it. You know that. He can't say any of it. That's slander."

She sighed again. "No, that's a campaign. And you need to refute all of it, immediately. The longer it sits out there unchallenged, the worse it is."

It couldn't get much worse than that. What had they dug up about his college days in Columbia? And they'd obviously figured out his mother was a Mexican immigrant. And— "What about Mandy Bryson? Screwed up her case? What the hell? The guy's already pleaded guilty. I got him to confess, damn it. How the hell is that screwing it up?" He realized he was yelling, and coming out of his chair again. He stopped both and tried counting to ten. It didn't work. Darcy let him go on for a while at slightly lower volume before she interrupted.

"Tucker said that the guy should have gone to trial," she said. "That the people of Branson County deserved to have the whole truth come out in public. Otherwise how are they to know that you got it right, because you probably got it wrong."

"He confessed!" The volume was back up. "I investigated, I proved it was him, and I got him to confess. Then he admitted it in court, which is a public forum, or doesn't that asshole know that? He—"

Darcy stopped him again. "That is the least of the three, frankly. We can prove that Roy Stanton pleaded guilty to murder. That the crime was solved while you were sheriff and the lead investigator. That should be enough to dampen it at least. It's the other two things I'm worried about."

Hank scowled. "What did he say about the stuff at Mizzou?"

"That's just it. He didn't say anything specific—just criminal conduct," she said, and then leaned forward. "What did you do?"

Just the one thing that St. Patrick's Day when he was a soph-omore . . .

"There . . . might have been some activities that seemed per-fectly valid at the time, which . . . might now be considered questionable as I look back on them."

Darcy groaned. Then she giggled. Hank flinched. Had he finally sent her over the edge? She giggled and giggled, fishing a tissue out of her laptop bag and dabbing at her eyes. "Oh, my. This is horrible. It will almost surely bite us in the ass. But, my dear, that was an absolutely perfect politician response. Perfect. I'm very impressed."

Hank slumped down in his chair in defeat.

"So, essentially, I just have to try every weasely way I can think of to not get you mad at me? Talk like that, and it's all good?"

"Well, it's better at least," she said. "We've still got a lot to do, though."

It took Hank only a split second to agree. His resentment over the Rotary luncheon was no match for how much he suddenly needed her help. He grinned at her. "You said 'we.' Does that mean you're not resigning?"

She tucked her blond hair behind her ears and adjusted her glasses. "I suppose it does. I can't let this go unanswered. It wouldn't look good. Plus, no one else on God's green earth would take you now. So, yes, I'm not resigning."

Hank tried not to look too relieved. They both rose from their seats, and he walked her to the door.

"Wait." She stopped short. "The Mexican thing. Is that true?"

"We talked about that," he said.

"No. No, no. We talked about you being from California. We did *not* talk about you being from Mexico. You didn't men-tion that."

"I'm not from Mexico. My mother is. She immigrated here

with her parents when she was four years old. She is a naturalized citizen. So are my grandparents."

That tightening around her mouth was back.

"That would have been pertinent to tell me, don't you think? Around here? To have that kind of ancestry?"

Hank doubted his mother would appreciate being called an "ancestor." And he didn't much appreciate being called a "Mexican" as if it were a dirty word. That must have been apparent from the look that crossed his face, because she quickly put up her hand in a "stop" motion.

"Just hold it. I am not maligning your heritage. Or calling you a dirty name. I am trying to work within the realities of the situation. And that situation is southern Missouri. Where, in case you haven't noticed, there aren't many Mexicans. And the ones there are, sure as heck can't vote."

How was it that this woman could send him from even-keeled to completely pissed off in less time than it took to exit a room? He scowled. "As a voting bloc, they're referred to as Latino."

She rolled her eyes. "I know that. You've got to have a thicker skin. You can't take this as a personal attack. That's what they want. We'll come up with some way to deflect it—try to say it's not a big deal. I'll figure that out. But you"—she jabbed a finger at his chest—"have to do your part. Keep your temper."

She left him standing there trying to do just that.

CHAPTER

15

The heat had just started, slightly earlier than usual. It shouldn't affect the grape vines too much. And for her tomatoes, it was wonderful, she told him. They would be *abundante*. She would send him salsa.

Hank leaned back in his chair and let the Spanish wash over him. How an accident just off the freeway had caused a detour right past the front gate. How the parish was almost done raising money for the new parish hall. How that friend of his from high school had just joined the Chamber of Commerce. How she missed him and her grandbabies. He hung up his cell phone feeling more at peace than he had in weeks. *Gracias, Mamá.*

"How's your mom?" Maggie sat down on the other end of the couch and tossed their battered copies of *Sheep in a Jeep* and *Goodnight Moon* onto the coffee table.

"Good. She says hi. Wanted to know how many lives you've saved since she talked to you last."

Maggie burst out laughing. "Really?"

"Yeah. She won't admit it, but I think she uses it as ammo in the bragging wars with the other ladies in the women's group at church."

"I love your mom." She stretched out along the couch, and Hank automatically drew her feet onto his lap and started rubbing. He stopped when she jerked back.

"Ow. Just not that spot. I've got a blister. I had to switch to dress flats today. My tennis shoes got trashed."

"You get blood on them again?"

"No. Vomit this time. Which is definitely worse. At least blood doesn't stink. They went straight in a biowaste bag." Hank gingerly took his hands off her feet and looked over at her. She gave him a lazy grin. "I washed them, silly, don't worry."

A loud snort came from behind them and they turned to see Dunc and Guapo. It was unclear which one had made the noise.

"You two finally have a night off together and you're in here talking about bodily fluids. Only in this house." He shook his head and shuffled off toward the stairs and his basement bedroom. Guapo contemplated his retreating back before deciding that the people on the couch had more attention potential. He waddled around and planted himself in front of Maggie. She gave him a pat, but kept her attention on Hank.

"At least we're talking," she said.

He concentrated on her feet for a while before finally speaking. "Yeah. I didn't like that, either. I'm sorry I didn't let it go. I just . . ." He shrugged.

Maggie looked at her husband, and her face softened. "I know, babe, I know." She drew her legs up and snuggled in next to him. He put his arms around her.

"And I'm not going to fire Darcy."

She drew back and stared at him in surprise. She hadn't expected his apology to extend to his campaign manager.

"I thought about it, and . . . you had some good points, and she does work really hard, so . . ."

There'd be ample time later to tell her about the Tucker radio interview. For now, quiet on the couch was enough.

Cigarette smoke still hung in the air. Kinney must have passed this way recently. Hank stopped at the edge of the woods and looked back toward the house, sitting low and silent in the clearing. He could guess at the original cabin front—a rough log wall on the left side of the structure sitting on top of a stone foundation—and wondered how many generations ago the Kinney clan had claimed this land in the Ozarks. And what they were doing with it now.

He took a last glance, then turned back to the trees. And froze. Jasper Kinney stood two feet away, unlit cigarette dangling from his mouth and twelve-gauge cradled in his arm. Jesus. Hank hadn't heard him at all. Nothing. Not a rustle of leaves or snap of a twig. He still made no sound as he stared at Hank. The only noise was the rush of blood in Hank's ears. He felt a little faint, actually. Thank God he hadn't stepped back or done something else to show that he'd almost startled out of his skin.

He slowly hooked his left thumb on his belt and relaxed his right arm down by his side, and his gun. A study in nonchalance. Kinney didn't buy it. He smirked, sending his cigarette dancing along his lips. He stopped it in the middle of his mouth and used the hand not holding the H&R Topper shotgun to reach into his shirt pocket and extract a book of matches. In a quick single-hand motion, he somehow pulled one free and dropped the book back in his pocket. Then he raked the match along his angular, stubbled jawline. It flared to life and Kinney, never taking his eyes from Hank's face, calmly lit his cigarette.

Jee-zus.

Kinney dropped the still-aflame match in the dirt and ground it into submission. Then he stilled his rail-thin body and gave Hank a look that quite plainly said he'd like to do the same to his county's duly appointed sheriff.

Hank bit back a sigh. Kinney might have all day, but he didn't. He'd have to speak first. Hell, he'd already lost the manliness competition, clearly.

"We are still examining your woods where the body was found. Our search warrant has been extended for an additional week. Do you need to see a copy of it?"

Kinney held out his hand. Hank drew the document out of his own shirt pocket and waited while Creosote examined it. He half expected the guy to light it on fire. But he gave it back to Hank and resumed his stance. Hank was forced to walk around him to access the path that led to the crime scene, almost stumbling as he hit a rotten stump.

Pissing contest: Creosote, 2; Worth, 0.

Descending into hell was almost a welcome diversion. He swung gently as they lowered him into the fissure. Alice had excavated up to what looked like the clavicle on the left side of the skeleton. The right arm and collarbone remained buried, as did a few ribs and most of the skull. Hank settled in and got to work. From above, he could hear Sam and the relief sentry chatting as they examined Bill Ramsdell's camping equipment. It was apparently good stuff, because both deputies sounded quite envious as they poked through it all. Some fancy kind of camp stove had them especially appreciative.

He'd sent Bill home that morning with orders not to return until night fell. The guy had seemed almost disappointed. Hank was just glad he had a deputy willing to camp out every night until the crime scene was cleared.

"Oh, he's always been like that," Deputy Orvan said in response to a question from Sam that Hank hadn't quite heard. "Known him since we were in junior high. Always rather be outdoors than in. His gear's sure improved, though. I remember a canoeing trip down the Buffalo River in high school where we turned it upside down and used it as a lean-to shelter because we didn't have a tent." He chuckled. "We did have beer, though, so nobody much cared."

That led to a spirited discussion about prime canoeing spots that kept Hank's mind occupied as his hands carefully uncovered Little Doe's broken right ribs. By the time he'd finished with those, Sam had gone back to the station and Orvan sounded like he was organizing the supplies Alice had left up top. Hank sat back on his heels and pondered what was left.

The right arm was almost completely covered with soil. The body had probably come to rest with it wedged underneath the torso. The weight and the many years had compacted the earth well. Just above where he'd removed the collarbone, the skull lay at an angle because the cervical vertebrae had settled and come apart. He snapped several photos and then prodded at the bones. They were pretty well trapped in the dirt, so he gently nudged the skull. The ground's hold was looser there, and the yellowed dome rocked under his fingers. He sighed. He hadn't wanted to do this yet. But better him than Alice.

He gathered his brushes and leaned forward into a crouch, ignoring his cranky back. The black sockets soon stared back at him, and then the smile emerged. He shifted and began to work around the crown, loosening soil as he slowly freed the rest of the skull from the earth. Finally, he was able to lift it up. The last clump of dirt fell off as he rotated it gently, one hand supporting the jawbone. He turned it further and stopped.

In a way, he was relieved. Little Doe hadn't died a slow, agonizing death of starvation at the bottom of a fissure. It had been quick. A bullet to the back of the head will do that.

Before Hank could say anything, Sheila reached across her desk and handed him a list of names in Sam's handwriting. Five men and one woman of various ages who drove for herbal companies in southern Missouri. Three had notations that they were out of state with their primary trucking jobs when the bark thefts occurred. One was halfway through a six-month stint for domestic violence in a jail two counties over. And one had been in the middle of delivering herbs to his company's plant in Colorado. The weeklong trip took place right as Vern Miles reported the theft. Sam had scribbled "unlikely" next to that name.

The last man, Forsyth resident Ned Bunning, had only question marks next to his name. Hank frowned.

"Yeah, I know," Sheila said. "Sam couldn't find him. His primary employer hasn't needed him for the past two months, and so has no idea where he is. And the address listed on his DL is a little duplex that Sam says looks lived in, but nobody in the neighborhood has seen him in more than a week. So him and Lloyd Taylor are the two herb drivers without alibis."

Hank stared at the list. "And we know that Lloyd is alive. We don't necessarily know that about Mr. Bunning, do we?"

Sheila leaned back in her desk chair and folded her arms.

"And you say I'm the one with a dim view of humanity," she said. "Here you are accusing some poor guy of stealing bark and getting killed over it."

"Not accusing. Just theorizing," he said. "But, yeah, my view of humanity is pretty dim at the moment." He tossed a clear plastic evidence bag onto her desk.

"It's a bullet."

Hank nodded.

She poked at the bag with one long, slender finger, and then looked at him—really looked at him—for the first time that evening.

"You're all dirty. You—wait. Oh, no. Little Doe?"

He nodded again.

She slowly put her hand over the bag and pressed lightly.

"That poor baby. Where?"

He explained the entry wound in the skull and his fine-tooth combing of the underlying dirt. The bullet hadn't been far, at least.

"I thought you'd want to be the one to change the designation on the file," he said.

She picked up the bag. "Yeah. I do." She raised it up to the fluorescent light. "You're not a death investigation anymore, kiddo. You're a homicide. And we're going to solve you."

She gave Hank a grim smile and picked up a pen to log the evidence.

"Now get out of here. You're getting dirt on my desk."

He hadn't realized he'd been holding his breath until then. He let it out in a relieved gust as he left the room, basking in her surliness. Maybe that meant things were back to normal.

CHAPTER
16

He'd fallen asleep with the heating pad on his back, and as the smoke alarm jolted him awake, he thought for a split second it had caught fire. It hadn't, and he bolted out of bed and ran down the hall toward the yelling in the kitchen. The skillet on the stove was shooting flames, and a Scotsman in a bathrobe was struggling with an upside-down fire extinguisher.

Hank spun around, saw the open package of bacon on the floor, ripped one of Maggie's decorative copper lids off the wall, and slammed it down on the burning pan. Then he grabbed the container of salt on the shelf above the range and dumped it on the grease that had spilled out onto the stove. The last of the flames immediately disappeared. He turned off the gas burner and backed away. Then he looked for his kids, whose screams and the dog's howls he could barely hear over the horrible peal of the alarm. He reached for it and jabbed the button, but the smoke was too thick to allow it to turn off. The sound was like a cleaver in his brain.

He yanked the fire extinguisher out of Dunc's hands, hefted it, and smashed it hard and fast into the circular case. Silence.

He lowered the extinguisher and turned to the kitchen table, where Duncan now stood with the kids, Guapo cowering at their feet. Benny was crying and clutching the bottle of syrup. Maribel looked close to hyperventilating. When Hank reached for her, she bolted out of the room, sobbing as she ran down the hall.

He scooped up Benny and turned to his father-in-law.

"What. The. Hell?"

Dunc collapsed into a chair, his robe askew and his thin gray hair sticking out in every direction. "Sweet Lord above. I couldn't get the damn thing to work. It jammed . . ."

Hank bit back a growl. "Good thing," he snapped. "You smother a grease fire. An extinguisher is the last resort. It could have blown the flames all over the place."

Dunc seemed to crumple even more. "Oh. I didn't know that."

He apparently didn't know how to cook bacon, either, without turning it into an inferno. Hank shot a glance at the stove to make sure the fire was still out and set Benny down.

"You think you can get him some Cheerios without setting anything else on fire? I need to go check on Maribel."

Dunc looked like he'd just taken a punch. He nodded and reached for Benny, gently stroking his grandson's sandy brown hair. "Come on, big guy. Everything's going to be okay," Hank heard him whisper as he left the kitchen.

He followed the sobs back to Maribel's room. She was huddled in a corner with her favorite stuffed animal. He knelt down next to her and patted the purple rabbit on the head.

"Honey? Everything's fine. The fire is out. It's not going to hurt you."

She drew away and squeezed herself into an even tighter ball. He spent five minutes coaxing her out, until she finally climbed onto his lap and buried her head in his shoulder. He was puzzled. She was usually able to shake things off pretty well. It was unlike her to be upset for more than a few minutes over anything. Even her fourth-birthday party, where Benny had demolished her My Little Pony cake in the split-second no one was watching—she'd raged for about the amount of time it took to haul Benny to his room for a time-out. Then she'd been off and playing with her friends again.

Granted, that calamity hadn't involved the possibility of the house going up in flames, Hank told himself. He wished Maggie weren't at work. She was better at the comforting thing than he was. He rocked his girl until she got her breath back and then he pulled her away so she could see his face.

"Sweetheart? It's okay. I know it was scary, but nobody got hurt. It was an accident. Grandpop didn't mean to do it. And it won't happen ag—" He stopped as she let out a wail that sounded almost as loud as the smoke alarm had. He bent forward and looked her directly in the eye. "All right. Enough. What is going on?"

She clamped her lips together and the noise mercifully stopped. Her teary brown eyes widened as she looked at him.

"I . . . I did it. It's my fault. I wanted . . ." She trailed off. Hank waited and tried to put on his impassive suspect-interview face, but found it a good deal harder to do when the suspect was clutching a lavender bunny.

"I wanted to turn on the knob. By myself. Grandpop . . . he said I couldn't. That he needed to clean something up." More tears. "I did it anyway. I . . . I wanted to hear the clicks. I . . . I'm sorry." She buried her face in his T-shirt.

Well.

He took a long breath and thought about what to do. What was the appropriate discipline when your five-year-old started a grease fire that ruined at least one skillet, a copper lid, a smoke detector—okay, technically he was the one who'd smashed that— and a whole lot of bacon? He sighed and patted Hoppy on the head again. It did not make him feel better, but it seemed to help Maribel. She gave him a cautious smile and wiped her nose with the back of her hand.

He tried to remember what Maggie had said about that parenting book she was reading. He probably should have paid more attention.

"Um, okay." Something about taking responsibility. "You know what you did was wrong, right?"

She nodded.

"And what do you think you should do now?"

Her little face scrunched up in thought.

"I should help fix it," she finally said. "I can sweep the stuff that fell on the floor." She looked at him hesitantly and he nodded encouragement. "And help wash the dishes that got burnt. Oh—and say sorry to Grandpop."

Hank nodded again and lifted her up off his lap. He needed to go say sorry to Grandpop, too.

It took an hour to clean up the stove. With Dunc's endorsement, he had Maribel "wash" the skillet, even though they both knew it was now unusable and would have to be trashed once she wasn't looking. Then they took a look at Maggie's ornamental lid, which had acquired several not-so-decorative scorch marks on the inside. Neither one of them had any idea how to clean it. So they hung it back on the wall.

The dropped package of bacon had disappeared. As had the dog. Hank left Dunc to solve the mystery of which piece of furniture the damn mutt was hiding under with his prize, and went to work.

He was almost there when his cell rang. The caller ID said *Padre*.

"Hi, Father Tony."

"There is a problem, my friend."

"Javier?" His *pájaro*?

No, no, the priest said. Javier was fine. Luckily, he had still been in bed when the visitors arrived this morning. So they had not seen him. "They" were two Branson County commissioners. And one of them had been quite impolite.

"Let me guess. He was named Fizzel," Hank said.

Oh, yes, said Father Tony. Edrick Fizzel had been there. He had wanted to know if the church was sheltering illegal aliens. He had replied that in God's eyes, no one was an alien. This had caused Mr. Fizzel to turn an interesting shade of red. Almost magenta. Father Tony had been a little concerned, but it soon became evident that his coloring was not the result of a physical ailment. Father Tony had an opinion about whether it was indicative of a moral one, but he was going to refrain from commenting further on his suspicion.

Hank grinned and steered the conversation back on topic. The commissioners had come to him, Tony said, because they had heard about a large group of illegals found in the northern part of the county.

"What? Did they think you have them there with you?" Hank asked.

"I think they do not know what they think, so they came to see the first Spanish speaker they could find," Tony said.

They did stop short of accusing Tony of harboring fugitives. They did not use such restraint when they brought up Hank, however. They said they did not trust local law enforcement to handle the problem. Tony had asked them why, and Mr. Fizzel had launched into an unkind litany of Hank's perceived failings. He had considered correcting the commissioner on several points, but decided that it would be more helpful to let the man go on so that he could find out exactly what kind of dirt he was shoveling. The stuff Tony listed off sounded a lot like the crap Tucker had ranted about in that radio interview.

"Why does he dislike you so much, my friend? Was he not one of those who appointed you sheriff in the first place?"

Oh, yes, Hank said, he sure was. But then Hank had tangled

with Henry Gallagher and found out that the commissioner had a mutually beneficial relationship with the county's leading businessman. Gallagher paid Fizzel's son a small fortune for a job as a routine clerical worker. In return, Fizzel looked out for the interests of Gallagher Enterprises with the devoted zeal of a yappy terrier. And he had yapped plenty during the Bryson murder case last February, interfering with Hank's investigation as it zeroed in on his benefactor.

Gallagher Enterprises had owned the showboat where the victim was found and that was destroyed soon afterward in an explosion—a big, fiery one that got rid of a barely afloat vessel and the responsibility for the many old, sick, and expensive-to-insure employees who lost their jobs when it sank. Hank was sure that Gallagher had ordered the destruction, even though fire marshals had ruled it an accident.

"I have a parishioner who lost her job when the *Branson Beauty* sank," Tony said. "It makes me very unhappy to hear that it was a deliberate act." He was silent for a moment. "And now, Mr. Fizzel is back, trying again to make you look bad. Hmm. I do not think it will work with most of what he said. People will see it for what it is."

Hank forced a chuckle. "You have more faith in people than I do, Padre."

"Well," Tony said with a smile in his voice, "that is my job."

Hank laughed genuinely this time. "I thought your job was to have faith in God," he teased.

"No," he said softly, "that faith is my privilege."

Touché.

There was a shuffling in the background, and a muffled *buenos días* as Tony covered the phone.

"Ah, now I must go," he said. "Both the cat and the boy need feeding." They set a time for Hank to come and interview Javier, and Hank thanked the priest for his call.

"*De nada*," said Father Tony. "Please take care of yourself, *mi amigo, y Vaya con Dios.*"

After a day of bone excavation and a dinner of soggy pasta and scorch-mark explanations, Hank left Maggie to bedtime-story duty and retrieved the stack of missing-children files he'd stuck in the corner of the living room. He would have rather read *Barnyard Dance* for the thousandth time. At least that had an ending. The sad collections of paperwork in front of him did not.

There were five cases. Once he knew Little Doe's age and gender, he could narrow it down considerably, but that wouldn't mean anything if the dead child wasn't local. The skeleton could be from anywhere. He sighed and opened up the first folder.

An eleven-year-old girl from Kirbyville. Missing since August 20, 1960. Taken from a parking lot while the parent's back was turned. Suspect was a local delivery driver, never charged.

A six-year-old boy from an unincorporated Branson neighborhood. Reported April 14, 1985. But no one outside the family had seen him for a week prior to that. Both parents questioned extensively and passed polygraph tests.

A nine-year-old boy from Rockaway Beach. June 5, 1976. Disappeared from the shore of Lake Taneycomo during a family outing. Multiple suspects. Not enough evidence to arrest anyone.

A seven-year-old girl from the city of Branson. July 12, 1993. Playing in her backyard. No suspects.

An eight-year-old girl from near Forsyth. February 22, 1994. Walking home from school in a snowstorm. Suspect, not arrested for lack of evidence, was an uncle who died two years later.

He closed the last of the folders and sat back. Each of the files was at least five inches thick. All of the disappearances had been exhaustively—desperately—investigated. And all of them had ended up in the same place. On a shelf, in record storage rooms, gathering dust. And he knew there were dozens more through-out the state. Just as dusty and just as impossible.

He gave himself a shake. He'd get information from the forensic anthropologists, narrow down the possibilities, and start getting DNA swabs from relatives. He could—he would—at least identify the bones. And allow someone the dignity of a burial.

"Oh. Sorry. I didn't know you were in here working," said Dunc as he walked in.

"No. It's fine. There's not much more I can do until I hear from the bone experts anyway."

"Is it that kid skeleton?"

"Yeah. Just looking through some files of kids it could possibly be."

Dunc sank into his easy chair by the fireplace and gestured toward the stack on the coffee table. "Is the Alton girl in there?"

The Branson PD case. Melissa Alton. He nodded.

"That was a big one. There were search parties and everything. She was in Marian's friend Judy's second-grade class. Tore Judy up something fierce."

Hank considered his father-in-law. "Did Judy ever say anything about it? What she thought happened?"

Dunc kicked off his slippers and flipped out his footrest. "Let's see. Not to me, certainly. Never much liked me, I think." He stared at the ceiling. "I'm trying to remember what Marian said Judy had told her. The backyard was big, an acre or something, and wasn't fenced. Everybody thought it had to have been a stranger, snuck in somehow."

Hank asked for Judy's last name and slapped a sticky note with it in the Alton file. He was so used to Dunc, and usually so exasperated with him, that he forgot how helpful his father-in-law's deep knowledge of Branson could be. The guy had lived here his entire life, leaving only for his stint in the Army and his time at Mizzou in the early '60s.

He asked if Dunc remembered any other child abductions. He vaguely recalled the other cases in Hank's stack, and an additional one the county over that involved a brother and sister. That was further back, he said, possibly the '50s. That had Hank scratching out another sticky note.

"You probably go through a lot of those, don't you?" Dunc said.

"Yeah. Way too many."

Dunc nodded and contemplated the stack for a moment, and then Hank.

"What?"

"Oh, it's just that you work real hard. And I know I bitch about that sometimes, but really, it's pretty impressive. You really do care about it. And you've come in here from outside and you're battling away and not giving in. I'm proud of you."

Hank was speechless. He'd never gotten anything remotely like that in the almost twenty years he'd been with Maggie. He stuttered out a thank-you.

Dunc stowed his footrest and pushed himself to his feet.

"I'm off to bed." He turned toward the hallway and the stairs down to the basement, then stopped, thoughtful. "You ever talk to Darrell Gibbons?"

That was a left turn. Hank stared at him. "Huh? Um. Yeah. Once." He paused. "The only time I've ever talked to him directly was about three months ago, right at the end of the Mandy Bryson murder case. He told me I was too rigid. That I needed to play the game better. And he made sure I knew how valuable his endorsement would be in the election."

Dunc smiled at Hank's bitter tone. "That sounds like Darrell. And yeah, his endorsement will mean a lot around here. I know he's been quiet so far, but that just means he's testing the wind. Which way it's blowin'. He'll figure that out before he endorses."

"Really?" Hank said. "I figured I didn't stand a chance. Tucker was one of his favorites when he was sheriff."

"Yeah," Dunc said, "but Darrell doesn't like to back losers. He likes to act like he knew what the outcome was going to be all along. Done that in a couple of commission races over the years. Ended up endorsing the guys he didn't agree with because they looked likely to win."

"And did they win?"

"Every time."

Dunc ambled off to bed, and Hank sank into the couch and thought about that. What a slick old bastard. Gibbons could say that his endorsement helped the candidate win. That he'd done the guy a favor. And someday, he'd come around asking for one in return. From a politician who never would have been a Darrell ally otherwise. Hank was sure Gibbons had accumulated a good number of those chits in his eighteen years as sheriff. Chips in the game. That was what he had called them when he had come to see Hank in February. He'd said that Hank had one after finding out Fizzel was taking money from Henry Gallagher in return for advancing the businessman's interests. Hank scowled. He was still trying to figure out a way to press charges for that.

He suddenly sat straight up. A chip in the game. Fizzel also would likely endorse a sheriff candidate at some point. And if Hank used his chip, his leverage over the Gallagher thing, could he get Fizzel to endorse him? And would that help—or hurt? Fizzel was an idiot, and a lot of people knew it. A lot of people didn't, though.

He started pacing the length of the living room, wondering about voter demographics and turnout rates. He could ask Darcy and—good God, what was he thinking? He stopped and sank down onto the stones of the fireplace hearth. Fizzel was a corrupt asshole who needed to be slapped with campaign-finance violations. *That* was his course of action. Not trying to operate like some kind of mafia don. What was this election doing to him?

CHAPTER

17

It seemed that Rotten Doe had some chipped ribs.

Hank and Sheila stared at the speakerphone and then each other. No kidding. He'd been flattened by a falling immigrant. Hank reminded Whittaker of this and got an amplified chortle in response.

"I know that, young man. I didn't say 'breaks.' The whole ribcage is broken ten ways to Sunday, thanks to your illegal landing on top of him. But—several ribs are also chipped. By small pellet projectiles."

Hank high-fived Sheila. Their theory, based on the shotgun pellets found at the scene, was correct. "Yes, indeedy," Whittaker continued. "X-ray showed a fair number of the little suckers, concentrated in the upper chest area. From the lack of dispersion, it's likely that the shot was fired at fairly close range."

Hank tried to contain his exasperation. Why hadn't the damn doctor started with that information in the first place, instead of chuckling about falling immigrants? This guy drove him more and more crazy every time he dealt with him.

"Course, I still don't have any idea who the fella is," Whittaker said. "So you'll need to start doing some investigating. I'd like to get him off my books."

"*You'd* like to—" A glare from Sheila stopped Hank before he could tell the good doctor what he really thought. Instead, he glared back and didn't bother to return Whittaker's cheerful good-bye. He leaned back in his chair and looked at Sheila.

"So was this guy killed there in the woods, or somewhere else and then dumped in that hole?" she said.

"Good question," Hank said. "Either way, it's a location the Taylor boys could have easily known about if they're the ones who've been out stripping down trees." He rose to his feet. "I think I'll go have a chat with the one we've got."

Hank walked out of the building and around to the main public entrance of the jail. He liked to come in this way every once in a while. Nothing gave him a better feel for how it was going inside than the people waiting outside to visit. But this morning the lobby was empty. He said hello to Earl, who had, as usual, a crisply ironed tan polo shirt that denoted him as a civilian department employee. He looked at two new pictures of the latest grandbaby, asked after the wife's bunions, and thanked him for the neatly kept visitor log.

No one had come to see Lloyd Taylor.

Earl buzzed Hank in through the two sets of security doors. They swung silently shut behind him, and all the ambient noise of the free world disappeared. Instead there were shouted cell-to-cell conversations, clanking as inmates rapped on the metal of their doors, and the smell of substandard food, which this morning was . . . he sniffed . . . likely biscuits and sausage gravy, judging from the odor of greasy meat and lack of any fresh-bread aroma.

He stopped at the guard station to see the inmate roster. There were meth addicts who'd been in and out so many times, they requested the same cells when they inevitably got rearrested. There were the drunk drivers in for a night or two until they could make bail. There were the poor folks who had been picked up on bench warrants because they hadn't shown up for a court date to settle a stupid traffic ticket. And there was always someone who'd beaten up his wife or girlfriend. Occasionally, there were ones who'd abused a kid. They had to be separated from the general population for their own safety.

He looked up Taylor's cell number, which, come to think of it, was the job of the duty officer, who was not there. Who—

Shit.

"You want something? *Boss?*"

Gerald Tucker sauntered up to the guard station, crossed his arms, and stared at Hank. This day really could not get any worse.

"You're not allowed smoke breaks while you're on duty," Hank said.

"I was takin' a—I was using the facilities. There's no rule against *that.*"

There wasn't, but Hank was sure the Good Ol' Boy spent more than a reasonable amount of time away from his post during his shifts. Hank had put him on permanent jail assignment since he'd left his post—the man did have a pattern—watching over the *Branson Beauty* showboat once it had been towed to shore without its paddlewheel. Shortly after he said he'd gone home (without permission), the boat had exploded. Accidentally, my ass, Hank thought. Someone had done it deliberately, and he knew exactly who it was as he stared at the man who wanted his job.

"Blown anything up lately, Tucker?"

Tucker smirked. "Just your campaign."

The day could get worse.

Hank forced himself to smile back, because he couldn't think of a response. He stepped away from the guard station and headed down toward where Taylor was kept.

"Heeeey, Sherf."

An almost inconceivably thin man rose from his bunk and came to the door of his cell, which was the one directly next to Taylor's. As tall as Hank, he looked like he weighed less than a hundred pounds. Drugs will do that to you.

"What'd you do this time, Gursey?"

Gursey's face split in a lopsided grin, and his spindly fingers reached up to scratch his nose.

"I don't right remember, Sherf. They say I stoled cough syrup from Nixon's Drug Store. I can't see how, though. I don't even like cherry flavor."

Gursey was a frequent flier. In and out of jail constantly. Forsyth businesspeople had given up pressing charges. If they did, they just ended up spending a lot of time in the courthouse hallway waiting to testify. And Gursey would be diverted into a drug treatment program that stuck—for a bit. Then it would be back to his old ways.

So instead, folks called the cops just to get him out of their stores, and he ended up here until he came off his high and stayed clean for a couple of days.

"How you feeling now? Doing okay? Did you eat your breakfast?"

"Oh, yeah. Biscuits and gravy. Tasted so good. The biscuits was like those throwed rolls at that place up by Springfield. I had them once. My mom took me."

If he was sober enough to remember things like that, it was probably about time to release him, Hank thought. He wondered where Gursey's mother was now. Nowhere he needed her, that was for sure. Maybe he could track down some other relative who would take the kid in and keep him away from cold medicines, oxy, and everything else he enjoyed consuming.

He gave Gursey a smile and turned toward the next cell. Compared with his neighbor, the reed thin Lloyd Taylor looked positively bulky.

"Get up, Taylor. We're going to go have a conversation."

Taylor glowered at him and didn't move off his bunk. Hank reached to the back of his belt and brought out his handcuffs.

"Easy or hard, Lloyd. You decide."

Taylor sat up and swung his legs off the cot. His right shoulder was still wrapped in bandages and he held it close to his body as he carefully rose to his feet. Hank unlocked the cell and took his left arm. Lloyd did not appreciate the courtesy.

"I'm gonna sue your ass. My shoulder hurts like a son of a bitch and . . ." He ranted all the way to the interview room. Hank sat him down on the far side of the table, locked his ankle into the shackle bolted into the concrete floor, and settled himself into the opposite seat. Cushioned and with arms, it was a much more comfortable chair than the molded plastic one Taylor was stuck in. He had a feeling they'd be in here awhile. Taylor showed no signs of shutting up, and he had no plans to make him. He leaned back and listened while Lloyd called him names, questioned his mother's virtue, mocked his haircut, accused him of having inappropriate relations with farm animals, and told him exactly where he could shove those "Hank Worth for Sheriff" election signs.

He started to lose steam after about fifteen minutes. Hank just continued to stare at him. He doubted any cop had let the bozo go on this long before, because Lloyd didn't know what to make of it. So then he did what any self-respecting sleazeball would do—proclaimed his innocence.

"You got no reason to hold me, man. All I done is earn a living. And I can spend my paycheck any way I want. Getting a tattoo ain't a crime."

Hank pretended to stifle a yawn.

"Look," Lloyd snapped. "I load up my truck and I drive it where they tell me. I don't even know what the shit is. Plants. And not pot. It's nothing illegal. I take it to the places they tell me and I get paid. That's it."

There it was. Hank kept his face impassive. "I thought you only drove for one company. Why more than one place?"

"One place." Lloyd shifted in his seat. "That's what I said."

"No." Hank leaned forward and rested his elbows on the table. "That was not what you said. You said 'places,' plural. You know, more than one."

Lloyd started twitching his foot and jangling the cuff.

"Who else did you deliver to, Lloyd?"

"Nobody."

"Well, where do you take the plants and bark that you've stolen?"

"That goes to—" He froze.

Hank bit back a smile and waited. Lloyd didn't move. Didn't even blink. Hank half expected him to roll over and play dead in a minute. He even looked a little like a possum, come to think of it.

They stared at each other for a bit, until Lloyd had to blink.

Hank switched tacks.

"Who's Ned Bunning?"

Lloyd was so surprised the "huh?" escaped his lips before he could stop it.

"Did you meet any other delivery drivers in the course of picking up those plants?"

Hank took Lloyd's sneer as a no.

He slid a copy of Bunning's driver's license photo across the table. It showed a thirty-four-year-old man with a lined face that suggested life up to that point hadn't exactly been easy. He had brown eyes, a scruffy goatee, and a full head of brown hair.

"I don't know no old dudes." Lloyd rattled his cuff.

"Really? Not even in the course of doing business, with the plant delivery? You didn't run across him?"

Lloyd folded his arms and slouched even farther down in his seat.

"I never seen him before."

"Was anybody trying to take a piece of your business? With the tree bark?"

"I don't know what you're talking about," the possum snarled.

They went back and forth for another ten minutes. Lloyd got steadily more agitated and jumpy, but wouldn't give up a name. Hank pushed until he lapsed into sullen immobility. He knew from his innumerable interrogations of Kansas City gang members that once suspects hit that wall, they were very unlikely to cough up any more information during that interview session. He got up without a word and left the youngest Taylor sitting there.

He grinned when he saw Sam standing in front of the two-way mirror.

"You really do take a special interest in him. How much did you see?"

"Most of it, I think," Sam said. "And I wouldn't put it past them to try to cut out any competition for their easy-money plant thieving."

"Yeah, but murder?" said Hank. "These brothers haven't ever done anything that bad. They're petty criminals. Besides, we don't even know who Rotten Doe is. It could be someone totally unrelated to the Taylors."

"Well, where's Ned Bunning then?" Sam's mouth became a thin, determined line. "Those lowlifes got it in 'em. I know they do. And I got an idea." He spun on his heel and walked out.

Hank was pleased with the Pup's initiative, even though he didn't know exactly what the kid was up to. And Sam's investigation into the missing driver left him free to pursue another line of inquiry. He buzzed for Tucker to take Lloyd back to his cell. Let the GOB deal with the youngest Taylor's charms for a while.

CHAPTER
18

Hank went back to his office and found the yellow pages listing of the business he wanted. Then he looked it up in the department records. A 1999 Chevy Camaro had been stolen from the parking lot four years ago. And someone was stopped for speeding on the road in front of it eighteen months ago. Other than that, the location generated no hits, which was patently absurd.

He switched over to a state-government database, typed in the business again, and jotted something down. That led to much more useful information than the one lousy vehicle theft. He logged off his computer and headed out for a drink.

The bar was not busy. Only three cars sat in the gravel parking lot as Hank pulled off of LL Highway. It was only midafternoon, he thought, as he threw a quick three-point turn and parked facing the way he'd come. He got out and stretched his creaky back. It had been a long drive out here. Not really on the way to anywhere, which was—if he had to bet—what made it a very popular place later in the day.

The building sat about twenty yards back from the road,

long, low, and windowless, with a shingle roof and a corrugated-metal awning over the entrance. The large, neatly lettered sign painted on the wall said he had reached the Redbone Bar. He crunched across the gravel, put his hand on the heavy wooden door, and closed his eyes to shut out the sunny sky. No need to walk into a dark room blind. He waited a moment and then pulled open the door.

Three faces turned toward him simultaneously, squinting at the blaze of light he'd let inside. He swung the door shut and optical order was restored. The two customers, who looked like down-on-their-luck construction workers, gave him a once-over and went back to their drinks. The guy behind the bar waved him closer.

"What'll you have?"

Hank hadn't expected this. He'd figured on hostility, threats, and quite possibly gun brandishment. He sat down half a dozen stools away from the two men nursing their beers and made a show of considering the line of taps against the wall while he got the feel of the place.

There was no one else in the long, rectangular room. The air had the lingering staleness of cigarette smoke and booze, but the place itself was spotless. The bar ran almost the whole length of the back, stopping about ten feet short of the east wall, where a small, shabby stage sat. At the opposite end were clusters of tables. The middle was clear and the wood floor shone smooth even in the dim light. Dancing? Huh.

The bartender waited politely. No matter how unexpectedly polished this place was, it was still a bar. No one was going to talk to him if he ordered a Diet Pepsi. He decided to play it safe and asked for a Budweiser. Served in practically every such establishment in Missouri. Anheuser-Busch might have sold out to foreigners, but its St. Louis roots still ran deep.

The guy banged a frosty bottle down in front of him. Hank

picked it up and saw what was underneath. Grains and knots swirled and spun down the enormous length of the slab of burnished wood. It wasn't smooth and slick and polished and uniform like a regular bar top. Instead it gloried in its bumps and whorls and color variations. It was the most beautiful piece of wood Hank had ever seen.

"Hickory."

Hank started in surprise. The bartender laughed.

"Anybody new always asks. It's made outta hickory."

"It's . . . wow. It's beautiful."

"Yup. My granddaddy cut it about a hundred years ago. Back when trees grew this size. Nowadays, you'd never see this kind of monster. . . ." He shrugged. Hank thought about all the forest he'd been in lately. Plenty of monsters, but no trees that looked like this. He set his beer back down very carefully.

That got a belly laugh and a flash of teeth through the guy's salt-and-pepper beard. "No need for that. It's tough as nails. Put my special varnish on it once a year. Nothing will hurt this thing."

Hank stuck out his hand and gave his first name. The guy was Willie Boyd, the same man listed in the state liquor-license database. He wished he could just sit there and shoot the shit for a while—find out where the guy's granddaddy felled that tree and how it had come to rest lengthwise in a genuinely rustic watering hole in the middle of nowhere, Branson County, Mo. But he'd learned from painful experience that establishing a rapport was one thing. Going beyond and getting friendly was another, viewed as a betrayal when it finally came out that he was there as a cop. People didn't like to feel used, and when they did, they sure as hell didn't feel cooperative.

The guy's eyebrows shot up when Hank added his title to the introductions.

"I guess I do remember hearing something about Darrell Gibbons running for something else. Congress?"

"The state legislature," Hank said.

"Eh. Just as bad," he responded. "They're all a bunch of ass-holes. I hope ol' Darrell doesn't go that way."

Hank, who thought his predecessor had gone in exactly that direction, just nodded and smiled. The owner offered no further opinion, and just stood there, comfortably waiting for Hank to continue. It was his bar, and he had all day. Hank was liking him more and more.

"I need to ask you about a couple of your customers," Hank said. Willie nodded, and waited. Hank decided to start with the low-hanging suspect fruit. "The Taylor boys—Lloyd and his brothers. They ever come in here?"

The scowl was obvious even behind the beard. "Are you kid-ding? That trash isn't allowed here. Ever. None of them." He sounded offended that Hank had even considered the notion.

"Okay," Hank said as apologetically as he could. That wasn't why he was here, but now he was curious. "Why's that?"

Willie looked at him like he'd ordered that Diet Pepsi after all. "If you're asking about 'em, then you know why."

Good point. Hank raised his bottle in agreement and took a swig. Now for the real reason.

"What about Jasper Kinney?"

Willie's eyes changed. Wary? Scared? Definitely cautious. "What makes you think he comes in here?"

"He carries around your matchbooks."

"Hmmm."

And that was it. Hank asked again. The barman got out a rag and started wiping down his bar. Hank let him for work for a bit, and then he put his beer down directly in the path of the cloth. The two men stared at each other for a good long minute. Finally, Willie shrugged.

"Sometimes. Every once in a while. Most everybody north end of this county and the next comes in every once in a while."

"Then why'd you hesitate?"

Willie shrugged again.

"He's not 'most everybody,' is he?" Hank said.

Willie turned away and went back to wiping the bar. Hank took another swig and shot a glance down the bar, where the two day drinkers were trying not to look like they were listening.

"What about you two? You know Jasper?"

One guy froze. The other one sputtered on his Bud Light. Neither said anything. Man, was he getting sick of this. He gave them his I'm-not-going-to-ask-again look. Finally, the sputterer cleared his throat.

"He's called Mr. Kinney around here."

"Oh, is he? And why's that?"

The guy started to doodle a pattern on the bar with his damp beer bottle.

"Dunno. Just is. That's how my dad always called him. That's how everybody calls him. He's deserving of your respect."

That last part sounded like the guy had heard it somewhere— it definitely wasn't a line he'd come up with on his own. Hank decided to play along.

"That's good to know. I'm new here, so . . . I'm still figuring this stuff out."

Willie had worked his way down to the far end of the bar with his rag, but Hank knew he was still listening to every word as the sputterer relaxed a little and turned toward him. It's good to know who's the important folks, the man said. And Mr. Kinney was sure important. He'd owned a whole lot of land, and folks still were obliged. So he was important. And respected.

He would have kept on, but his companion thawed at that point, firmly set his half-full drink down on the bar, and walked out the door. The sputterer whirled around in surprise and then hopped off his stool and scurried after his friend. The door slammed behind them, and Hank was left again in the dark. He left his barely touched Bud and walked down to the end where Willie was standing.

"You seem like a nice fellow," the barman said. "So I'm going to tell you—don't go there."

Hank laid a five on the bar. "You seem like a nice guy, too. Someday, I'd like to hear more about your granddaddy. But right now, I have a job to do."

Willie gave him the appraising look of an older, wiser man, and shrugged. "So be it."

"Yeah," Hank said. "So be it." And he walked out of the comforting gloom into the hot glare of the early-summer sunshine.

He'd been told that someone who declined to give her name wanted to see him. He walked into the office lobby and stopped. A short, plump woman rose from the molded plastic seat to meet him. She had steel gray hair and a smooth face, except for the lines that radiated out from her eyes, deep and craggy ones not caused by the sun.

Hank knew immediately what she was. He glanced over at the receptionist, with her tan polo shirt and blatantly curious expression. Not here. He silently motioned the woman through the door and down the hallway leading to his office. He followed her inside and shut the door. He smiled and held out his hand. Whose mother was she?

"Thank you, Sheriff. I didn't want to give my name out there. People still . . ." She gathered herself. "My name is Patty Alton. I'm here about the skeleton in the woods."

He guided her to the seat in front of his desk and pulled his own chair around the furniture to join her. He leaned forward and put his elbows on his knees.

"Melissa?"

She nodded. "I'm her mother."

Hank very carefully explained that the bones would be sent to specially trained forensic anthropologists, where they would be analyzed and any information gleaned would then narrow down the search for an identification.

"But you'll do the DNA, right? Ours is on file. You'll be able to tell if it's her. You can do that right off."

No, he said gently, they couldn't. That wasn't how it worked. They first needed to know how old the child was when he or she died. That was fairly easy to determine from the teeth and the bone growth plates. Then they would try to determine the gender, but that was more difficult, because the pelvic differences that made it easy to distinguish in adults were not there in children. Then, and perhaps most key, they would try to figure out how long the skeleton had been there.

"So you mean how long ago the child died?" she said softly.

"Yes."

She nodded slightly. This wasn't the first time law enforcement had told her that something was more difficult than she thought it should be. She thought for a moment.

"Do you know yet how the child died?"

The skull flashed through Hank's memory. He shook his head.

"We're still working on that," he hedged.

He answered a few more questions as best he could, and then said that he'd be happy to come to her next time. He jotted his cell number on a business card and pressed it into her hand.

"Just call me. You don't have to make the drive all the way here to Forsyth from Branson."

She gave him that little smile again. She hadn't come from Branson. They'd moved to Springfield five years after Melissa disappeared. They couldn't take everyone constantly asking how they were doing, or if they'd heard anything new about the case. They couldn't take the sympathetic whispers that erupted as they left a room. They couldn't take her empty room, and they sure couldn't take their backyard. So they moved up to Springfield, where they could be anonymous and not get asked about it every time they turned around.

She still lived there, in the house with the second bedroom, just in case Melissa came home. Her husband had passed on eight years ago. A stroke. He'd never been really healthy again after Melissa disappeared. So now it was just her.

She shrugged and stood to go. Hank walked her out to her car and promised to keep her updated.

"And, ma'am," he said, bending down to talk to her through the open window as she buckled herself into her little Corolla, "your daughter is an open case, so no matter what happens with this skeleton, we're going to keep looking for her."

Patty Alton gave him a smile so small it spoke volumes. She knew full well her daughter's file had been pulled off a dusty shelf. And she knew that was right where it would end up again if this child in the woods wasn't hers.

"Chief, can you meet me over on Creekbend Road?"

It was less than a mile away. And it was Ned Bunning's duplex. Hank, wondering exactly what the Pup was up to, climbed into his cruiser and took the two-minute drive.

He arrived at the dilapidated unit to find Sam leaning over the hood of his own squad car, paperwork scattered over the flat surface. Kurt was next to him, and frowned when he saw Hank pull up.

"—preliminary identification. You should've waited to call him," Kurt was saying as Hank got out of the car.

Sam was bouncing on the balls of his feet.

"You said it's highly likely. We just have to run it through the computer to make double sure your match is right."

"What match?" Hank asked as he picked his way along the weedy dirt shoulder of the road in front of Bunning's front yard.

"Lloyd Taylor," Sam said.

Hank stared at the fingerprint sheets on the hood of the car and then at his deputy.

"Sammy, you didn't go into the house, did you?"

"No, no," he said quickly. "I know we don't have probable cause for a warrant, cuz nobody's reported Bunning missing. I did try the landlord, but he said Bunning is paid up on the rent, so he doesn't much care where he is. He also said he doesn't like cops, so he wouldn't give me permission to go inside. But he did say we could go in the yard."

Hank raised a skeptical eyebrow, which made Sam dig a notebook out of his back pocket.

" 'You want to walk around in weeds and a bunch of dog shit, go ahead, you moron.' That's a quote." He shoved the notebook back in his pocket. "So I started thinking."

"And then he called me," said Kurt. "And we dusted the front doorframe."

Hank had a feeling he was about to be very happy. Kurt saw the look on his face and held up his hands in a "slow down" gesture.

"You're as bad as Sam is," Kurt said. "I've eyeballed it, but I'm not going to give you a definite yes—or no—until I get back to the office and run it proper."

"But you think it is, right?" Hank said. He had to refrain from bouncing the way Sam was doing. Kurt rolled his eyes.

"I'll go do it right now, before you all explode." He started to pack up his gear. "And I did all the windowsills, too, and the back door, so don't go calling me back here thinking I forgot something."

He trundled off, and Hank took a turn around the house.

The other half of the duplex was in the same bad repair, but whoever lived there at least took some care. The small concrete pad
in front of the door was swept, and neat yellow curtains were visible through the windows. Bunning's half was nothing but ripped
window screens and a glimpse of a messy kitchen through a dirty
window.

And the landlord hadn't been wrong about the yard, which
had plenty of evidence of dog habitation. Hank managed not to
step in any of it as he made his way back to the street. He and
Sam were starting to head to their cruisers when a beat-up Ford
Escort lurched to a stop in front of the tidier half of the duplex.
They immediately changed course and met the poor woman as
she hefted herself out of the car.

"Uh, hi?" she said.

Sam introduced them both and pointed to the duplex's lesser
half. She nodded emphatically and started talking. Her name was
Tracy Dugan, she worked at the Ozarker Lodge Motel in Branson,
she'd lived here for three years, and she hated her neighbor.

"I know that ain't what the Bible says, but I do," she said.
"He's always got horrible music playing, he don't got no
housekeepin' skills, and he's mean as a constipated goat."

Sam asked when she'd last seen Bunning. She wrinkled her
nose in thought—or maybe distaste—and said it had been about
two and a half weeks ago. She hadn't seen the dog since then,
either.

"That poor little thing. I don't know how such an awful man
coulda had such a nice dog. He left her outside too much. I'd feed
her some, when he weren't home."

They listened to another several minutes' worth of Ned
Bunning's failings, then carried her groceries into the house.

"So he must have taken the dog with him," Sam said as they
walked back out to their cars. "Or got himself murdered, and the
dog's disappeared who knows where."

Hank nodded. "See if Bunning has anything like a locker at his seasonal job that his employer would let us into. It might have something in it we could get DNA off of. I'd love to know if he's our Rotten Doe."

"I'll get right on it," Sam said. "But DNA takes a while, and . . ."

Hank grinned. "And you want those fingerprints to get put to use right now, don't you?"

Sam nodded eagerly. Hank leaned against his open car door and thought for a moment.

"Okay, there's an argument to be made that possible homicide evidence at the Taylor property could disappear during the time we're waiting for DNA results. If Kurt does definitely match Lloyd to those prints on the door, that should be enough to get a judge to give us a search warrant."

Sam beamed. Hank started to get behind the wheel, then stopped.

"And good job," he said. "That was a really nice piece of detective work."

Sam's smile doubled in size.

"Now go home," Hank ordered with a smile. "Tomorrow's looking like it's going to be a busy day."

CHAPTER
19

Now that he was actually on the property, Hank realized that the place not only looked like shit, it smelled like it, too.

"Oh, my God. What is that?" Sam gagged from behind him.

Ted Pimental pointed to the left, past the rusted-out engine block, to a pile of lumber and trash and beyond it a ramshackle shed semi-screened by trees.

"I think it's coming from over there."

Ted was one of the winners of the tagalong competition. Every deputy on duty, and two on their days off, wanted to come. A county judge had quickly approved the search warrant once the computer confirmed Kurt's visual match of Lloyd's criminal-record fingerprints and the ones lifted off Bunning's doorframe. And everyone was as giddy as Sam. They'd never been able to secure a warrant for the Taylor place before, and the whole department was itching to get on the property. That had resulted in a free-for-all argument that morning—with the two off-duty guys chiming in by phone—that stopped only when Hank cut up his leftover Whipstitch Diner straws and made everyone draw one. The three shortest got to come. He couldn't justify using any more manpower than that. Pimental and Doug Gabler had picked the first two. Sam had drawn the third. Sheila had growled and stomped back to her office.

He wished she were here. Those three were fine—Sam especially was shaping up very nicely—but no one could match Sheila's observational skills. Or her attitude. Which he had come to appreciate more and more the further into this job he got. He'd never been in a position before where people just did what he told them to, and he was finding that it had its drawbacks. Having someone who questioned him, prodded him, and made him get his own coffee was turning out to be a good thing.

The smell faded a bit as they made their way to the mobile home on the right. Gabler had stayed in a squad car, parked to block escape via the dirt driveway. The other two were uniformed and Hank had his badge clearly displayed on his shirt. He pulled the search warrant out of his back pocket and loudly announced their presence.

They'd taken only a few more steps when a crash came from the far side of the mobile home. With a whoop, Sam took off around one side, and Ted took off around the other, following after the person now stumbling noisily through the dense undergrowth behind the trailer. Hank stayed out front. He wanted to see who was behind the curtain in the front window that had just twitched and then fallen back in place.

He switched the warrant to his left hand and dropped his right one down to rest on his Glock. He climbed the cinder-block stairs, gave the flimsy door a quick pounding that left indentions in the metal, then hopped down and waited. After sixty seconds, he identified himself again—loudly. After sixty more, he drew his gun. Time was always very distinct for him in situations like this. He knew exactly how much was passing, and exactly how long he was going to give the reluctant recipient of his warrant.

At two minutes and twelve seconds, he moved a broken ax

handle away from the door and tossed it out of reach. Then he made sure he was in view of the curtained window and raised his gun. There was a shuffling sound and the door swung slowly open. This Taylor was as thin and surly as Lloyd, but older. Dark bags hung under his eyes, and lines were starting to pull down the corners of his mouth. His widow's peak was barely visible on his shaved head. That was about all the skin Hank could see. Everything else was covered with tattoos. Mostly standard black single-hue ones, with a few mixed in that looked like the same drunken pen-ink designs Lloyd sported. They must have an artist in the family, Hank thought. And he might have been halfway sober when he did the spider that took up most of this Taylor's chest, with legs stretching up onto his neck and down into the ratty boxers that hung at his waist.

"Come outside," Hank said.

This Taylor scowled and didn't move. Hank trained the Glock on the middle of the spider. Its owner growled and stepped down the cinder blocks and onto the dirt.

"I wanna get dressed. I know my rights." It sounded like he hadn't used his voice in a while.

"No. You have no right to a pair of pants. Not at the moment." He moved back a step as the smell of unwashed Taylor hit him. "Is there anybody else in the house?"

Taylor smirked at his backtrack. Hank didn't care. The guy stunk. He waved to Doug Gabler, who got out of the squad car and jogged down the dirt driveway to gleefully cuff whichever Taylor this was. None of their rap sheets listed a spider tat like that, so it must be relatively new. Hank needed to find something old enough to have been added to the descriptions in the law-enforcement database. He took a look at Spidey's calves. The left one didn't have a tattoo of a fist with its middle finger up, so it wasn't Jackson Taylor, the oldest brother. And the right calf didn't have a Gothic cross stretching from knee to ankle, so it wasn't third-oldest Boone Taylor, who ironically was rumored to be the meanest of the bunch.

That meant the gentleman currently hocking a loogie at him must be the second of the four Taylor brothers. "Hello, Leroy," Hank said as Gabler backed him away and made him sit cross-legged on the ground. That did not help the fit of Leroy's boxers. Hank averted his eyes as he suggested Gabler put him in the back of the cruiser until they'd made sure there was no one else in the trailer.

He climbed the cinder blocks again and stepped inside. He should have brought one of those respirator things that Alice and Kurt used. Years of BO accumulation, stale pot smoke, and uncleaned toilets made him gag. The only thing that made it the least bit bearable was the cross breeze created by the other open door on the opposite side of the trailer. He glanced out that way but saw no sign of Sam or Ted Pimental.

Gabler joined him and they quickly went through the double-wide. They confirmed that no one else was there and fled outside. When Hank had finished choking, he promised Doug that they'd get respirators before going back in to inventory the contents. They were both still gulping in fresh air when the shooting started.

They froze. Hank spun toward the squad car, but the back doors were still closed, and through the window, Leroy looked as shocked as they were. He spun again, trying to pin down where the shots were coming from as the reports echoed around the clearing.

The next volley was followed by Sam's voice, yelling incoherently. Hank and Doug bolted for the trees in back of the trailer, both of them drawing their guns as they crashed through the line of bushes that separated the woods from the clearing. Once past it, Gabler turned on speed Hank didn't know he had, racing past him and into the gloom of the untended forest in front of them.

Sam's yelling grew more distinct as he got closer. Then he heard an explosion of swear words from Doug. Hank didn't think he could've run any faster, but he did. He breached the last screen of trees between him and his deputies and skidded to a stop. Ted Pimental lay on his back, drenched in blood.

Sam knelt over his legs, his hands around the middle of Ted's thigh. He was yelling something about an artery. Hank dropped to his knees and scrambled forward as he undid his belt. He wrapped it around Ted's leg above the wound and cinched. Tight.

The gush of blood began to slow. Hank fell back and looked at Ted's face, which had lost all color. They elevated his leg so that his ankle rested on Sam's shoulder. Sam shifted and readjusted his grip on Ted's thigh as Hank yanked the radio mic off Sam's other shoulder.

"Deputy down. Deputy down. All units. Hogsback Hollow. Shooter at large. Ambulance needed. Repeat, deputy down."

He turned to Sam, who was starting to shake as he continued to press down on Pimental's wound.

"Which one was it?"

Sam stared at him blankly. Hank put his face directly in front of him and repeated the question, more loudly than he probably should have.

"Which brother was it?"

Sam blinked. "I don't know. Average height, blond hair . . . tank top and shorts . . . jean shorts. I didn't get a look at his face."

Hank turned back to the radio and issued the BOLO, listing the suspect description and repeating the location. Then he looked at Ted again. He was turning gray. "And get that bus out here now. We need medical assistance immediately."

He dropped Sam's radio and stood. Where the hell was Gabler? And where the hell was his gun? He spun back toward the screen of trees and saw it lying in the dirt. He must have dropped it when he saw Pimental. Definitely not a pro move. He was getting angrier and angrier at himself every second. He picked it up and shoved it in his holster just as Gabler came huffing back from the other direction.

"I lost him," he puffed. "Never saw him, but I heard him crashing around ahead of me. He was headed toward Bear Creek. He had too much of a head start, though."

Hank nodded. "I need you to get back up to the road and show the paramedics the way back here. I don't want to move Ted until they get here."

Doug turned and looked at his friend, who was going from gray to almost translucent. His face hardened and he took off toward the trailer where it had all started.

Hank picked up the radio again and started issuing orders. Roadblocks. Mutual aid. Highway patrol. Regional fugitive task force. He would have called in Air Force bombers if he could have.

Finally, after a string of minutes so long Ted could have died twice, he heard the sirens and then the shouts and thudding footsteps as the paramedics rushed through the woods toward them. They gently eased Sam away, checked Ted's vitals and the tourniquet, and lifted him onto a gurney. The wheels were no good on the forest floor, so they carried him out without putting the legs down. Thank God for strong young backs, Hank thought as he followed their brisk trot.

They didn't stop, sliding the gurney into the ambulance in one smooth motion and leaping in behind it. He watched the doors swing shut and the rig peel away down the dirt driveway. There was only one thing he could do to help now. He reached for his cell.

Maggie picked up immediately. She didn't say hello.

"I know. We're getting ready for him now. I'm going to take care of him, honey. We're going to do everything we can."

Hank couldn't speak. Maggie waited a moment and then continued when he didn't say anything. "Hank? Honey? I'm going to do my job. You go do yours. You get this son of a bitch, okay?" There were sounds of commotion in the background. "I gotta go. And Hank—be careful, babe."

She ended the call. Hank put the phone back in his pocket, closed his eyes, and took a breath so deep it felt like it reached his toes. When he opened them, Sam was standing in front of him. His uniform pants were soaked with blood, and spots of it covered his shirt where he'd held up Pimental's leg. Someone had given him a rag and he'd cleaned off his hands but not his face. What was there had streaked down his cheeks from tears he was trying to hold back. He looked like a ghastly Halloween decoration.

Hank stepped up to him. He had to get a grip on things, because the poor Pup was about to lose his.

"Sammy? Sammy, it's going to be okay. Ted's in good hands now. They're going to do everything they can."

He steered his deputy toward a Branson PD squad car parked near the trailer. The officer hurried to open the passenger door, and Hank sat Sam down in the full blast of the air conditioner. The officer pulled his own bottle of water out of the console and pressed it into Sam's hands. Sam stared at it as Hank pulled the burly blond Branson guy away from the car.

"Thanks for coming out here," he said.

"Hell, yeah," said Officer G. Fesse, according to his nameplate. "I just started my shift when I heard it on the scanner. I radioed in and they told me to get straight out here."

"How long do I get you for?"

"As long as you need me. My department is sending more your way. So's Forsyth PD. They're helping man the roadblocks until the highway patrol gets out here to assist."

Good. Thank God for emergency protocols.

He glanced over at Sam, who thankfully was drinking the water and looking slightly more alert. He dug his phone out of his pocket again and called Sheila.

She also picked up immediately. "Don't bother me. I'm co-ordinating." The line went dead. It rang back two seconds later.

"Who was it?"

"Ted."

"Shit," she said, and hung up again.

CHAPTER

20

Sam was still sitting immobile in the Branson PD cruiser, his eyes glazed with tears and his white knuckles strangling the plastic water bottle. Hank knelt down so they were face-to-face. "Sam?"

"I've been to his kids' birthday parties. Ava just turned ten. He got her a phone. With a *Doctor Who* case. They love *Doctor Who*." He turned his head toward Hank. "Who's going to watch it with her now?"

There was no time for this. No time to sit and think and worry. Only to act.

"Sammy, I need your help. He hasn't shown up at any of the roadblocks. So he's still out there. You're the only one here right now who can track him. The state conservation agent can't get here for another hour. You're a hunter. You've tracked all kinds of animals. We need your experience.

"We need to go into the woods."

Sam looked down at his blood-soaked pants. "I was in the woods."

He stared at Hank. A tear on his cheek rolled slowly down, cutting the smear of blood on his jaw in half. It dropped onto his collar, adding a pale red splash to the rest of his stains. Hank forced himself to wait.

It was the worst possible thing he could do to Sam right now—make him go back to the scene. He should be sending him home so he could take a nice hot shower and call his mother. How hard could it be, to follow the trail made by a man who'd bull-dozed through the woods at a full run? Even a city idiot like him should be able to do it.

But if he couldn't, the chance would be lost. And that would be more costly than the price he was about to ask Sam to pay.

"And now we have to go back in the woods, Sam. We have to track the man who shot Ted. Do you understand me? We have to go."

Sam's head moved—the slightest of gestures. Hank saw it and focused on the ground so he wouldn't have to look him in the eye.

"Get out of the car, Sam."

The plastic bottle slowly crackled into shapelessness. Sam swung his big feet out of the squad car and stood up. He didn't meet Hank's gaze either, just turned and plodded back toward the trees. Hank waved Doug Gabler over, told him to get his twelve-gauge out of his squad car and follow Sam. He turned back to find G. Fesse getting his own shotgun out of his Branson PD cruiser.

"I went to school with Ted," he said. "Our moms still go to River Baptist together. I'm coming with you."

Hank nodded and pointed to the gun. "Grab mine out of my car for me. And I want four more guys. Everyone else stays here. I want this place torn apart."

"Gladly." Fesse strode off.

Five minutes later, the group—bristling with firearms—plowed into the woods. When they caught up with Sam, just beyond where Ted had been shot, a dumpy, balding officer in a

Branson uniform who looked like he should have taken a medical retirement years ago stepped to the front of the line of men
and stopped. He scanned everyone's faces and muttered something
profane. Hank, who was with Sam at the head of the group, started
to protest at the delay.

"Shut it, kid," he said. "All you assholes are too young. So
you'd better listen good. This is how it's going to work. You"—
he pointed to Gabler—"are going to run point. That means your
job is to protect the scout. You"—this time his finger jabbed
toward Fesse—"you bring up the rear. This bastard could be anywhere."

Hank shot Fesse a look. *What the hell is this?* Fesse patted the
air. *Calm down.* He fell in next to Hank as the line, cowed into
silence by the Commando, filed forward on high alert.

"He's a Vietnam vet," Fesse whispered. "Led raiding parties
into the jungle. I don't know much about it, but I do know he
always came out. Never even got injured. He might have let himself go since then, but in this particular kind of situation, he
knows what he's doing."

"No talking," the Commando barked. "Get back in position."

Hank and Fesse reflexively obeyed and the whole group shuffled forward, following Sam as he walked along the still very
obvious trail of the shooter. They came to a tiny clearing and
stopped as Sam knelt down.

"This is where I lost him," Doug said from his spot in front.
The Commando growled at him.

Sam swept the small open space twice, then pointed to the
left, uphill toward the ridge. As they followed him, Hank saw the
barest of circular indentations from a shoe heel. The chances that
he would have found that print on his own were about nonexistent. He started to feel better about having ordered Sammy into
the woods.

They hiked through stands of spindly pines that were dotted with the stumps of far bigger trees. Hickory, maybe, or oak. The grooves where the trunks had been dragged off through the leafy mulch of the forest floor were still visible. Discarded branches littered the ground and made walking difficult, but no one dared grumble—first for fear of the Commando's wrath, and later as they realized that the jostled tree limbs and broken twigs were telling Sam exactly where to go.

They pushed on for half an hour, making the same haphazard turns as the Taylor brother had on his escape up the ridge. The forest grew thicker as the logging petered out. Unharmed deciduous trees soared above them and shaded a riot of ground cover, some of which looked like the flowered stuff Hank had walked through at the Rotten Doe crime scene and some of which looked like poison ivy. He ground it all under his boots as if it were Taylor's face.

After several switchbacks near the top of the incline, they hit a tangle of brush that stretched in front of them in an unbroken line. Sam stopped and stared at it. The Commando silently waved the rest of them into positions along the thicket, alternating whether they faced it or the trees behind them. Everyone stood on the balls of their feet with their shotguns at the ready, gripped by itchy fingers.

And Sam stood there. For a good long time. Hank finally dropped his heels back onto the ground and saw the others do the same. And still Sammy stood. Hank was just about to walk over to him when his deputy dropped into a crouch and sidled to the left along the thicket. Everyone froze. Sam moved about ten yards along without taking his eyes off the ground and then suddenly darted through what looked like an impenetrable wall. Everyone stared after him, then swung around to look at the Commando. With a blast of expletives, he raised his shotgun and plowed after him.

Hank gestured for the other three to stay put and dove into the tangle. Branches snagged on his clothing and lashed across his face as he climbed a steep few feet. And then he was through.

It was the summit of the hill they'd been climbing—a gently sloping dome that was mostly meadow, but spotted here and there with trees and more of that ground cover. It sat above all of the surrounding forest. The endless view of green ridges and rocky crags wrapped in tendrils of misty fog was beautiful. And no one cared.

"What the hell are you doing?" the Commando said to Sam in a whisper that was quite clearly intended as an angry shout. "You could have been ambushed. Shot."

"I knew he wasn't up here." Sam didn't bother with the whisper and instead went directly to the shout. "No one would be stupid enough to stay up here in the wide open. He's long gone."

"Yeah? And what if he's hiding down there training his gun on us right now?" The Commando flung his arm out in the opposite direction from which they'd come. And then stopped as his gaze followed. "Oh."

"Yeah. Oh," Sam spat.

As the hilltop ran down toward the far side of the ridge, the meadow turned to stone. Cracked sheets of limestone fell steeply downward for more than a hundred feet before the forest started up again. The bald expanse had no place to hide, and no surface that would hold any sign of a person passing through.

Sam stomped over to where the rock started to drop off, drew his arm back as if he were fixing to throw a fastball, and let fly a long, thin object that glinted in the sun as it shot toward the trees far below. As it spun in the air, Hank realized it was the plastic water bottle, crushed into an angry tube that Sam hadn't let go of the whole way up the ridge.

Sam spun around and headed back toward the thicket. The

Commando started to say something, but Hank put a hand on his shoulder. Sam disappeared into the brush.

"What the hell are you letting him go for? We need to keep on with it." The Commando again pointed down the rocks.

"No," Hank said. "He's done. We'll have the conservation guys take over from the other side when they get here, but there's nowhere else we can go from here. And Sammy's done enough." He headed for the thicket.

The Commando disagreed, loudly, for about thirty seconds. Then Hank turned around and gave him the vitriol he knew he should be directing at himself.

"Look, whatever your name is, I appreciate your help. And your expertise. You quite clearly know what you're doing. But no one here is equipped to go down that rock face. I'm going to leave two people to guard it for now, but everyone else needs to head back and be put to better use elsewhere. Including you."

The Commando clearly did not view Hank as a superior officer. The two men stared at each other for a minute before the older man grunted and turned back toward the trees. Hank followed. Sam was already gone.

CHAPTER

21

Ted was still in surgery. The family—his wife, three kids, all six of his siblings, and his mother—had camped out in the upstairs waiting room at Branson Valley Hospital. The highway patrol had sent one of their chaplains to sit with them. They were allowing him to stay, the duty nurse told Hank, even though the pastor from River Baptist was already there. They figured the more prayers the better.

Hank wished they would send some his way. They had, so far, not been able to find the escaped Taylor, even with a conservation agent now working the other side of the ridge. A couple of tracking dogs were on their way from up near St. Louis. Maybe they'd have better luck.

He shoved his cell, with its latest no-progress update text, back in his pocket and turned toward the mobile home. Kurt had "accidentally" busted out a couple of windows, which improved ventilation tremendously, although he and the Branson PD tech helping him still wore heavy-duty 3M respirators. They'd emptied the place of its rickety, stained furniture and were starting on the kitchen cabinets.

Alice and the other Branson tech had started with the junk in the yard and were slowly working their way over to the small shed off on the left side of the property. When they got about twenty feet away, they came staggering back.

"Oh, my God," Alice gagged. "That is horrendous. Worse than a decomp. I don't think we can go any closer without the full suit."

She retched for a minute before heading for the van and the suits they used to go into meth labs. The Branson PD equipment was in transit, so B. Handlesman, the slim, athletic-looking city tech helping Alice out, put on Kurt's voluminous gear and waddled back over toward the shed.

"We got a couple buds of pot in the kitchen," Tech Number Two hollered from inside the mobile home. Hank walked over to the open doorway and gave him a grim nod. That would allow them to hold Spidey for a while at least. He stepped down off the cinder-block steps just as the whole damn building started rocking.

"What the hell?" he yelled as he dashed back inside and down the hallway toward the bedrooms. He found Kurt in the very back one, stomping his sizable feet all over the floor.

"You're messing it up," Kurt garbled through his mask. "Go back outside." He shooed Hank away. He walked out and cleared his lungs of the inside smell and watched the tin can tremble as Kurt hopped from room to room. The shaking stopped as abruptly as it had started, and Kurt appeared in the doorway.

He climbed down the steps, grabbed a crowbar and a flashlight out of the gear bag sitting on the trunk of a nearby cruiser, and walked confidently around to the back side of the trailer. Hank followed, because, well, who wouldn't? Kurt counted out his steps until he came to a spot about halfway between two windows. Then he went to work. Sixty seconds later, five aluminum strips of skirting were on the ground and Kurt's Maglite was shining in the gap. He peered in cautiously and then let out a long, low whistle.

"Well, I sure wasn't expecting that. Not with these jokers."

He sat back on his haunches and waved Hank over. Hank took the offered flashlight and slumped down next to Kurt. The tech elbowed him forward. "Don't worry. Nothing's going to bite you."

Hank leaned in and saw nothing in the beam of light but three full black garbage bags. He groaned at the thought of what disgustingness could be inside. Then off to the right, he saw the fourth bag, which had come untied at the top and spilled its contents on the packed dirt. He sat back, stunned.

"Yeah," Kurt said. "I know. That's a lot of cash."

Bills, in what looked like all different denominations, poured from the bag. Many of them were crumpled and bent, like they'd just been pulled out of somebody's jeans pockets and dumped on the dresser after a night out. Hank stuck his head in the gap again and played the light over the other bags.

"Holler for someone to bring your camera," Hank said. Kurt began to stand up. "No. Stay here." Kurt shrugged and started shouting. They waited until Gabler hustled around the corner of the trailer with the equipment.

"I want every dollar documented and witnessed by all three of us," Hank told them.

Gabler shook his head and pointed toward the other end of the property and the small shed. "They need you over there."

Hank nodded and said he'd send someone else over to witness the collection. Then he took a deep breath of the comparatively clean air and headed off toward olfactory hell.

Where Alice was smiling. He thought. It was hard to tell with the full face mask on. She met him about twenty feet from the shed and went through a series of gestures he didn't understand in the slightest. He frowned at her.

"I'm breathing in this stink. You can too. Take off the damn respirator."

She pulled it off and grinned at him.

"They might be smarter than we think," she said. "They are definitely as nasty as we think, but I gotta say, as far as a defensive plan goes, it's pretty good."

Hank's scowl deepened. He was not in the mood. She quickly adjusted, clearing her throat in serious fashion as she pointed to the sides of the shed.

"See that trench? It goes all the way around. About a foot and a half deep. That's a guess, though. I haven't measured it yet, because, well . . . it's full of shit."

Hank was so surprised his jaw dropped. Alice never swore. She saw the changed look on his face.

"I don't know how else to say it, really. Human, dog, probably cat. And goodness knows what other kinds. It's a feces fence."

At one point, she continued, it also served to mask the odors of meth manufacturing. But that didn't appear to have been done in there for quite a while. She handed him a regular ventilator and led him to a piece of plywood that lay over the shit moat like a drawbridge. The door to the shed was wide open, and B. Handlesman looked up as they entered. He pointed out the empty tubs and containers. The place might have had the old-cat-piss smell characteristic of meth manufacture, but it was hard to filter out the exterior stench to be sure. Dust and pollen had settled on the wooden workbench, and motes caught in the light from the single window as they drifted through the air.

"We're taking samples to see how contaminated the soil is. It's possible the whole site needs remediation. But there's no immediate danger."

Hank nodded and left as quickly as he could. He got in his own squad car, turned the AC on high, and stuck his head in front of a vent. As the canned air gradually diluted the foulness in his lungs, he tried to clear his mind as well. At least there was one positive to report. He'd get to tell Sammy that his meth suspicions were right on. He hoped—fervently—that it would make a difference.

The poor kid had been driven home by Earl Crumblit, who had gotten off his jail shift and called in to see what he could do to help. Hank told him to stay with Sam and make sure the kid showered and ate something. He had a feeling that if nobody was there to insist on it, Sam would just sit his bloodstained self in a chair on his back porch and not move for days.

Hank did not have that luxury. He had a huge mess to clean up. A mess of his own making. He never should have allowed the two of them to run into the woods after that thug. He never should have brought only three men for the initial raid. He never should have—

His cell beeped with Maggie's special tone. He ripped the phone out of his pocket and looked at the text.

Out of surgery. Still touch and go. Can't talk now. Will call later.

He never should have taken this damn job.

CHAPTER

22

Sheila had been tied to the office all day. Hank knew she was aching to get out and join the search, but someone had to be the point person for the multi-agency response that was flooding southern Missouri with law enforcement. When he staggered in at nine o'clock that evening, she was still working the phone and the computer simultaneously. She had a whiteboard marker jabbed into her no-longer-tidy French-twist hairdo and more worry lines etched in her face than he had seen before.

She hung up the phone and turned to him. "Why the hell has your cell been off?"

He'd stopped by the hospital to see the Pimental family. They hadn't been allowed into the recovery room yet, and everyone was getting more and more upset. Ted's prognosis was not good.

They sat still for a second, Hank thinking about Ted's three kids and Sheila muttering about the war on cops. Then the computer dinged with an email notification, pulling them both out of their ruminations. Sheila turned toward Hank and her worry lines eased.

"I do know which one we're looking for."

Hank almost leapt out of his seat.

"What? How? Which one is it?"

"You don't have to be yelling about it," she said, looking like a cat who'd just polished off a bucket of cream. "I just had a little chat with Lloyd Taylor. I thought I should take advantage of his isolation, before he hears what's been going on today."

Hank's own grin spread slowly across his face. "What'd you get out of him, Sheila?"

She was about to respond with the phone rang. She glanced over and swore.

"That's the marshals. I got to take this. I've been waiting for them to get back to me all damn night." She reached for the receiver with one hand and pointed toward Hank's office with the other. "Go call up Interview Room B. I videoed the whole thing."

Hank hustled into his office as Sheila answered the phone with her best sweet-talk-the-feds voice. He called up the digital recording on his computer, sat back, and hit play.

"Who're you?" Lloyd slouched lower in his plastic chair, oozing contempt and sweat in equal measure. Probably sat like that in school—however much of it he actually attended.

"My name is Deputy Turley." She sat down across the table.

"You don't look like no deputy." He rattled the shackle around his ankle. "You look like a cashier at Kmart."

Sheila didn't bat an eye, merely made a notation on the pad of paper she'd brought in with her. Lloyd shook the shackle again and poked at the Styrofoam cup half full of cold coffee on the table. He'd been gnawing on the rim.

"What? What you writing? About how long I been in here? Hours. That's cruel and unusual, man. And I already talked to somebody. That tall dude. No reason for me to be in here again."

"There is, actually," she said. "We went out and took a look around your land."

Lloyd's posture stiffened and the jangling stopped. "What?"

Sheila made another note. Lloyd lunged forward. She didn't flinch, just stared coolly at him.

"You can't do that. You gotta have a warrant." He tried to get up, but got nowhere with his ankle bolted to the floor. He fell back into his chair. "That's private property, you bitch."

Sheila pulled a sheet of paper from underneath her notepad and slid it across so he could see it.

"Signed by a judge. Access to every inch of your land." She drew the paper back under the notepad. No need for him to see the particulars.

His pointed chin jutted forward. "I want a lawyer. We want a lawyer. Where are my brothers?"

"Well, I can answer that for you, but that means that I'm going to have to keep talking to you. Do I have your permission to do that, keep on talking—you and me—without a lawyer?"

Just like that, smooth as Ozark honey.

"Yeah. Answer my damn question." The metal around his ankle began to rattle again, slightly. He was trying not to shake. "Where are my brothers?"

"Of course," Sheila said, and smiled. "Leroy was there when we searched. We brought him down to the station, just to talk. Normal procedure, you know."

She stopped and jotted another note. Lloyd looked like he wanted to ram the pen down her throat.

"What about Jackson and Boone?" he yelled.

"Well, they weren't there," she said. Lloyd lunged again.

"Where are they?"

He was worried. This was going quite well. She laid her palms flat on the laminate table and tried to sound concerned.

"Now, Lloyd, you sound upset. Are your brothers in danger? Do we need to help them?"

He froze.

"Nah. They're fine. It's cool." He forced himself into a slouch again, but he wasn't able to stop his hands from trembling.

Sheila started writing again. Without looking up from the paper, she casually asked, "When was the last time you saw Jackson and Boone?"

"I see all my brothers all the time," he snapped.

"Oh, okay," she said soothingly. "I guess I didn't realize you all were that close."

He growled at her. An actual growl, like a dog. She had to stop herself from rolling her eyes.

"Course we are, bitch."

She put down her pen and looked directly at him. "Then, well, why don't you know where they are? 'Cause if you don't, well, now I'm worried, too. Where could they be?"

His eyes got very large and his breathing very fast. And Sheila got very interested. She waited a few beats and then lobbed her question like a firecracker into a fish pond. Curious to see what floated to the surface.

"Has your business gotten dangerous?" The same concerned voice.

He blinked rapidly. "No. What business? We don't got no business."

"Really? That's not what we found during our search."

He smirked. "You didn't find nothing."

"Then what has you so worried?"

"Nothing."

"Then where are your brothers?"

She was running him around in circles. He looked like his head was about to explode. He rubbed a hand over his face, glared at her, and clamped his lips shut. Time to shake things up a bit. She pulled her phone off the clip on her belt and checked the screen. Her eyes widened in surprise and she grabbed her papers and left the room.

As soon as the door clicked shut behind her, Lloyd started savagely yanking his cuffed leg. Sheila, watching from behind the two-way mirror, let the tantrum continue for exactly two minutes and then let herself back in the room.

He immediately fell back into his standard slump. She sat back down and patted at her hair.

"Well, I guess we're done here. They found them."

"What? Found who? Who found who?"

"We did," she said briskly. "We found your brothers. They're in custody. Getting brought in now. I should go process the paperwork." She made as if to stand.

"Wait." The word exploded out of him as he leaned forward, his dirty hair falling across his forehead and into his eyes. "Both of them? They're here? You have Jackson, too?"

He fought back a grin and sagged against the molded back of his chair. She smothered her own smile.

"I guess those worries were for nothing," she said. "Of course, they'll be charged with evading arrest, you understand."

Lloyd waved his hand dismissively. "That's nothing." He stopped. "But . . . since they're here, can I talk to them?" He tossed it out like it was no big thing, but the undercurrent of little-boy pleading came through clearly.

Sheila started to say no, but then pretended to argue with herself for a moment. She let out a sigh. "I maybe could . . . seeing as you've been in here awhile, and aren't making bail. Probably only one, you understand. It's not exactly regulation. If I could get you one of your brothers, which one would you want to talk to?"

"Jackson," he said instantly, then took ahold of himself and casually swept his palm across the table. "Yeah. Jackson, I guess. Or whoever."

Sheila made a show of fidgeting a bit. "I'll see what I can do. I have to process everything first, though, you understand." He nodded eagerly. She tapped her paperwork into a neat stack and stood up. "I just can't believe we found them there. What a hiding place."

He pushed his hair out of his face and eyed her suspiciously. "They weren't there. If they had been, you wouldna found 'em."

She arched a perfectly curved eyebrow. "Oh, really?"

"Yeah. Really." Now he was a snot-nosed kid gloating that he knew more than the grown-ups.

"We know this area pretty well."

"*We* know them hills better than anybody. You musta caught 'em out. No way, otherwise."

"Where possibly could anyone hide that we couldn't find them?" she taunted.

"You're just trying to get me to tell. And I ain't gonna." He sat back.

Sheila shrugged. Let him think he saw through her questions. She gave him a smile and swept out of the room.

Hank hit the stop button. Brilliant. She was just brilliant. He walked back out into her office just as she was hanging up the phone and told her so. She nodded graciously in response.

"It seems that he hasn't seen or talked to Jackson in a while, so it's got to be Boone who was in the trailer and took off when we showed up. And he's got to be still in the hills," he said.

She nodded. "I just sent his record to the marshals. They're going to take over coordination of the manhunt." There was no small amount of relief in her voice. "They're already hunting down known associates."

"Good," he said. "Now go home. And tomorrow, you're out of this building. How about you get out to the scene, then start tracking the money. Kurt should have finished counting it by then."

Sheila grimaced. "I wish I'd known about you finding that

before I interviewed Lloyd. I never would have guessed those losers could amass that much cash. And he must think it's still safely hidden, because he didn't seem worried about it. Just worried about Jackson."

"Yeah," Hank said slowly, raking his hand through his hair. "About that brother . . ."

Sheila shut down her computer and sat back with a gleam in her eye. "I know. If they all live together, and Lloyd hasn't seen his scumbag, itinerant brother Jackson in a long enough time to actually be worried about him . . . how long you think that'd take?"

Hank gave her his first actual smile of the day. "Ten to fourteen days, I'd say."

She reached into her bottom desk drawer and pulled out a clear evidence bag. Inside was a Styrofoam cup, chewed around the rim. "I thought some familial DNA might be useful."

Hank's grinned widened. "Like I said. Brilliant."

CHAPTER

23

BRANSON CO. DEPUTY SHOT

Massive manhunt underway for suspected gunman; opposition sheriff candidate questions judgment
By Jadhur Banerjee

A Branson County sheriff's deputy is in critical condition after getting shot during an investigation in the northern part of the county yesterday morning. Local, state, and federal authorities have flooded the area in a search for the suspected shooters, two brothers with a long string of local arrests.

Boone Taylor, 21, and Jackson Taylor, 25, are wanted in connection with the shooting of Deputy Theodore Pimental, and are considered armed and dangerous. Authorities declined yesterday to disclose which brother they believe fired the shots that hit Pimental.

"We urge the public to be on the lookout for these individuals," said Deputy U.S. Marshal Wesley Dixon.

"They are armed, and have shown that they have no respect for life. If anyone sees or hears anything about their whereabouts, we urge you to call 9-1-1."

Authorities said the Taylors were at the family's property near Hogsback Hollow when Pimental, 35, accompanied Sheriff Hank Worth and two other deputies to question them in connection with an ongoing theft investigation.

The Taylor brothers fled, shooting and wounding Pimental in the process. The deputy was rushed to Branson Valley General Hospital, where he remained in critical condition last night.

While law enforcement officials throughout the state expressed support for the Branson County Sheriff's Department, some questioned the decision to take only four deputies to such a potentially dangerous location.

Worth's opponent in the upcoming sheriff election, Gerald Tucker, said that deputy safety is paramount.

"These Taylors are known threats to law enforcement. To go out there without full backup is incredibly stupid," Tucker said. "This just proves that Hank Worth doesn't know who the bad guys are in this county. And he doesn't know how to keep our deputies safe."

Worth was leading the shooting investigation yesterday and could not be reached for comment.

Kaitlyn Murphy of the Eye on Law Enforcement League said that situations vary, but commanding officers must always be aware of how quickly an incident can turn deadly.

"That is their most important duty—the safety of their officers and of the public," she said. "Imagine if this had occurred in a crowded area. More people could have gotten hurt, and that is unacceptable."

However, Kevin Cox, a member of the national Police Chiefs Fraternal Organization, said that the facts in this case appear to support Worth's actions.

"All the deputies were out there for was an interview, not a raid. These guys were criminals, but they didn't have violent records. I think four officers was a very sensible contingent to take."

Taylor is the son of Merlon Taylor, a longtime north county resident who was killed in a 2002 car crash while fleeing sheriff's deputies who were attempting a traffic stop. When paramedics pulled Merlon Taylor from the wreckage, they discovered a kilo of cocaine in his car.

Despite multiple investigations, authorities have never been able to link Merlon Taylor's four sons to his drug trade. All of them, however, have had their own problems with the law.

Jackson Taylor has multiple arrests dating back to his juvenile days. He was convicted three years ago of identity theft and stealing from the Branson Wal-Mart, and served two years in prison.

Boone Taylor also has almost a dozen arrests for misdemeanor stealing and DWI. He is wanted for failing to appear in Greene County associate circuit court on a traffic violation.

Leroy Taylor, 22, recently served 11 months in county jail for possession of marijuana. He also has several misdemeanor convictions for shoplifting and other stealing offenses, including the theft of a neighbor's pig. He was taken into custody at the family property yesterday without incident.

Lloyd Taylor, the youngest brother at 19, also has misdemeanor convictions for stealing and for possession of marijuana. He is currently on probation. He has been held without bail at county jail since last week on a charge of assault in connection with an incident at a city of Branson tattoo shop.

All four live at the Hogsback Hollow property where yesterday's shooting occurred. Deputies worked well into the night processing the crime scene and removing evidence.

Pimental, a graduate of Branson Valley High School, is a 13-year veteran of the department. He is a resident of Hollister and a member of River Baptist Church.

"We continue to pray for Ted, and we ask everyone out there to pray for him as well," said Brian Wilcox, River Baptist minister. "We know that with the Lord's help, he will get through this."

Hank forced himself to read the entire article. As usual, Jadhur had talked with everyone even remotely relevant to the story. Hank hated that.

He and the deputy marshal heading the manhunt had decided yesterday afternoon to put both brothers out as wanted, since they didn't know which one had done it. It was only after Sheila's evening interview with baby brother Lloyd that he'd become confident he knew which Taylor it was. And he was going to keep that piece of information to himself for the moment. It wouldn't hurt to have a large contingent of federal marshals looking for Jackson as well.

He tossed the newspaper on the table just as Dunc walked in from the garage. Guapo trotted beside him. He had dirt on his nose and looked very pleased with himself. Dunc had dirt on his hands and did not. Hank knew what that meant.

He waited until Dunc had turned off the Johnny Cash blaring through his earbuds before speaking.

"What'd he do this time?"

Dunc snorted. "Mrs. Crawford's geraniums. Demolished two of them before I could get him away from the damn flower bed." He glowered at the dog, who plopped down at his feet with a satisfied grunt. "Thank God it's five in the morning and nobody saw it happen."

Hank rolled his eyes. By now, the entire neighborhood knew exactly who was responsible for the overnight "landscaping work" that had reshaped numerous front yards in the four months they'd owned Guapo.

"I didn't mean it that way," said Dunc, misinterpreting Hank's look. "I'm going to replace them. I'm not trying to get out of it. I'd just rather not actually talk to Mrs. Crawford."

Hank hid a smile. The long-divorced Mrs. Crawford never passed up an opportunity to talk to eligible widower Duncan McCleary. But Hank knew better than to tease him about it. It was still too soon after Marian's death. Her fatal heart attack had been less than a year ago.

Dunc poured himself a cup of coffee and then filled the empty travel mug sitting on the counter. He crossed the kitchen and handed it to a surprised Hank.

"I'm sorry about your deputy," he said. "I know you'll find the bastard who did it."

"Thanks, Dunc. I appreciate it."

Guapo had settled on Hank's feet. His tail softly thumped against the linoleum floor. Hank gently nudged him off.

"You headed back out there?"

"Not yet," Hank said. "There's someone I need to check on first."

The house was dark, except for a faint light in the kitchen window. It was a tiny cottage in an older neighborhood near downtown. Hank knew Sam rented it almost solely because of the sizable, and heavily secured, shed in the back where he was able to keep all of his hunting gear.

He knocked quietly on the front door. He saw a shadow block the kitchen light and then heard the deadbolt slide back. A woman in her mid-fifties swung the door open and gave him a wan smile.

"Hello, Sheriff."

"Mrs. Karnes?" Hank had never met Sam's mother.

She nodded and gestured him inside. He followed her through a small living room dominated by a huge TV and a long green velour couch and into the kitchen, which smelled of coffee and bread. She made him sit at the table as she bustled in the little space—pouring coffee, checking the oven, straightening the dish towels. She finally settled into the one other chair and told Hank he should call her Leslie.

"I couldn't sleep, so I thought I'd start a batch of raisin bread. It's his favorite."

Hank nodded. Her raisin bread was legendary at the office. There was a mad scramble for it whenever Sam brought it in.

"How is he doing?"

"Well, I hope that he'll be better today," she said. "He didn't fall asleep until really late. And he certainly didn't want me here. I wouldn't have known if Carrie hadn't called me." She stopped at Hank's confused look. "Oh, she's in our church. And her sister over in Forsyth is married to Earl Crumblit. He's worked at the jail for I don't know how long."

The small-town grapevine comes through again, he thought.

"And he wouldn't talk to me," she continued. "Just took a shower twice, even though Earl said he'd already taken one."

Hank guessed that it would take more than that to wash away what had happened yesterday. He pulled out a business card, wrote his personal cell number on the back, and asked her to call him with an update whenever Sam woke up. Or if she needed anything. He slid the card across the small table between them.

She ran her finger over the raised sheriff's logo. "Sammy really likes you. He says that you're kind. Not weak, nothing like that, but kind. I don't think he's ever worked for anybody like that before. It's not a very . . . common . . . law enforcement characteristic." She picked up the card. "I hope you win the election."

Hank was stunned. He had no idea Sammy felt that way. He had always worried that he was too hard on the kid.

He must have looked surprised, because Leslie laughed. "Don't worry. I won't spread that around. I know you got to be tough to be considered sheriff material. I won't say anything when I'm going door-to-door."

"Well, I appreciate—wait, what? You're going door-to-door?"

She nodded. "It's actually kind of fun. I've never done it before. Cindy and I have done four neighborhoods so far, and we're doing another two soon. Handing out your pamphlets and talking about you. Most people even give us a listen."

If he was stunned before, now he was speechless. He stared slack-jawed at her for a moment until he realized he was being a jackass. He thanked her profusely and was about to ask her to thank the Cindy he didn't know when Sam staggered into the kitchen in a T-shirt and boxers. His brown hair, which had obviously been wet when he went to bed, stood up in all directions.

He stopped short and glared at Hank.

"Samuel," his mother said in a finely honed remember-your-manners tone. "The sheriff just came by to see how you're doing."

Sam's glare stayed put.

"How's Ted?"

"They took him in for another surgery about four this morning," Hank said. "He's not out yet."

Sam sighed and lurched over to the coffeemaker.

"Honey, maybe you should go back to bed."

Sam whipped around, knuckles white around his coffee cup. Hank stood quickly to leave. He did not need to see a grown man argue with his mother about taking a nap.

Apparently Sam didn't need to see it, either. He smacked the coffee cup down on the counter. "I'm coming with you."

"What?" Hank and Leslie said at the same time. Then they both started in.

"I don't think—"

"Honey, you need to rest—"

"We've got this handled, Sam, and—"

"Am I going to have to call your father? He wants to bring over Pastor Tom anyway."

That did it. Sam slid the mug into the sink so forcefully that the handle broke off.

"I am going to go to work." He pointed to Hank. "You stay there. I'm going to get dressed."

Leslie let out an exasperated sigh. "Fine. Let me wrap up the raisin bread for you."

"I don't want it." He stomped into his bedroom and slammed the door.

Hank frowned. Now, that was over the line. Leslie apparently thought so as well. She pulled the bread out of the oven, put it in a foil-lined container, and covered it with a towel. She handed it to Hank with a wink, then turned serious.

"Take care of my boy, Sheriff. Please."

"I promise, ma'am. He's not even going to go out to the site. I'll have him do paperwork all day."

"Like hell you will," Sam shouted from the bedroom. That was followed by several thuds and a stream of loud and incoherent grumbling.

"Maybe I'll wait in the car," Hank said. He thanked Mrs. Karnes again, went out, and settled into the cruiser. Daylight was starting to crack across the sky to the east, heading his way and toward the northern county woods where the shooter was hiding. And where two people had died and moldered in the dark earth.

He tore off a hunk of the warm bread. He had a feeling it was the best thing that was going to happen to him today.

CHAPTER
24

No one said a word. It sat on the table in Interview Room B like a halfheartedly tossed salad. Sheila reached out to touch it, but then reconsidered and withdrew her hand. Sam shifted from foot to foot and almost gave up his scowl. Kurt leaned wearily against the wall with a clipboard in his hands. Hank stood in front of it and wondered where the hell he was going to keep it.

Finally, Doug Gabler spoke.

"One million, five hundred forty-seven thousand, five hundred and twelve dollars."

Unbelievable.

The Branson County Sheriff Department's evidence room was not equipped to hold that much money. Setting aside the actual value and the security needed to protect it, that much in small bills took up an extraordinary amount of room. It looked like about a fifth of it was in bank-stacked order, neatly bound by denomination. That wasn't so bad. The rest, though, was crumpled, wadded, and ripped.

"We counted it twice on site and again here this morning,"

Gabler said. "We tried to get it into stacks"—he waved at the wrinkled pile—"but, geez, it was hard."

Kurt stepped forward and handed Hank a sheet of paper. It was a breakdown of denominations and which bags they'd been found in. He and Gabler took them through the whole list. Toward the end, Hank noticed that both men still had dirt on their knees.

"Have you guys been home yet? Since yesterday?"

They shook their heads.

"Neither has Brian Handlesman from Branson PD," Kurt said. "Partly because once we got it all here, we didn't want to leave it alone. It's a lot of money."

Sheila mentally calculated the overtime, frowned, opened her mouth, and then stopped, looking at both men's exhausted faces. "You're right," she said, "and you did the right thing. That was a hell of a lot of work. You guys are going to make it possible to kick some Taylor ass. For Ted." They stood a little straighter at that. He really did love her sometimes.

"Okay, you guys are officially off-duty," Hank said. "Go down to the Whipstitch and eat breakfast. A good one. Tell Nan to put it on my tab. Then go home. Don't report back in until tomorrow morning."

They all filed out of the room. Hank locked the door and rounded up two fresh deputies to stand guard. Then he headed to his office. The crime scene would have to wait. Figuring out what to do with a fortune in cash had just become his priority.

"We could take it to the bank," said Sam, who had followed him into his office.

Hank shook his head.

"I wouldn't trust them to keep it separate," he said. "We've got to have the exact bills back. It's got to be in an evidence locker somewhere. With better security than we've got here."

Sam looked wounded. Hank thought fast.

"I'm not being critical. We're pretty good here. But that's

enough money to make any gang of idiots want to overrun this joint. And if there are enough of them, they just might be able to do it."

Sam gave a weak grin and lackluster chuckle.

"We do have a history of that around here," he said.

Hank looked puzzled.

"All that Bald Knobber stuff back in the 1880s. They were breaking people out of jail all the time. Course, it wasn't the 'state-of-the-art facility' we got now." He made air quote marks and grinned.

Hank hadn't known that bit of local history, but it worked to his benefit. He'd come up with that rationale so he didn't have to divulge his real reasons for finding somewhere else for the case. There were a whole lot of people with access to the department's evidence locker, and he didn't want any of his employees being tempted to peel a few bills off the top of that monstrous pile. Better to not put people in that position at all. Plus, if it were in someone else's custody, any theft couldn't be blamed on him.

Dear God, he was thinking like a politician.

He asked Sam to get them both coffee, wanting to keep the kid's body active and his mind off yesterday's events.

As soon as Sam disappeared out the door, Sheila came in. From the scoffing look on her face, she'd heard what he said. And knew it was bullshit.

"Look," Hank said. "I didn't think I needed to go into it with the poor kid that some of his fellow deputy friends might not be too trustworthy. Would *you* keep that"—he waved his hands in the air—"that mountain of money here?"

"No. I most definitely would not. But you need to come up with a better reason why you want it moved. No one but Sammy is going to buy that you're worried about an armed takeover of department headquarters."

He sighed and sat down at his desk. Sheila shot him a pitying half smile, said she'd be out at the scene, and sailed out of the
office. He spent the next ten minutes waiting for his coffee and
trying to track down the correct person to talk to at the regional
Missouri State Highway Patrol office in Springfield. When he finally got her on the phone, she didn't believe him. Until he sent
over a picture of Mt. Greenback, with his two deputies standing
next to it—for scale.

Yes, it was currently in his interview room. Yes, he agreed
that was not an ideal place for it. No, he didn't have room for it
in his evidence locker. No, he didn't have the personnel to drive
it up to Springfield. He didn't have the right kind of vehicle, either.
You know, one of those armored ones, that banks like to use? The
highway patrol did not find that funny.

After ten more minutes of back-and-forth, she finally agreed
to come pick up the money. Presumably in some kind of reinforced vehicle. Hank hadn't asked for specifics. He just wanted
the damn pile out of there. He hung up the phone and turned to
a cold cup of coffee and a glowering deputy.

He sat hunched in the chair in front of Hank's desk. He had
on faded jeans, a worn T-shirt for some band Hank had never
heard of, and a flannel button-down that was missing all of its
buttons and much of its color. His hair still stood at a dozen different trajectories.

"Look, I think we need to talk about this," Hank said.

Sam's mouth stayed shut.

"How are you feeling?"

"Fine."

"No, you're not. Obviously. This was a really big deal,
Sammy, and—"

Sam made a chopping motion in the air.

"Look, I'll write my report later," he said. "Now I need to
be, you know, helping find the guy who did this."

"The report's important, Sam. You know that. You're going to be a key witness when this goes to trial."

Sam slouched lower in the chair and mumbled something that sounded like "if." Hank stifled a sigh.

"Don't worry. We'll catch him," he said firmly. He had hoped that the more he said it, the more he'd believe it, but it wasn't working. And Sam's stony glare said he wasn't fooled. Time to redirect.

"Why don't you take some time and go see Ted in the hospital?" Hank asked.

The scowl slowly melted away and Sam's eyes filled. He slowly shook his head.

"Why not?" Hank asked softly.

"I can't. I just can't. He wouldn't be in there if it weren't for me. It's all my fault. I should've run faster. I should've been in the lead. I should've drawn my gun. I should've fired. I should have shot the bastard. And I didn't. I didn't do anything. I didn't save him."

He curled up upon himself, full of heartbreak and recrimination. Hank could relate, but he couldn't very well go over and give him a hug. That might send Sam over the edge. He tried desperately to think of something to say, and his eyes fell on a file teetering at the corner of his desk. He grabbed it and tossed it forward. At least he could do for Sam something he couldn't do for himself.

"I'm reassigning you."

Sam's eyebrows shot up. He picked up the file, and nodded when he saw what Hank had scrawled across the top. Little Doe.

"The missing-person case files are in my car," Hank said. "Go through them and prioritize them. Otherwise we're waiting on the forensic anthropologists. So . . ." He quickly cast around for another task. "How about in the meantime, you keep trying to track down Ned Bunning."

Sam nodded. "Oh, yeah. I forgot to tell you. I got permission from the business owner to search his work locker. I haven't had a chance to yet, though. I'll go do that now. Hopefully find something with DNA that we can run against Rotten Doe."

"There you go." Hank nodded encouragingly. "Great idea. The more progress we can make on ID'ing both of the victims, the better. And—"

He stopped talking, because Sam was no longer listening. His head was bent over the Little Doe file. He stopped near the end and held up an evidence photo of the skull, with the bullet hole clearly visible.

"I guess I didn't realize it was in the back of the head," he said.

Hank nodded. Sam slapped the folder shut and stood, straight and solid again.

"I'm on it," he said in a decent approximation of his normal voice.

He strode from the office, and Hank felt like a competent boss for the first time in days. But, man, was he in some kind of business, where getting handed two homicide cases improved an employee's morale.

Hank slowed the cruiser as the road curved about a quarter mile before the Taylor driveway. And swore when it straightened out and he could see the line of satellite trucks parked on the shoulder. The Springfield news stations had found the place. Damn Google Maps.

He rolled slowly through the gauntlet, trying not to look as annoyed as he felt. He saw Jadhur chatting with a brunette he was pretty sure worked for a KC station and a slicked-back blond guy he recognized as a columnist for the St. Louis paper. So the whole state was interested. He sighed.

And down at the end, parked slightly away from all the

activity, was a light blue Prius. A mop of gray curls was visible behind the dash. At least Lovinia wouldn't try to interview him.

He made it to the driveway and through the crime-scene tape before anyone realized it was the actual sheriff in the squad car and started banging on the windows. Alice met him outside the trailer and gave him an update. They'd found no more cash and only two handguns. Otherwise, the only thing of note, she said with a grimace, was the high number of decaying rodent carcasses in the moat around the shed.

Hank shot a disgusted glance toward the shed and did a double take as he saw Lovinia emerge from the woods behind it. She stopped and waited calmly as he strode over.

"How'd you get in here?"

She waved vaguely toward the woods. "Oh, you know."

She wasn't usually this assertive with her crime-scene bystanding. And she'd definitely never snuck past the roped-off boundaries before. He waited for an explanation. She gave him a cheery smile.

"You can't be in here, Lovinia."

"I know," she said unapologetically. "It was the only way to talk to you without the press seeing, though."

"And why do you want to do that?" His surprise was turning to exasperation.

"Well, Darcy is a little scared to contact you right now. She knows what a traumatic thing all this is, and she doesn't want to get you even more upset." She put her hands out, palms up, to stop the protest about to come out of his mouth. "So I thought I'd come out and tell you what you need to hear."

Sweet Lord. He wanted to just crawl into one of Guapo's holes and stay there until all of this was over with.

"You have to talk to them." She pointed toward the road and the media, who were mercifully blocked from their view by a row of trees. "And here is perfect. At the scene, showing that you're in command. Good visuals, too."

"I have work to do." It sounded like whining, even to him.

"And reassuring your constituents isn't part of that work?" Now she was the exasperated one.

He stood there, his good sense warring with the desire to hide somewhere. Lovinia took a very firm step toward him.

"And Tucker has been all over the morning news, ranting and raving. You, my dear, need to counter that. You can't let him be the only voice people are hearing in regards to this shooting."

She let that sink in. Which it did. Hank took a deep breath and nodded at her. She smiled at him and with a bounce of her curls, turned back the way she'd come.

"Hey. Wait a minute," Hank said. "How do you even know Darcy?"

She shot him a sly grin. "I'm a campaign volunteer. What'd you think?" She gave him a wink and disappeared into the woods.

"I am pleased to announce that Deputy Ted Pimental is making progress and has been upgraded from critical to serious condition. He is a very valued member of our department and we're all praying for his full recovery. I ask for all those watching this to do the same."

Hank self-consciously bowed his head for a moment and then looked back up into the camera lenses focused on his face.

"As for the suspects in yesterday's shooting—an extensive manhunt is currently underway for both Jackson Taylor and his brother Boone. Because we immediately set up roadblocks that cut off vehicle access to this entire portion of the county, we believe they are still in the woods. We are asking that residents living in outlying areas use caution when going about their business. These men are armed and dangerous. However"—he paused for effect—"I want to assure all of my residents—all of my *constituents*—that we will find these men and bring them to justice. Two Taylor brothers are already in custody, and these two will be soon. Thank you."

He began to move away from the bristle of microphones poking at his face, but the questions started almost instantaneously. He couldn't sort out who was asking what, so he just pointed at Jadhur.

"You must know which brother was the shooter," Jadhur said. "I've heard that there is only one person's trail that is being tracked through the woods. Which brother is it, and where's the other one?"

How did he find this stuff out? "We are searching for both Jackson and Boone Taylor."

Jadhur opened his mouth to protest the non-answer, but Hank quickly pointed at a lady from one of the Springfield stations.

"What ongoing investigation were you investigating when you went to interview the brothers?"

Hank tried to look apologetic. "That case is now part of the shooting investigation, so I'm going to have to decline to comment. When we have any kind of update that we can release to the public, we'll do so as quickly as possible. I *will* keep my constituents informed."

More shouted questions. He pointed to the St. Louis columnist.

"Should you have known that these guys were dangerous? Your election opponent, Gerald Tucker, is saying that you didn't use enough backup yesterday, and the whole incident was your fault."

He had known someone would ask that question. He put on the worn-out-parent look he'd practiced in his car's rearview mirror.

"Mr. Tucker is assigned to the Branson County Jail. He has

been since well before he announced his candidacy for sheriff. His assignment as a deputy has not brought him into contact with this investigation. At all. Not once. Anything that Mr. Tucker has said is a result of conjecture. He has no actual knowledge." That was probably a good spot to stop, so of course he didn't. "And I'd hope that Mr. Tucker would spend his energy wishing Deputy Pimental a speedy recovery, instead of hoping that we don't catch his shooter."

Tucker had not actually said that last part, but he could deny it on his own time. This was Hank's turn.

He pointed to a man from a different Springfield station.

"What kinds of prior theft convictions are we talking about here? At gunpoint?"

Damn, it was hard to keep his temper.

"No. That would be robbery," he responded. "Theft means that property was involved, but no violence to persons. In fact"— and thank God and Leroy's idiocy—"I believe the highest-value item taken by any one of them was a pig stolen by Leroy Taylor about a year ago. The owner had planned to show it at the fair, and pressed charges."

Some of the cameramen snickered. Lovinia gave him a surreptitious thumbs-up from her spot off to the side of the crowd.

That seemed like a good spot to end the whole damn thing. Hank gave a thank-you nod and backed carefully away from the swarm.

CHAPTER

25

Rapturous. Incredible. Absolutely pitch-perfect.

Darcy gushed on, and Hank made no move to stop her. It was the first time she had a reason to be complimentary during the campaign, and it'd probably be the last so he decided to enjoy it.

They sat in the Worth living room with glasses of iced tea as the sunset burnished the tall windows on either side of the big river-rock fireplace. She had been adamant that no one see them together, so she'd met Maggie at the hospital and hid in her minivan for the ride to the house. Hank had thought it was absurd.

"No," she'd said with exaggerated patience as she took the sugar bowl from Maggie, dumped an enormous scoop into her drink, and stirred it in with a meticulous swirling motion. "It's fine that people know you have a campaign manager. But this press conference you just did isn't related to the campaign and if people think I'm behind the scenes on it, feeding you lines or maneuvering things for political gain, it'll ruin the wonderful sheriff-in-charge image you've got going. I just need to lay low for a while on anything regarding the shooting." So she'd crouched among the crumbs and God knew what else in the back of the minivan until the garage door had closed and she was safely inside. And now she was singing his praises.

"You managed to smack Tucker down without it seeming like it had something to do with his being your opponent. I'm so proud that you didn't bring him up at all until someone asked you a question about it. That made it look like your focus is the investigation, and not the election."

Hank started to protest that his priority was indeed the investigation, but she waved him quiet.

"*And* you managed to make it seem like those Taylor brothers were just a bunch of stupid yokels who steal laughable things like pigs. Which totally undercuts the criticism that you should have known they were big, violent, scary threats. Just excellent." She sat back and took a sip of her aggressively sugared tea. "Now we just need to build on this momentum."

Hank started to speak again, but stopped when Maggie laid her hand on his arm.

"What do you suggest?" she asked Darcy.

"Well, we ignore all media requests for a couple of days at least. He needs to look like he's concentrating on the shooting."

"That's what I *am* concentrating—" He stopped when Maggie squeezed his arm.

". . . Battenberg's radio show. I'll set that up when the time is right. And then . . ."

Darcy went on, but Hank stopped paying attention. He stared out the window and wondered if Boone Taylor was looking at the sunset right now from his hidey-hole in the woods. He wondered if that was actually Jackson Taylor lying on a slab up in Springfield, his rotting decay suspended by heavy-duty refrigeration. And he wondered about a set of little, fragile bones that had been sent up to a forensic anthropology expert who would hopefully be able to tell him something about the child whose bulleted skull haunted his sleep.

He looked away from the darkening sky to find both his wife and his campaign manager staring at him in exasperation.

"Well?" Darcy said.

Hank looked to Maggie for help, but got only an eye roll in response. She let him stutter for a moment before taking pity on him.

"We're going to commit to some more campaign appearances. And we need to have a fund-raiser. Maybe a barbecue," Maggie said. "Tucker has a lot more money than we do, thanks to Gallagher and all of the donations from his employees."

Darcy nodded and waved a spreadsheet at him. He was glad he'd tuned out for that part. He nodded solemnly. He really had no choice.

"Okay. I agree. You can commit me."

Maggie smothered a grin. Darcy didn't catch it. She was busy tapping notes into her phone.

"All right," she said, dropping the phone into her mammoth tote bag and standing up. "This is great. We'll use this momentum and keep rolling right along. More supporters, more donations, more success. We're on our way."

Hank wasn't too sure about that. He glanced at Maggie, who shot him a look back that said, *Don't you dare stomp on her enthusiasm with your pessimistic-ass grumpiness.* So he slapped on a smile and walked them both to the garage, where Darcy again climbed in the back of the minivan for the trip back to the hospital to retrieve her car. Maggie gave him a quick kiss and a wink before getting behind the wheel.

He watched them leave from the front window, hoping that Darcy's faith in the campaign—and Maggie's faith in him—wasn't misplaced.

He was turning back toward the living room and his iced

tea when he saw it—a brown Nissan Sentra, model year between 2004 and 2007, parked across the street three houses down. It had not been there when he got home an hour and a half before. The man in the driver's seat was a study in nonchalance. Leisurely scrolling through his phone, as if he were merely killing time waiting for someone to come out of the house. But Hank knew the Conways had gone to see her mother in Florida and weren't due back until next Thursday. And the way the guy was parked gave him a very good angle from which to aim his phone's camera directly at Hank's front door.

He needed to start giving Darcy more credit.

He slowly backed away from the window, grabbed the big Mag flashlight from on top of the fridge, and slipped out the back door. Thankful it was almost completely dark by now, he jogged through his neighbors' backyards until he had passed where the Nissan was parked. Then he cut through Mrs. Crawford's side yard, dropping into a crouch as he crossed the street and came up behind the sedan.

He rounded the back bumper, stood, took two strides forward, and turned the flashlight on directly in the driver's face. The guy jumped a foot. Some professional.

"License and registration, please."

The guy was solidly built. Broad shoulders, very short dark hair, olive skin. He was innocuously dressed in a gray polo shirt and jeans. And his phone had a telephoto lens attached to it.

"License and registration," Hank repeated.

The guy recovered quickly. He put both hands on the wheel (smart) and tried looking at Hank (not smart). He couldn't see through the glare of the flashlight.

"I'm not driving, Officer," he said.

"You're sitting in the driver's seat. License and registration. Slowly."

Hank couldn't ticket him for anything, but he did want to

confirm his suspicion. This had to be Kondakor, the off-the-books private investigator for Wikson & Clancy, Gallagher's St. Louis law firm.

The gumshoe slowly pulled his wallet out of his front pants pocket and extracted a license. I'm batting a thousand today, Hank thought. Carl Kondakor on Cleveland Avenue in St. Louis. Next came the registration. The car belonged to a woman named Cecilia Liu, out of Florissant in the St. Louis area. He'd track down information on her later.

He handed back the paperwork and asked what Kondakor happened to be doing on a quiet neighborhood street such as this. Gumshoe waved toward the Conways'. Waiting. They were late getting home. Hank shook his head, but the guy couldn't see him because the flashlight was still aimed full in his face. So he vocalized it.

"That's funny, because they don't get back from their trip until next Thursday."

He was thinking fast, Hank could tell, but he wasn't used to operating in a place where people actually knew their neighbors.

"Well, sir," he said, "I was given this address. It might be the incorrect one if it's as you say. I'll check it with my . . . mother. She's the one who asked me to stop by here."

"Oh, really?"

"Yes, sir. She sometimes does get things confused. I'll check with her." He reached down toward the ignition.

"I'm sure you will," Hank said, lowering the flashlight so Gumshoe could see his smirking face. "So who's your momma—Wikson or Clancy?"

Gumshoe gaped at him. And then burst out laughing. Hank raised an eyebrow.

"You are definitely not as dumb as they told me you were," he said. "You had me thinking you were just some Branson PD patrol with nothing better to do. And you snuck out of your house without me seeing you. Very nice."

Hank scowled at him. The compliment at the end had not negated the insult at the beginning. Gumshoe started the car.

"I'm going to have to up my game. Excellent." He reached down and shoved the car into gear. "I'll be seeing you, Sheriff."

His laughter floated out the open car window as he gunned the engine and sped away. Leaving Hank standing in the middle of the street with the uneasy feeling that he'd just given away a major advantage.

Maggie was not pleased to hear that their house had been under surveillance.

"You really shouldn't use those kinds of words around the kids," Dunc said.

He gave her a very parental frown and turned back toward the dishes in the sink.

"The kids are brushing their teeth." She waved toward the hallway, where suspicious splashing sounds were starting to come from the bathroom. "They didn't hear anything."

Dunc didn't deign to turn around again. He started his own splashing, tossing plastic kiddie cups into the soapy water with theatrical reproof. Maggie rolled her eyes and turned back to Hank.

"What are you going to do about it?" she asked.

There wasn't much he could do. The PI hadn't broken any laws, he told her. He was pretty sure the guy wouldn't be watching the house anymore, he added. He did not mention that his decision to confront the guy might mean increased scrutiny on other fronts.

"I'll tell Darcy, and I'll keep an eye on things," he said. "It'll be fine. He's not going to *do* anything."

He found his cell phone on the little built-in desk in the corner where they tossed everything when they came home from work and was making a show of finding Darcy's number when it rang. Maggie raised a questioning eyebrow and he shook his head. Not Darcy. She grumbled and headed toward the kids as Hank answered the unknown number.

A forceful male voice asked if he was speaking to Sheriff Hank Worth. Hank answered in the affirmative, and wondered how his private cell number had fallen into this man's hands.

"I am calling regarding the skeleton in the woods," he said stiffly. "I would like any information you have regarding the identity."

Hank moved into the empty living room and away from Dunc's background noise. He stood in front of the tall window by the fireplace and fought back a swell of anger at the night's second intrusion into his family life.

"And who are you?" he said in as even a tone as he could manage.

"My name is Calvin Holm."

Hank's anger instantly evaporated. Holm was on his list.

"I am," the man continued, "the brother of Jeremy Holm, who was kidnapped on June 5, 1976, in Rockaway Beach."

It was a sentence worn smooth with time and repeated use. So was this one:

"Do you know yet who the child skeleton is?"

How many times had this man asked that question? Every time a body was discovered anywhere in a ten-state region, Hank guessed. He explained the same things to Mr. Holm that he had to Mrs. Alton, who had indeed been the one to give Jeremy's brother Hank's phone number.

Calvin confirmed that his DNA was on file, as was his parents', both of whom had passed on. "Good thing," Calvin said. "I don't think they could have survived another body—another possibility that it was Jeremy, only to have it not be. It does kill you a little bit, every time."

Hank didn't doubt it. He sank onto the couch and asked a few questions, holding the phone away from his ear. Calvin's voice was still almost belligerent, but Hank now had a feeling it was a protective measure. Maybe the more loud and forceful he made his voice, the easier it was to get through his story.

The Holm family went on a picnic that Saturday. Festivities were really starting to crank up for the national bicentennial in July, and the parks and lake shorelines were already crowded on the weekends. They had all packed up the station wagon and headed down to a stretch by the lake that was privately owned, but that everyone used as a beach and picnic spot.

Jeremy was nine, and he was twelve. Their dad was an electrician and their mom had a day care. They took ham-and-cheese sandwiches and chocolate-chip cookies. And grape soda, special. Their parents stayed put after a long week's work while the boys ran around, darting through trees and chasing squirrels. And then Jeremy disappeared. Just . . . disappeared. There wasn't shouting, or the sound of a car driving away or anything. He just turned around, and Jeremy was gone.

He had wandered back to his parents and the picnic fixings. They all figured Jeremy'd be back. He never strayed far without Calvin. But after about fifteen minutes, their mother started to worry, and they started to search. After fifteen more, they went for the police. Another picnicker who they knew from church ran to his car and drove quick into town to use the phone.

By then, everyone there was looking. He was a skinny, little beanpole of a kid with a mess of black hair and big ears and probably a collection of rocks in his pocket. What he wasn't was sneaky. He'd never play a trick and hide. He wasn't that way.

They told that to the police, who didn't believe them. He'd probably just run off, they said. Were there problems at home? That one destroyed his mother. It wasn't until their pastor arrived and confirmed that Jeremy was not the type of boy to pull something like this that the cops started taking it seriously. They turned that property and everyplace else along the lakeshore inside out. And the only thing they ever found was a torn shred that matched the American-flag T-shirt Jeremy had been wearing. And more than forty years later, that was still all they had.

He still had nightmares about that day, Calvin Holm told Hank as he thanked him for his time. Hank promised to keep him updated and told him to call again if he needed anything. He hung up and hauled himself to his feet. He turned to find Dunc standing in the kitchen doorway and Maggie at the entrance to the hallway. Both of them were staring at him. Dunc's chin trembled, and Maggie's eyes brimmed with tears.

He gave them a sad smile and headed with a heavy step toward the bedrooms. It was his turn to read the bedtime stories.

CHAPTER
26

He'd already gone through an entire pot of coffee and it was only 8:00 A.M. He hadn't slept well at all last night. He'd finally given up, gotten dressed, and gone to see his deputy at the hospital. Ted was still in ICU but might be moved to a room later today if he remained stable. Hank prayed that would be the case.

He took a sip from the first cup off the second pot and leaned back in his squeaky desk chair. He had several things to do before heading out to the Taylor property, which had become the staging point for the manhunt. He picked up the phone.

"Wikson and Clancy, attorneys-at-law. How may I help you?"

He asked for Cecilia Liu and got an impatient sigh in return.

"Is this her boyfriend again? Look, file clerks are not supposed to get personal phone calls. You'll need to call her once she gets off work. You're going to get her in trouble."

He tried to sound like a chastised boyfriend as he hung up. Excellent. The Gumshoe had, just as he suspected, borrowed a junior employee's car for his reconnaissance trip. He hoped the jerk returned it in good condition. He resisted the temptation to use the department computers to look up what kind of car Kondakor actually owned. It wasn't an official investigation, and he shouldn't be using official avenues. But it would make it so much easier, he groused. Then he imagined Edrick Fizzel, spiky hair all aquiver, standing up at a campaign event with proof of Hank's illicit use of county resources. That doused his urge to misappropriate the way a cold shower doused—

He heard the door to the outer office bang open, followed by a set of unmistakably heavy footsteps. Kurt poked his head around the doorjamb.

"Got a sec, Sheriff?"

Hank waved him in.

"I was just curious that the money was safe," Kurt said. "You got it out of here, right?"

Well, that was proof right there he hadn't overreacted. If someone with a lot more county experience than him was also worried about it staying in this facility, then Hank had made the right call.

He reassured Kurt that it was now in Springfield, and then asked about the processing of the rest of the Taylor evidence. Kurt had just talked to Alice, who said that with the help of the Branson PD techs, it was almost complete. He was heading out to the scene now to help with packing everything up.

Kurt was almost out the door when a thought popped into Hank's head.

"Hey, wait a minute. Can I ask you something?"

"Course, Sheriff. What do you need?"

"I, um, I was just wondering about the stomping. You know, when you were in the Taylor trailer. I . . ."

Kurt started laughing. "I guess that did look mighty strange. I probably shook that thing something fierce."

He settled himself into the chair across from Hank's desk. He'd searched so many of those kinds of mobile homes—all of them rickety, cheap, old, or a combination of all three—that he'd developed a feel for them. The floor didn't feel the same if there was something hidden underneath it. Maybe it didn't have as much give to it, maybe it didn't feel as hollow. He shrugged. He'd never really thought about exactly why—he just knew it when he felt it. Originally, it had taken forever, slowly going over every square foot. But eventually, he developed a quicker system. He stomped. Hard. And that let him "feel" whether there was anything underneath the floors.

And that helped a whole ton when they had to pry off the metal skirting that shielded the space between the raised trailer and the ground. It was usually only about a foot and a half high and packed with all kind of bugs and gravel and such. Knowing where something was hidden meant they could crawl straight to it instead of searching the whole thing. So that's what he'd done yesterday. And bam, if it wasn't right where he knew it'd be.

"It's usually guns or drugs, though. It's never been cash. Not like that." He shook his head. "I never in my days thought I'd see something like that."

"Yeah," Hank said. "Me, either."

Kurt hefted himself to his feet just as Sheila called out that it was time to go. He grinned.

"She can holler at me all day long. She's doing the search warrant return paperwork, which means me and Alice don't have to." He gave a wave and headed out the door.

Five hours later, they saw him. Deputy marshals radioed in that they had spotted a man deep in the woods. He had slipped away, but all search teams were converging on the coordinates.

Hank and Sheila stood at the command center located upwind of the Taylor trailer and listened to several federals—at this point hot in temperature and in temperament—debate how Taylor had gotten away. Then things really got heated.

"It wasn't him," came a voice over the radio. Hank recognized the drawl of the state conservation agent attached to the northwestern search team.

"Well, who the hell else could it be?" a deputy marshal snapped. "Nobody's out for a day hike in this area right now. It has to be Taylor."

"It doesn't match the description of the suspect," the agent said calmly.

"How do you know? He was too damn far away." This from another deputy marshal on the team.

There was the sound of some shuffling and then a liberal amount of swearing.

"You brought a camera?" the marshal sputtered with rage. "We're not out here hunting a goddamn Sasquatch." More swearing. "Maybe that's why we didn't catch him. You're too busy taking his picture."

"I always bring a telephoto camera," the agent drawled. "Camera, gun, and hat. And I'm very good at using all three at the same time."

There was the briefest of pauses, and then Marshal Number One shouted in surprise. "Hey, put that away. What the hell? You don't draw on a federal marshal."

The agent chuckled. "Just makin' a point, boys. You may know fugitives, but I know these woods. So let's get on with a little bit more respect, shall we?"

There was a good deal of loud grumbling that didn't stop until a fourth voice cut through it.

"So, your picture doesn't match Taylor's description?" barked the Commando.

"Nope," said Wayne Pondo, the conservation agent. "Lookit." There was rustling as everyone crowded closer to the camera's view screen. "I can enlarge it up to here. That is not a dirty-blond guy with an average build."

"That's a skinny, little guy with black hair," the Commando from Branson PD said.

"Son of a bitch," growled Marshal Number Two.

"Well," shouted the clearly still pissed-off Marshal Number One, "does Taylor have an accomplice? That's got to be it. There's no other reason for someone to be out here in the middle of God-infested, bug-forsaken nowhere."

Pondo snickered. On their end of the radio, Sheila did, too. Hank picked up the mic and identified himself before Marshal One went headfirst off the deep end.

"The unknown individual is not working with the suspect," he said. "The unknown is likely a member of a work crew dispersed last week. He is not a threat."

Sheila shot him a puzzled look. Then comprehension dawned, and she hooted with laughter. Hank shushed her as Marshal Two started talking.

"'Dispersed' a work crew? What, into the woods? What the hell does that—oh, shit. They're illegals. And they escaped into the woods, didn't they?"

"Their status has not been confirmed," Hank said. "And they are not currently wanted by my office."

Marshal Two sighed. "How many are we talking?"

"Possibly up to ten."

He was pretty sure the strangled growling sound on the other end was Marshal One trying to keep from losing it completely.

"So . . ." Marshal One said once he had calmed down enough to form a sentence, "we have a forest full of people, essentially—who might or might not be innocent bystanders, who might or might not be illegals, and who might or might not know where the suspect is. Is that correct?"

When he put it that way, it did not sound that great, Hank had to admit.

CHAPTER
27

He was on his way back to the office when Sheila called. As the nearest deputy not actively searching the woods for Taylor, she had just been dispatched to a trespassing call. Hank was headed in the opposite direction and told her so.

"Yeah, but the RP is Donna Kolpeck." She paused for effect. "And she said her brother is going after Kinney—and he's armed." Another pause. "So I'm thinking trespassing doesn't quite capture the nature of—"

"I get it, Sheila. I'm on my way." He hit the lights and siren and aimed the cruiser back north.

Twenty minutes later, he pulled up next to Donna's Audi in a cloud of dust. When it settled, he could see Vern and his sister walking out from the trees. Followed by a shotgun-toting Sheila. This ought to be good.

He leaned against his cruiser and watched them make the last two hundred yards to the house. Donna was clearly pissed off, stomping along several feet in front of the others. Vern walked along with his head bowed and his hands stuffed in the pockets of his canvas pants. His hatless head was starting to turn pink.

Sheila had Vern's rifle slung over her shoulder and looked delighted. Out in the fresh air, no paperwork in sight, taking control of a situation. He thought about finding a reason to send her back into the woods for a while. Anything to keep that smile on her face.

Donna reached him first and suggested, quite loudly, that he arrest her brother. Vern started to argue, but fell silent as Sheila and her twelve-gauge drew even with him. Hank felt a little sorry for him. He wouldn't want to be bookended by those two, either, especially if he'd done—well, whatever the hell it was.

"What'd you do, Vern?" he said.

Sheila unslung the rifle and handed it to Hank.

"It's a longer story than standing out here can support," she said breezily. "How about we go inside and settle down, and Vern can tell it proper."

She waved the siblings ahead of her and gave Hank a wink. He grinned. This was shaping up to be better than good. They filed in through the narrow entryway and the two gun racks and the faded wallpaper and into the living room. Donna turned toward the kitchen but Sheila gently guided her to a seat, saying there'd be time for sweet tea in a bit. Then she casually leaned against the wall by the door, propped her shotgun up next to her, and gestured toward Vern.

He sighed and ran his hand over his sunburned head.

"I thought he was on my land. So I went out there."

Donna snorted. "Yeah. Yelling and screaming and waving your rifle."

Vern shot her a dirty look. "Doesn't mean you needed to call the cops. You always overreact and—"

"Me?" She was on her feet now. "Me, overreact? What do you call what you did? You damn—"

"Oookay." Hank, who was still holding Vern's rifle, stepped

forward from his own place against the wall. "We're going to let Vern talk here, and then it'll be your turn, Donna."

She slowly sank back into the chair, her back straight and eyes blazing. Vern turned his own chair away from her and toward Hank. He did not appear eager to open his mouth again.

"Who did you think was on your land?" Hank prompted.

Donna snorted again. Sheila caught her eye and shook her head. Donna pressed her lips together and fell silent.

"Jasper Kinney, of course," Vern said.

"And how would you know if he was on your property that far out in the woods?"

Well, he'd installed some motion-detector things, Vern explained. After the, ahem, activity that had gone on recently. And one of them went off. Right at the creek. So he went out to see what was going on. With his rifle, just like his daddy had always told him to do.

And Kinney had been out there, just as he'd thought. In the creek. So he'd stood at the edge of the water and demanded to know what the bastard was doing. Kinney had refused to say.

Which surprised exactly nobody.

"Is the creek your property? Or his?" Hank asked.

Vern fidgeted slightly and finally shrugged. The creek had always been considered the borderline between the properties, so if you were standing in the middle of it, well then, he wasn't exactly sure. So he'd stood on his side of things and yelled at Kinney some more. The bastard had waded out of the water onto his own side and gotten his shotgun from where it was leaning against a tree. At that point, he might have accused Kinney of stealing his slippery elm bark.

"That finally got him riled up," Vern said. "He turned around and fired that damn Topper in the air and told me I didn't know a goddamn thing about these woods. That I should sell the

place and take the worthless Mileses out of Branson County for
good."

He stiffened his spine. "Hell, no."

Hank folded his arms across his chest. "Then what'd you do,
Vern?"

Vern stared at his shoes. "I might have fired my gun, too."

Donna rolled her eyes. Clearly, her restraint was about de-
pleted. Hank turned to her.

"Kinney's been saying that for years. Since before we were
born. That's nothing new," she said.

"Oh, yeah, like you're so concerned with family pride and
history. Up in your fancy house in St. Louis."

"Hey, who came down to take care of Dad when he was sick?
Not you, you selfish jerk. You were 'too busy.' You left everything to me. Dumped it all in my lap."

"I offered," Vern yelled. "You just blew me off. Said I'd just
muck it up. You—"

Hank decided it was time to step in, before it became necessary to arrest Donna for assault. He held up his hands and shut
them both down.

"That's enough. Vern—quiet. Donna, your turn."

She straightened in her chair and clasped her hands in her
lap. She had waited in fright until the officer arrived—she pointed
at Sheila—and they both went after Vern.

At that, Sheila cocked an eyebrow and aimed it at Donna,
which meant she was calling bullshit. Hank scowled at Donna. The
woman looked over at Sheila and sighed.

"Okay. She told me to stay here, but I followed after her anyway," Donna said. "Which . . . was actually good, right? Because
I knew where he'd gone."

She snuck a glance at Sheila, who clearly intimidated her,
then took a deep breath and continued. They heard a good deal
of yelling as they approached the creek, and then a gunshot. Officer

Turley started running and made it there pretty quickly. They'd gotten to the creek right as Kinney said something and Vern fired his rifle. Officer Turley ordered them both to put their guns down. Vern lowered his but didn't drop it. Kinney laughed at her and disappeared into the trees on his side of the creek.

Then Officer Turley took Vern's rifle, which should just be tossed in the trash as far as she was concerned, Donna said, and they all walked back up to the house. "And now, here we are."

Yes, indeed. Here they all were. Stewing in a room that was stale and stuffy and full of hot air. Might as well use it.

"I want to know more about the feud between your family and the Kinneys."

They both stiffened at that, like cats that had seen a dog but not yet decided whether it was a threat. Vern decided it wasn't.

"We bought this land from Kinney's granddad, after World War I. They sold it. It was their choice. And they've been assholes about it ever since."

Donna nodded. It was thirty acres, and no, they didn't know why the elder Kinney had sold it. But soon after, he'd died and his son, Jasper Kinney's father, had come into the homestead. And he wasn't happy that a third of it had fallen into the hands of the Miles family. They'd hated each other ever since.

"Is that why Jasper said you didn't know the woods?" Hank asked.

"Yeah. We haven't been here a hundred and fifty years, so of course, I can't know the woods." His tone made clear what he thought of that line of logic.

Hank thought a moment.

"Is your land the only parcel that the Kinneys sold off?"

Vern thought so, but Donna hesitated.

"I remember Daddy saying once that the Old Kinney had sold some other land, before he sold this to our great-grandfather," she said. "He needed the money. I remember something about gambling, but I don't know whether that was about the Old Kinney or someone else, to be honest."

"So what does Jasper Kinney do with the land that's still in his family's possession?" Hank said.

"Guards it like it's a damn fortress," Vern said.

That was not very informative, and since these were the first two people Hank had come across who actually wanted to talk about the Kinneys, he was not going to leave it at that. Had Jasper ever farmed it, logged it, mined it—anything? They both shook their heads. He'd never done anything with it. He'd made his living as the manager of a tractor dealership until about five years ago, when he retired.

Hank turned to Vern. "And why do you think Jasper's the one who stole your bark?"

Vern started to fidget and then hem and haw. "I guess I don't really have a—"

"Just to screw with us."

They all swung toward Donna. "And look. It's worked. Vern's a mess. Which is just what Kinney wants." She shrugged. "I have no doubt he did it. But we need to just let it go. *You* need to let it go," she told her brother.

They were back to giving each other dirty looks, and that was how Hank and Sheila left them twenty minutes later. They walked out into air much cooler than what was inside and strolled over to Sheila's cruiser, which was parked farther away from the house and closer to the woods. Hank leaned against the hood as she secured her shotgun in its spot between the front seat backs and the partition that separated the backseats.

"What do you think? About Kinney being the thief?" he said.

She slammed the car door and looked back at the house, where a thick green curtain moved in one of the tall windows.

She rotated so she faced away before she started talking. And laughing.

"That man has no sense when he gets mad. Because anybody who goes waving a gun at Jasper Kinney like that and expects to walk away in one piece is a damn fool."

"So you saved a life today."

She gave him a wicked grin and pointed at the lettering under the sheriff badge on her squad car door. " 'Working for your safety and security,' " she drawled.

"But honestly," she continued in her normal voice, "I don't know. I don't know if Kinney would have bothered to shoot him. He obviously enjoys messing with him. If he shot Vern, who would he have left to hassle like that?"

She brushed a speck off her otherwise immaculate uniform. "So, I think Kinney might have done it, if he'd thought of it. Just to piss off Vern. But it's more likely it was the Taylor boys' operation. Plus, Jasper's got stripped trees of his own. And if there's one thing I don't think that man would do, it's destroy his own property."

Hank agreed. He inclined his head slightly toward the Miles farmhouse. "What do you think? Have we stood here long enough to get him worried? Worried enough that he'll think twice before doing something stupid again?"

They both laughed, careful not to let the watching Miles siblings see.

"Now," Hank said, "how about we keep the fun going and go talk to Jasper Kinney?"

Kinney did not answer his door. The brown-paneled house sat silent. The Confederate flag had been taken down. Hank knocked again. Nothing. They walked back to their squad cars.

"I got one more place to look," he said. "Follow me."

Fifteen minutes later they pulled into the gravel lot of the Redbone. It was later in the day this time, and the sun painted the shingle roof with orange glow instead of pounding it with white heat. There were many more vehicles, most of them pickups, parked along the front. The workday must be finished.

Hank didn't realize he was instinctively checking that his gun was ready in his holster until he saw Sheila doing the same as they walked up to the door. He opened it and she stepped inside with him right behind her. Then they walked up to the bar, the silence and the stares spreading behind them like a boat wake.

Creosote sat at the hickory plank just right of center. He was the one patron who had not turned around at their entrance. Hank took the empty barstool to his left and Sheila sat down immediately to his right. Hank looked down the bar toward barman Willie Boyd, who did not look pleased that they'd added themselves to his customer base. He stood for a moment, considering. Whatever decision he was weighing must have come out in their favor, because he finally started to very slowly walk their way. He stopped directly in front of Kinney.

"What'll you have?"

Sheila passed an admiring palm over the wood of the bar and then folded her hands in front of her. "Whiskey. Dickel No. 12."

Well, damn. He couldn't very well order a Budweiser now. He asked for a bourbon and didn't move until the bartender set it in front of him. He took it and casually turned around, leaning back against the bar. He wanted to see what the clientele thought of his temerity.

It was as if he'd spit on the altar at church. Men averted their eyes. They stared at the floor or at the ceiling and fidgeted uncomfortably. A few of the younger ones gaped at him in open disbelief. And then two older guys at a table near the dance floor got up and headed for the door. And every last customer followed them out.

The door clicked shut after the last of them. Hank turned back around. Willie retreated to the other end of the bar. And Kinney calmly took a sip of his drink, which looked like a pretty decent bourbon. Better than what he'd been served, Hank thought as he settled against the bar.

"So, that dead guy in your ravine was killed by a shotgun," Hank said.

Kinney said nothing. Sheila twirled the whiskey in her glass and nonchalantly shifted closer to Kinney. That made him finally turn his head. Toward Hank.

"Lots of folks got shotguns."

Hank nodded. "Yep. 'Lots of folks' don't have access to your property, though. But you do. So do your sons."

Kinney scowled. Hank took a drink and idly glanced around the empty bar. He knew that neither of Kinney's older sons had been anywhere near the area in the past six months. One was career military stationed in Okinawa, Japan, with his wife and three kids. And the other was working as a hunting guide in Montana and hadn't been off the resort's land since January. The third son, of course, was in prison for killing his wife.

"So I got people looking into them, 'cause of course, anyone with access to your land is suspect."

The ropy muscles in Creosote's lean arm tightened and the knuckles wrapped around his glass whitened. Good. Hank wanted to force the man to talk to him.

"Jeff's in the Air Force, you moron. He ain't been in the country in a year. And Jed is hunting goddamn bear and buffalo in Montana. They're not your suspects."

"Well, I guess that just leaves you," said Hank, still relaxed and easy against the bar.

Creosote chuckled and said he couldn't possibly patrol the boundaries of sixty acres of land. So yeah, his woods could have been used as a dumping ground.

Hank shook his head.

"So you're telling me that someone has so little respect for the Kinneys that they used your property as a trash can?" he said.

The knuckles stayed white against the bourbon glass as Creosote brought it to his lips.

"Well?" Hank pressed.

Kinney put down his drink and turned to face Hank, because Sheila, genius that she was, had been inching toward Kinney and was now so close that he was forced to turn fully toward Hank in order to avoid seeing her.

"Yes." It was a growl and a curse at the same time.

"Huh," Hank said. "That's not what I'd been hearing about you and your kin, but . . ." He shrugged and took a very enjoyable swallow of bourbon.

Kinney's eyes looked like smoldering coals. His hand instinctively drew toward his shirt pocket before he stopped it and nonchalantly rested it back on the bar. So Creosote needed a smoke. Excellent.

"Come to think of it, your land must have been a dumping ground for a long time. There's that other body we found in your ravine. The kid."

The smolder flared into a full-blown fire.

"You goddamn son of a bitch. You come in here—to my favorite place—and you insult my family, insult my land, and call me a murderer. A child killer. Fuck you." He slammed his drink down on the hickory plank. "I'll ruin you. I'll make it so you'll never get elected."

Hank smiled and leaned in. Close enough to smell the nicotine bourbon of his breath.

"Not if I catch you first."

Creosote rose to his feet, barely missing Sheila as he stepped away from the bar. He drew himself up to a full six-foot rail and slowly walked out of the Redbone. As soon as the door clicked shut, Sheila pointed to the emergency exit door in the back.

"Is that alarmed?" she asked the barman. He shook his head. She was instantly through it, leaving Willie with only an unelectable sheriff for company. The sheriff wasn't much bothered. He sat down.

"I'm sorry about that—everybody leaving on you. I didn't mean for that to happen."

Willie moved slowly down his long plank toward Hank. He removed Kinney's glass, washed it, dried it, put it away, and then finally spoke.

"I never seen him angry like that. And I've known him for forty years. . . . I don't know if that's good or bad for you—just that it's a first." He started in on Sheila's glass. "You sure got a way about you. First time you came in here, I thought you were a nice fellow. New to the area obviously, because otherwise you wouldn't have been asking those kinds of questions in a place like this. Then you come in here today and do the same thing, but in front of twenty people who are probably armed, and probably vote. And you don't give a damn." He finished with the glass and put it away. "I don't know if you're stupid or crazy, but I'd recommend that you not come back here again during business hours."

Hank took a final swallow of bourbon and stood. "Fair enough." He placed a twenty on the bar and stuck out his hand. "Regardless, it was a pleasure to meet you, and I appreciate your time."

The barman eyed him like a coffin maker sizing up a prospective client. Then he silently shook Hank's hand and went back to wiping down his plank as Hank crossed the room. Just as he reached the door, the bartender straightened and spoke.

"I'd just watch your back when you're walking to your car."

CHAPTER

28

The several search teams had made no progress in the search for Taylor. The conservation agent had taken some lovely pictures, though. Trees, craggy granite outcrops, swaths of white-flowered ground cover. Hank had them up on Maggie's laptop, which was open on the cereal-strewn kitchen table. He clicked through them and stopped on the Sasquatch photo. The grainy man-figure was scrawny and dark. It had to be one of his *aves de paso*. His birds of passage. That's what his grandmother always called them. When they passed up through the Central Valley in small fearful groups, looking for work. She would pull them into the little ranch house, feed them, and send them on with water and *bendiciones*.

And now he had a flock of them in the Ozark Mountains.

His cell rang. Wayne Pondo gave him a hearty hello.

"You got some pretty pictures here, Wayne. I especially like the little flowers."

"That's the goldenseal. It's blooming all over. White flowers everywhere. I took those just to tick off the marshals. They're awfully fun to tease." They both chuckled.

"But seriously," Wayne said, "I'm going to take them a little farther west today. That seems the most likely spot to me. It's steeper and more wild, and likely known by somebody like Boone Taylor. We've been all over these woods, and I think we've probably forced him back into that section."

"You think the marshals can handle that?"

Wayne laughed. "It'll be fun finding out. My goal today is to get a picture of one of them trying to take a leak in the woods. City boys. Plus, I got two more of my own comin' down. So even if the federals can't make it, we'll get back in there. Don't you worry. Missouri Conservation is on the job."

That did make Hank feel better. He hung up just in time to referee an argument over the morning cartoons, and then Maggie walked in from the garage. Her scrubs weren't stained and she appeared to have on the same shoes she'd left the house in yesterday. She caught him looking at her feet and grinned.

"Yep. An entire shift and nobody bled or vomited on me. I did have a kid pee on me, but he was only eighteen months old, so that was nothing."

"I guess it's safe to kiss you then," he said, and did just that.

She hadn't expected him to be home this late in the morning. He said Duncan was out at some Kiwanis meeting. He was about to add that the kids were just chilling in front of the TV when there was a shout from the living room, and two sets of feet pounded toward the front door.

"Mail!" Benny hollered, and the door banged open.

Hank and Maggie both raced to the front window in time to see their children hurl themselves at the mail truck. By the time they got outside, Maribel was trotting back toward the house clutching a stack of letters. Benny followed behind her with a fat catalog in his hands. And Guapo, who had escaped with them, was throwing himself against a tree in pursuit of a squirrel. Hank corralled him and got him back in the house and then began to interrogate his daughter.

"We get the mail every day. Grandpop lets us, cuz Benny wants to be a mailman."

Benny held up L.L. Bean and beamed.

"Grandpop lets you go racing into the front yard? With the dog?"

Maribel shook her head. Grandpop always held on to Guapo, she told him very seriously. Everybody knew that he couldn't be trusted outside without a leash on, Daddy.

Yes, Hank had to agree, everyone did know that. And he and Mommy would talk to Grandpop all about it when he got home. He thanked them and took the mail into the kitchen. Maggie put the kids back in front of the TV, switched the channel to a documentary on dolphins, and joined him.

"I did wonder why the mail has seemed kind of crumpled lately," she said.

"I swear . . . your dad . . ."

"Oh, come on. He obviously keeps an eye on them. And the mailman didn't seem surprised. He probably knows to expect them," she said.

Hank, absently flipping through the stack of mail, stopped halfway. And swore. Maggie looked over his shoulder and laughed.

"We already adopted a dog," she said. "We sure as hell don't need another one. I can see why the animal shelter sends us donation requests, but an invitation to Adoption Day?" She rolled her eyes and set about clearing cereal bits off the table.

Hank turned to her and wordlessly held up the unfolded mailer. Full color and glossy, it was much nicer than the usual shelter solicitation. And smack in the center, a large photo of two adorable puppies getting cuddled—by Gerald Tucker.

Maggie swore.

"'Come meet local celebrities and see the dozens of dogs and cats ready to be adopted,'" she read. "'This special event will be held at the shelter's Gallagher Animal Rescue Hall from noon to six P.M. this Saturday.' "

And that was it, right there. Henry Gallagher's massive cash infusion had saved the chronically strapped shelter two years ago, and now he apparently could concoct a major event at short notice and choose his own cover model for the advertising.

"That jackass doesn't even have a pet," Maggie said, grabbing the flyer.

"Which jackass are you referring to—Tucker or Gallagher?" Hank asked as he sat down wearily at the kitchen table. His wife started to pace.

"This has got to violate something. Some kind of campaign law."

Hank shook his head. She waved the flyer at him anyway. "Call Darcy."

So he did. And then Maggie took the phone out of his hand and talked for a half hour, ranting about deceitful advertising and bad money in politics. He slumped in his chair and browsed through the junk mail. The classified-ad circular had a seventeen-foot bass boat for sale. Pretty decent price. Maybe he could try his hand at fishing once he was out of a law-enforcement job.

Suddenly his phone was shoved under his nose.

"Here. She wants to talk to you now. We have a plan."

That did not make him feel better. He took the phone.

"I have to admit, Hank, this is a genius play," Darcy said. "There's no election information or anything that identifies him as a candidate. So we have no standing as far as campaign violations go. And I just got an email back from one of your campaign volunteers who also works at the shelter. She says the flyer went out to the entire mailing list. Usually they pick and choose because they can't afford to send to everyone, but this one was paid for by Gallagher."

No kidding. Hank didn't want to know, but he asked anyway.

"Almost seventeen thousand addresses," she responded.

Fantastic. That was more than a fourth of the entire county population. And even more disheartening, it was more than the entire number of residents who had voted in the last election. And he had a feeling that the shelter mailing list had very conveniently been expanded to match the current registered-voter rolls. He forced his attention back to Darcy, who was still talking.

". . . going to do is have you show up at the event."

Hank tried to interrupt, but she was having none of it. He would go to the event, with the family and the dog, to show his constituents how great pet adoption was.

"You want us to take the dog?" Hank paused and tried to think of the most diplomatic way to continue. "He's . . . he's not fully trained yet. And he's not really photogenic. And . . . he tends to pee on people."

Nonsense, she said. She had every confidence Guapo would do just fine. He absolutely had to come. It was too perfect that they'd adopted a dog long before the election—they could accuse Tucker of pandering while they paraded their longtime pet in front of the voters.

Hank tried to tell her they'd only had the devil dog for four months, but she just kept talking.

"This means they're scared. The election is next week. They're putting this thing together at the last minute because they're worried."

No, they're doing this at the last minute so they can put the final nail in my coffin of a campaign, Hank thought. He had the phone snatched away before he could say so, and his wife tossed him a glare before walking away with Darcy still talking. Hank sighed and turned the pages of the circular to the want ads. Maybe the Steak 'n Shake was hiring.

Sheila held up her hand to shush him and continued speaking into the phone. He flopped down in the chair opposite her desk and gave her a dirty look. She commiserated with the person on the other end of the line and finally hung up.

"Well?"

"That was the marshal in charge of the manhunt," she said.

His look worsened, and made her grin.

"Oh . . . you want to know about me following Kinney yesterday."

"Yes, Sheila, that's what I'm referring to. And a voice mail yesterday that you're fine and you'll tell me about it in the morning is not okay. I needed a report last night."

"No," she said. "You *wanted* a report last night. But Tyrone's sister and our little nieces were coming over for dinner, and I was already late. And so I decided that—based upon my training and experience—what I witnessed could wait until this morning."

Her raised eyebrow dared him to contradict her. Which he knew better than to do when she was right. He waved his hand in the air in a "go on" gesture.

"He went home."

"That's it?" Hank didn't bother trying to hide his disappointment. "You could have just said that in your message."

He'd taken an odd route, though. Gone up and around, completely out of his way, she said. He didn't stop anywhere, just drove slow and steady around the northwestern part of the county and then turned into his driveway, parked, and went inside.

"Did he see you?"

"Nope."

Now it was Hank's turn to raise an eyebrow.

"Well, I don't think he did. Hard when you're the only two cars on the road, but I'm good. Lots of curves to lag behind, and I didn't have my headlights on."

"Did he pass by the Miles place?" Hank asked.

She nodded. "And the Taylor property, too."

They both contemplated that for a moment, but driving by

your enemy's homestead and the county's cesspool property didn't make you a murderer.

"We've still got nothing that points to him except that it's his land," Hank said. "And, that he totally seems capable of it."

"Agreed," Sheila said. "If he did do it, it wasn't a hair-trigger kind of thing. He did it because he benefited from killing whoever Rotten Doe is, and the benefit was big enough to take the risk."

"But, the risk was small, really. I mean, what were the chances that the body would be found? It could have moldered there for forty years, too."

"Well, okay, so if we throw in access to the dump site, we should throw in Vern Miles, too," Sheila said, steepling her fingers and pressing them to her lips. "He doesn't carry around a shotgun, but he sure as heck owns one. And his head is definitely hot enough to kill somebody, say if they were messing with his trees."

"Yeah," Hank said, "but I don't think he has the balls to then call me out there to investigate the theft. I think he would have left well enough alone. Especially if he knew he'd taken care of the problem."

Her fingers tapped together. "But . . . he still was responsible for a shipment to Old Mountain Natural Herbs. And he didn't have it. A police report would help explain that to the company."

Hank nodded, and then they both sighed at the same time.

"It would sure help to know who that body is," he said.

"Yep," she said. "But give me some time. There's something there. I can feel it. And we're going to figure it out. Just wait."

Hank smiled at her and rose to his feet, then stopped. "Oh, how was dinner?"

She looked at him in surprise, and her face split in a genuinely pleased smile.

"Good. My little babies are growing so fast. They live down in Little Rock, so we only get to see them once every couple of months."

They were eight and five now. And Tessie had finally kicked that no-account husband of hers to the curb, so all three of them were much happier, not to mention how glad she and Tyrone were about it because—well, anyhow. They'd had pork chops, which Tyrone had managed not to ruin, thank the Good Lord. The man could fix any mechanical thing on God's green earth, but ask him to fix a meal and he turned into a helpless ninny. So putting meat in the oven and managing not to burn it was quite the success. And he hadn't had to bother with dessert. The girls had brought cookies they'd baked themselves.

"Oh, I almost forgot," she said, opening her desk drawer. She pulled out a sealed sandwich bag with two misshapen lumps inside. "They sent one for you and one for Sam." She undid the zip closure and handed the bag over to Hank. He picked out the bigger of the two and bit right in.

"For that young an age, these are excellent," said Hank, who had not insignificant experience with kid-made treats. This one was not only edible, it had enough chocolate chips packed inside to even be tasty.

He thanked her through a mouthful of cookie and headed for his office.

"Wait." He stopped. "What'd the marshal want?"

She rolled her eyes. "To complain. I told him you'd go out later today with some extra-strength bug repellent."

He glared at her.

"Well, if you're making me do that, I'm taking the other cookie, too."

He grabbed the bag off her desk and stomped into his office, her laughter trailing behind him.

CHAPTER
29

It had been four days since Ted was shot. He was out of ICU, but still in very serious shape. Maggie came up from the emergency department to check on him several times during her shifts. Hank stopped by on his way to and from work every day.

The fugitive search groups felt they were closing in on Boone Taylor.

The radio-show host guy had been hounding him for an interview.

The animal-shelter event was two days away.

Hair inside a ball cap found in Ned Bunning's work locker had been submitted for DNA testing.

Patty Alton had called four more times, always with additional suggestions of people to interview. He'd given up telling her the investigation wasn't at that stage yet.

And now Sam was sitting in his office with a lot of case files and even more theories.

". . . was this one, cuz the timing matched pretty well. But the last place she was seen was pretty far away down near the Arkansas border, so I—"

Hank held up a hand to stop his earnest itemization. Sam immediately closed his mouth and looked at him with eager brown eyes. Hank hauled his own scattered thoughts back from all the far corners of his brain and focused on the kid. He leaned forward and rested his elbows on the desk.

"When you take a report at an accident or a crime scene, you do it chronologically, right? Either in the order of what you saw, or in the order of what the witness says happened, right?"

Sam nodded.

But when you lead an investigation, Hank continued, you get to treat it less like a book and more like a puzzle. You lay everything out, and you decide what is most important and what fits together. You can move the pieces around and examine everything from different angles. There might be pieces you have that don't fit anywhere, and you can put those to the side for the moment. And more pieces come in all the time. You need to keep track of them, but you also get to do the prioritizing. You decide which ones are the most important.

And some pieces change, as you get new information. That's why it's best to start with the pieces that are absolute facts. That aren't going to change. Then you use your judgment on the other ones, the pieces that do change.

Hank finished and sat back to watch the Pup. Sam pondered for a minute, scratched his ear, and then put his stack of files on the floor. He straightened and took a deep breath.

"We know for sure that we've got a dead kid. And, because of the hole in the back of the head—and the bullet—we know for sure that it was homicide. We know it was found on Jasper Kinney's land . . . but that doesn't mean the shooting happened there. It might have, it might not have."

He was warming up and the words started flowing faster. "I think the next most important thing is what the bone guy said."

"What? The anthropologist got back to you?" Hank said.
"When?" The guy hadn't returned Hank's calls at all.

Sam grinned.

"I called up there, and said that my boss was going to kill me
if I didn't come through with that forensics report." He paused.
"I figured you wouldn't mind that."

Hank agreed emphatically that he did not.

"Then," Sam continued, "I said that I had five families down
here with missing kids who were living in agony that the skeleton might be their son or daughter. Then I told a little bit of a fib.
I said that they might take matters into their own hands soon and
start calling him directly."

"That's brilliant," Hank said. "And it worked?"

"Oh, yeah. I don't think those folks up there are used to deal-
ing with live people. And definitely not used to having to deal
with grieving parents. They said they'd have the report for me
within twenty-four hours, and they did."

Hank smacked the desk in delight. "Fantastic. Great job."

Sam dug a slim file out of his stack and flipped it open. He
cleared his throat.

"I'm going to skip the measurements and stuff." He turned
to the second page.

There were no bones missing from the skeleton. Several bones
in the left foot had been broken quite recently, which must have
happened when the immigrant kid fell on it, Sam said. And then
there was the fibula that Alice had stepped on and snapped. Otherwise, the only sign of trauma was the hole in the back of the head
and the exit wound in the right cheek. The bone guy was quite
confident in stating that the injury would have been fatal.

Age of the subject at death was approximately seven to eight.
Gender was undetermined.

"I called him back on that one," Sam said. "Did you know

that when it's a kid, they can't tell so good? Only with adults. But they can pinpoint a kid's age within like six months to a year." He shook his head. "Amazing."

"Now, for how old the skeleton is—I mean how long it's been out there in the woods," Sam said.

Hank leaned forward. Sam fished out a sheet of paper and read directly from the report.

"'Taking into account the rate of decay, based on soil composition and the porous nature of the bones due to the young age of the decedent, this office estimates the length of burial at approximately forty years.'"

Patty Alton's heart would break all over again. And Calvin Holm's nightmares would continue.

Hank's vision blurred and the space behind his eyes suddenly felt like it was splitting apart. He dropped his head into his hands. None of them matched. All of his missing kids—none of them matched. The skeleton was too old.

"It could still be the Holm kid," said Sam, a little freaked out by his boss's obvious despair.

Hank's head, still buried in his hands, shook out a no. "Jeremy's outside the age range."

"Not by much," Sam said quickly. "He was nine and small for his age. None of this stuff is exact. You know that." He realized his tone. "Um, sir. Chief, sir."

The bone dude had said that his forty-year guess could go as much as ten years either way, Sam added. That could include the Kirbyville girl, but she was eleven, which was probably too far off the age range and—

Hank waved him quiet. They'd run all the families' DNA against the sample from the bones, but it would just be a formality. And even that wouldn't happen for God knew how long. He'd have to plead with the highway patrol DNA lab to move a forty-year-old homicide up on its list of priorities. And the odds of him being able to pull that off were about as low as his success rate with everything else lately.

Father Tony was in the nave of the church, plucking trash out of the slots in the pew backs that held the Bibles and hymnals. He greeted Hank with a broad smile.

"I just need to see Javier for a minute," Hank said. "No one answered at the rectory."

"Oh, good," Father Tony said. "I've told him not to come to the door. You never know who it could be. I'll go get him for you."

He picked up a pile of wadded papers and gum wrappers and headed toward the exit. Hank looked at him quizzically.

"Don't I have someone to do this for me?" Father Tony chuckled. "Sure. But then I'd lose out on all sorts of information."

He fished around in his pile and pulled out a piece of notebook paper.

Tom + Angie.

"Their parents think they've broken up. Worth keeping an eye on."

He held up another. A grocery list made up of canned beans, hot dogs, and macaroni and cheese.

"This is where the Corletti family sits. I'm pretty sure this means he's lost his job again. I'll stop by with some food tomorrow."

He put it back in his pile and smiled. "There's no better way to keep up with the congregation."

He said he'd be right back with the teen. Hank glanced around the big, empty church and said he might as well just come with him. The two men walked out of the building and across the parking lot to the rectory. They found Javier in the living room playing with the cat. Hank hardly recognized him. He looked happy, for one thing. And healthy. He must have put ten pounds on his gaunt frame in just the two weeks he'd been there.

"I know," Father Tony said at Hank's surprised look. "I made two pounds of *carnitas* last night, and he ate almost all of it by himself." He patted his own broad middle and grinned. "Better for both of us, actually."

Hank crouched down to pet the cat, trying to make Javier comfortable. The poor kid had gone all uneasy and tense when he walked in.

"*¿Qué es el nombre del gato?*" he asked.

The cat's name was Francisco, he was five years old, and he preferred the feather on a stick over the stuffed mouse toy. He was the first pet that Javier had ever had the chance to play with.

They talked about the cat until Father Tony offered Hank a seat and headed to the kitchen for some iced tea. Hank ignored the proffered chair and followed him.

Groceries were piled everywhere. There were enough sandwich fixings to feed the Corletti family for a year. Several jumbo packs of beef jerky sat in a bag on the floor. And a huge pot of soup bubbled on the stove. From the smell of green chilies and onion, Hank guessed it was *chile verde*. He took a peek to confirm it and then leaned against the counter.

Father Tony sighed.

"You were supposed to wait out there." He looked around. "I don't suppose you'd believe this is for the food pantry?"

Hank shook his head. He'd also seen the stack of blankets and cans of bug repellent down at the end of the hallway.

"How many of them are you helping?"

Tony shrugged. He'd only seen two—an older man, very short but powerfully built, and a young, slightly chubby man about Javier's age. Javier had confirmed that they were part of the work crew.

"How did they make it all the way back here?" Hank asked. "It's miles from where they were cutting down the trees."

They'd snuck along the roads at night. The older one had

remembered seeing the church as they drove through Branson in the van. It was the only place they could think of to go for help.

"And did they get back to their friends the same way? Or did someone drive them?" He arched an eyebrow at Father Tony, who made a great show of checking the soup. Finally he muttered into the pot.

"I'm trying to get them into a city. Where they can find a network. Get help. Until then, I don't have anywhere else to put them. I didn't want them here"—he smiled ruefully—"because you might find out. And that county commissioner. He's been showing up repeatedly since last week."

He straightened and faced Hank. "But they must be supplied. So that is what I'm doing."

"Tony, I can pretend I never saw any of this stuff," Hank said, "but it's crawling with federal agents out there. If the men come out of the woods to meet you, the agents are more likely to find them. And then there's nothing I can do. The marshals could very well arrest them."

"But I must help. *Es mi obligación.*"

The two men stared at each other through the steam coming off the pot.

"*Señor, por favor.*"

Javier stood in the doorway, cradling Francisco and looking terrified.

"*¿Qué pasa con mis amigos?*"

"*Sí,*" said the priest. "What about his friends?"

They, well, they were in a lot more trouble than Father Tony and his secret foodstuffs. They had federals *and* an armed killer out there in the woods with them. And yet no one had found them. The only whisper of contact was a grainy, Bigfootesque photo. Someone in that group had to know more about outdoor survival than Hank had initially thought. Someone that good might have noticed a hiding spot no one else could find. Someone that good was worth talking to. Hank looked at the *pájaro* and then Father Tony.

"I'm coming with you. When do you meet them?"

CHAPTER

30

The priest sent Hank off with a stomach full of *chile verde* and a solemn oath that he was telling the truth about the meeting time and place. At midnight a mile west of the Stout Oak Road turnoff.

Hank got there first. He'd driven Dunc's Toyota Camry, which was the most nondescript car he had access to. He didn't want anyone knowing what he was doing. If the voting public discovered he was "soft" on illegal immigration, it wouldn't bode well for his campaign. He pulled off the road at eleven o'clock, onto a little dirt track that petered out after about twenty yards, which was just far enough to hide the car from the view of anyone on the road. Then he hiked a half mile north and stopped just short of the semicircular gravel turnout Father Tony had said was the meeting place.

He had on dark jeans and a black shirt. His badge was in his back pocket. He didn't want it glinting in the meager moonlight and giving him away. He slipped into the trees and circled the turnout, trying to get a feel for how the forest extended out from the clearing and the road. He had no idea which direction the birds would come from, so he chose a clump of undergrowth about halfway between the road and the apex of the turnout. He'd settled himself behind a tree and among the plants before it occurred to him he could be sitting in the middle of a leafy sea of poison ivy. Brilliant. He was as dumb in the woods as that hopping-mad marshal.

He looked around as best he could, and all he saw were some waist-high shrubs and more of those short plants with the broad, maple-looking leaves. Only these had a single purple flower in the middle instead of a white one. Definitely not poison ivy. He made sure he was surrounded on all sides by foliage, turned off his phone, and sat back to wait.

It was torture. All he could think about was Ted Pimental's condition, which had only incrementally improved. He hauled his mind out of the hospital room where Ted was hooked up to too many machines that were doing too many things he ought to be doing for himself. But then his thoughts landed on Sam, and then the election, and then . . .

He shook his head and fought the urge to look at his phone for the time. He had no idea how long he had until midnight. He decided he'd occupy himself with picking Maribel a bouquet of the little purple flowers within his reach. He had a dozen of them in his fist when he heard the snap of a twig off to his right. He froze. There was a slight scraping sound even farther right and then silence. Father Tony's flock was here.

No more than a few minutes later, a battered Dodge Caravan puttered into the turnout with its headlights off. Father Tony got out and stood uncertainly by the driver's-side door. A dark shape in the passenger seat meant he'd brought the *pájaro* with him. Hank was not happy about that. The wood dwellers made no sound.

The priest fidgeted for a moment and then seemed to realize that the immigrants did not know it was Javier in the van. He gestured through the window and Javier hopped out. A collective sigh arose from the trees, and men began to step forward.

Hank used their noise as cover to shift his own position for better viewing. Father Tony stepped forward and shook hands with a short man built like a washing machine—so broad he was almost square—who had to be the one who had hiked in to Branson to ask for help. He was also quite clearly the leader. The other eight men hung back near the tree line as the Maytag finished greeting the priest and turned to Javier. He wrapped the kid, who was six inches taller and at least a hundred pounds lighter, in a bear hug.

That seemed to grant permission for the rest of the group to step forward. They clustered around Javier, peppering him with questions and playful joshing. Most of them appeared to be about the same age as the *pájaro*. They hadn't had the benefits of Chef Tony's cooking for the past two weeks, though. Their gaunt frames rattled around in filthy clothes and lousy shoes. Two of them didn't have anything on their feet at all.

Father Tony started to unload the food. He'd packed it well, and handed each worker a full satchel. He pulled Maytag off to the side and gave him a soft-sided cooler that Hank would bet held containers of still-hot *chile verde*. But the soup wasn't as important as the conversation. Maytag leaned closer as Father Tony began speaking quietly. When he stiffened and drew back, Hank knew the priest had brought up the cop who wanted to talk to him.

Maytag shook his head and started to back away. He collided with one of the younger workers, who had approached with Javier. The kid gave Father Tony a shy little bow. Javier pointed to him and then over to the others, who had finished pulling the blanket packs out of the van and stood waiting.

His friends humbly ask for the father's blessing, Javier said in Spanish. Before they go.

Maytag scowled and scanned the woods. Father Tony put his

hand on the leader's shoulder and said something that sounded like "Not here yet." Maytag made to move toward the trees, but Tony's grip tightened. He told the leader that he would bless the men before sending them back into the unknown.

The ragtag group immediately lined up behind the first young man, all of them looking relieved. Maytag relented and stepped to the side. Father Tony straightened to his full height and stepped to the front of the little line.

Hank quickly rose from his nest in the undergrowth and stepped from behind the tree. He needed to get to them before they were fortified with God's grace and disappeared back into the woods.

Father Tony saw him and froze halfway through the sign of the cross. The line of supplicants broke and the young men started to scatter. Hank moved into the clearing with his hands out and his Spanish rapid.

"*Por favor.* Everyone stop. I am not here to arrest anyone. No one is in trouble."

Maytag took a step backward toward the tree line.

Hank pointed at him. "*Por. Favor.*" It was not a request.

Maytag stared at him. *What are you going to do, pal, chase me?* Hank's Spanish got even faster.

He needed their help. There was a fugitive in the woods, a very dangerous man, and he—the police—couldn't find him. He needed to know if their group had seen the man, seen any sign of him, while they were out in the woods. That was all Hank wanted. He didn't want them, at all. He wasn't Immigration. All he wanted was the man. The man was a killer.

"*Es muy importante,*" he finished.

Javier nodded solemnly. The younger men shuffled their feet and considered what he'd said. Maytag clearly thought he was full of shit. And then the kid who'd been first in line for blessing spoke up.

"We saw a man. In the valley near the hill." He pointed to the east. "We thought he was police, because he shot at us."

The physical description matched Boone Taylor, although no one had gotten particularly close, for obvious reasons. That didn't matter to Hank. He only cared where they'd seen him. The young men's vague pointing wasn't helping. He strode over to their leader.

"You need to help me. Now. You obviously know how to cover your tracks, which must mean you're pretty good at picking up somebody else's. Where is he?"

Maytag shifted the soup cooler from hand to hand. Finally he decided that the risk of giving Hank the information was outweighed by the risk of continuing to stand out in the open. He pivoted toward the east.

There was a rocky hill about two miles east, Maytag said. It was not high—from far away it did not appear above the normal rises in the forest. But up close, it seemed very tall, because it was surrounded on all sides by ravines and deep gullies that probably were carved by the rain running off the rocks. They had not been able to find a way up the hill. Also, it did not provide what Maytag believed to be a sufficient amount of cover. So they had skirted it—and that was when they ran into the blond man. They immediately went into avoidance procedures, but when the guy fired at them, they changed direction again, heading—

Maytag stopped. Hank figured he was refusing to say which direction they'd gone because they likely were still holed up in that area. Then he heard it, too. The crunch of car tires on gravel.

He spun around just as a spotlight lit up the turnout, searing his eyes. He could hear the workers scatter behind him, but he could see nothing. Behind the light, a door slammed and someone started shouting orders.

Father Tony moved toward Hank until they stood side by side, each of them with an arm up to shield his eyes. Hank squinted and was barely able to see a small man walk in front of the vehicle, his porcupine hair outlined by the enormous wattage behind him.

"Goddamn it, Fizzel," Hank roared, "turn off the damn light."

Next to him, Father Tony swore under his breath. Hank yelled again. The Porcupine ignored him and kept shouting at the now-long-gone workers. Hank strode to the right of the light, toward the driver's-side door of what turned out to be a jacked-up Ford F-250 truck. He pointed up at the young man behind the wheel. Who immediately jerked into action and cut the light.

The fall back into darkness also extinguished the Porcupine's tirade. Hank stomped back around to the front of the truck, grabbed Edrick Fizzel by the front of his shirt, and lifted him up on his toes. Fizzel yelped.

"What the hell do you think you're doing?"

The Branson County commissioner squirmed, trying to get his heels back on the ground and failing. "You're harboring fugitives. Illegals. You're breaking the law. I'll have your badge."

Hank gave him a hard shake. He was so furious he could barely see straight, even with the spotlight off.

"Let's talk about my badge," he snarled. "I was using it to investigate a shooting. The attempted murder of a police officer. You remember that? A real crime? Yeah. And you just interfered—massively—with that investigation."

Fizzel wiggled enough to get his feet back on the ground, but he couldn't loosen Hank's grip on his shirt. So he leaned in, his red nose just inches from Hank's chin.

"It doesn't matter," he said. "The feds will find him. But you—you hypocritical bastard—you're going down. You won't win the election, *and* you'll go to jail. I'm going to tell everyone that you let a bunch of illegals loose in our county. See how many votes that gets you."

Hank lifted him up again. "You little—"

"And Sheriff Worth was just about to arrest them."

They both spun toward the priest. He stepped forward and nodded.

"Yes. The sheriff was about to arrest those men."

Hank was so surprised he let go of the commissioner, who quickly stepped out of his reach.

"I was the one who provided them aid," Tony said. "Only me. The sheriff was here to apprehend them."

Fizzel clearly looked like he suspected that Tony was lying. Hank tried not to look like he knew that Tony was lying.

"I don't believe you," Fizzel snapped.

Father Tony shrugged. Hank started to speak, but Tony held up a hand and turned to Fizzel.

"I am done with the Lord's work, and I am going home now."

He turned around and walked gingerly to the van, carefully placing his stocking feet on the gravel as he went. He climbed in, navigated around the huge pickup, and drove off alone. Javier had flown with the rest.

Hank watched him go and tried not to think about punching Fizzel.

"I don't believe him," the commissioner said to Hank's back. "You were harboring fugitives. I'm going to tell everybody. You won't win the election."

Hank didn't turn around. "What'd you do, follow him out from the church?"

He sensed Fizzel nodding. "I knew he was up to something. He'd been very evasive in our previous dealings. Plus, he's Mexican."

Hank sighed. Antonio Morales Alarcon was from Chicago. And his parents had immigrated—legally—from Guatemala. Any breath he used to correct Fizzel would be wasted, though. The little twit didn't give a damn.

Fizzel could never prove Hank had intended to let the workers go. But he certainly could allege it, and in a campaign, that
was good enough. Hank almost didn't care. He just wanted to
find Boone Taylor. And solve two murders. He turned toward the
south and started walking back to his car.

Fizzel started yelling after him. He'd make sure Hank never
worked in this county again. He'd see to it that good American
values returned to the sheriff's department. He'd have immigration police out here first thing to hunt down this dangerous gang
of illegals.

Hank stopped. And very slowly turned around. Fizzel took
a step back.

"I . . . I mean it. I'm going to have them all rounded up. And
that priest arrested."

Hank rolled his eyes. Father Tony had merely handed out
food, which was not a crime.

"He can't get away with that," Fizzel ranted on, arms flap-
ping angrily. Hank bit back a retort and strode toward him. Fizzel
flinched and scooted back until he bumped into the massive
chrome grille of the truck.

"It's mighty pretty," Hank said, reaching over Fizzel's head
to touch the hood. "Whose is it?"

"I don't have to tell you." It came out as a snarl.

Hank smiled. "Well, then I'll just have to take a look at the
registration. And run the license of the nice young man behind
the wheel."

He ordered the kid to climb down, with Fizzel protesting
the whole time. Hank knew exactly who he was, but made him
dig out his wallet anyway.

"Eddie Fizzel. Well, I've heard a lot about you. This is an
awfully nice ride. Mind if I take a look?"

Eddie glanced over at his father, but Hank was already lift-
ing himself into the driver's seat. He searched the glove box, which

sadly contained all the proper registration paperwork, and then the rest of the cab, which was the opposite of the gleaming exterior. Mud and leaves and flower petals, some crushed to a fine powder, littered the floor. A half-eaten Sonic burger of indeterminate vintage was stuffed in the ashtray. Candy-bar wrappers were scattered everywhere.

The more he dug around, the more nervous Fizzel got. The kid didn't look worried, though. Interesting. Did Dad think the Prodigal Son had something illegal in the truck? Hank redoubled his efforts, but still couldn't find anything, except an empty sandwich bag and several wads of gum stuck under the seat. And what looked like a dead lizard. The kid was a total slob.

And he was barely a high school graduate and still lived at home, yet he had managed to land a four-thousand-dollar-a-month job with Gallagher Enterprises. Hank knew the kid paid his dad several grand a month in rent, which was a nice way to funnel money from a prominent businessman to a decidedly pro-businessman county commissioner.

Hank climbed out of the cab. Face-to-face, Eddie got a little more nervous. He shifted from foot to foot, but answered Hank's questions readily enough. Yes, he was the one who bought the truck. Three months ago. From a dealership up in Springfield. He'd put a lot down, but he hadn't paid in full. He'd used his paycheck. Dad had cut him a break on the rent for a couple of months, cuz, well, it was his dream car. You know?

Hank glanced over at Fizzel, who was trying to look like an indulgent parent. Time to wipe that off his face. He motioned Eddie over to the side of the truck and told him to stay there. Then he slung his arm around Fizzel's shoulder and steered him away.

"That was nice of you," Hank said, gesturing toward the truck, "but it doesn't change the fact that you're getting a monthly kickback from Henry Gallagher."

Fizzel started to protest that Eddie was worth that kind of

money, but the words died on his lips as they both turned back to
see the Prodigal Son staring up at the sky and picking his nose.

"You can't prove anything," Fizzel said. "It's all aboveboard."

Hank leaned in. "That doesn't matter when you're running
for election, does it?"

Fizzel started laughing. He slipped away from Hank's grasp
and pointed at him.

"So the choirboy wants to play ball. Trade your election for
my election? How very politician of you."

What? Wait. That wasn't where he was going with this. He
was threatening Fizzel's re-election, sure. But in exchange for his
laying off the immigrants and Father Tony. He wasn't trying to
make some kind of deal for himself. Fizzel couldn't do anything
for his election, anyway. He'd just endorsed Tucker yesterday. As
Gallagher had weeks ago. And the corrupt little hedgehog would
never do anything that went against his patron. So there wasn't
really a point to—

Dear God. All of this made his head want to explode. He
stepped forward, startling Fizzel silent.

"I . . . I . . . you. You are not going to go after those men."
He pointed to the woods. "They are not your business. And neither is Father Tony Morales. You will leave all of them alone. Do
you understand?"

Fizzel's beady eyes narrowed, and behind them, his political
calculator started working. His gaze swept the forest. Then he
spun on his heel and ordered his son to start the truck. They
backed out in a roar of exhaust and crunched gravel and rumbled
off. Leaving Hank standing in the dark.

CHAPTER
31

"I'm happy to be here, Dick."

Nothing could be further from the truth. Hank forced a smile at the man across the table, who looked as ridiculous as he felt. They were both crowned with giant radio headphones. Big microphones dangled in front of their faces. The station staff stood in the hallway, looking through the window like he was an exhibit in a zoo. He should have worn a tie.

"So now, Hank, let's talk about this election. You were appointed sheriff last year after our own Darrell Gibbons got himself elected to the state legislature. Now you have to run to keep the job. How do you feel about that?"

It was so hard to keep the smile going. "Well, Dick, I'm happy to do it. Sheriff is a very important position that is quite properly an elected office. I'm glad to take it to the voters."

"What makes you the one we should vote for?"

"I'm the only candidate with leadership experience, Dick. My opponent has never held a command position, he's never been in charge of a budget, he's never led complex investigations. I'm currently serving as your sheriff, and I think I'm the voters' best choice to continue in the job."

He'd rehearsed that one. Darcy had told him to use every opportunity to stress that he was the current sheriff. She'd also emphasized a whole lot of other things, most of which he didn't remember, and all of which stressed him out.

"Let's talk about that for a minute," Dick said. "You led the investigation into the Mandy Bryson murder a few months back. Why didn't that murderous killer go to trial?"

Hank was beginning to understand why politicians started every sentence with "Well, interviewer name . . ." It gave them that extra split second to gather their thoughts.

"Well, Dick . . ." he said, "that killer confessed—to me—and then he pleaded guilty in a court of law. He got the same prison sentence he would have if the case had gone to trial. And it actually saved county taxpayers a lot of money."

"But what about justice for Mandy? And her parents? They did not get their day in court."

This idiot had no idea how it worked. "Actually," he said, trying to keep his voice even, "they did. Mandy's parents got to stand in front of the judge, and in front of the killer, and talk about how the crime had destroyed their lives. They were given their day in court. And they agreed with the decision not to take the case to trial."

Radio Dick deflated a little at that. Unfortunately, he rallied.

"Let's turn to current events now," he said. "One of your deputies was shot in the line of duty and lies near death at the hospital. Why was he in such a dangerous situation? You say you're a leader—he was gravely wounded under your command."

Darcy had known this one was coming, too.

"We are all praying for Deputy Pimental's full recovery. He's making remarkable progress." Hank continued in that vein for a

minute and finished with a solemn nod at his interviewer. It didn't
work.

"Why didn't you take enough deputies to secure the area?
Why didn't you ensure the safety of your men?"

Hank was becoming more and more thankful that Darcy
had made him rehearse beforehand.

"Unfortunately, Dick, with the current levels of staffing in my
department, we don't have enough deputies to send a full contingent to serve every search warrant we need to. I sure wish we did."

They went back and forth about the Taylor brothers' criminal records, how dangerous they should have been considered, and
whether pig theft was a violent crime for the purposes of evaluat-
ing whether neighborhood hoodlums might turn homicidal.

They couldn't come to agreement, and Radio Dick went to
commercial. Hank leaned back in his chair and relaxed his hands,
which had somehow balled into fists. He took a deep breath and
glanced over at Darcy, who apparently thought he was doing
okay—there was only a slight frown on her face as she watched
through the window.

"And we're back, on Branson's own talk radio station. If
you're just joining us, we're talking with Hank Worth, candidate
for sheriff. Let's get back into it, shall we?

"Now, Hank, the county commission appointed you sheriff
last fall. Yet now, none of them have endorsed your candidacy.
What do you have to say about that?"

That the commissioners were spineless weasels who . . . Hank
stopped himself and pasted on another smile.

"Actually, Dick," he said with a forced chuckle he hoped
didn't sound too fake, "two of our honorable commissioners have
said they're remaining neutral in this race. They aren't endorsing
anybody."

Dick frowned and agreed that was true. Then he brought up
the Porcupine.

"Edrick Fizzel has endorsed your opponent. So has Henry Gallagher, one of the county's major employers and philanthropists. What do you have to say about that?"

A lot, and none of it would pass FCC regulations. Hank's smile was starting to hurt.

"I don't want to be beholden to any business interest. So I'm perfectly okay with not getting Henry Gallagher's endorsement. I prefer to serve individuals, not corporations."

Dick smiled back. That wasn't good. "You don't think it's because you accused him of blowing up the *Branson Beauty* showboat for the insurance money? In this part of the country, them's fightin' words, especially when you had no proof."

"Well, Dick . . ."He drew it out as long as he could. On the other side of the soundproof glass, Darcy was throwing signs at him like she was the third-base coach for the Cardinals. He had no idea what she wanted him to say, but he knew what she wanted him to do. Keep his temper. He took a breath.

"In my business, accusing somebody means charging them with something. And Henry Gallagher hasn't been charged with anything." He put his hands in his lap so no one would see they were clenched into fists again.

Dick blinked. And frowned. Hank had left him with no follow-up. He hit the show's theme music and shuffled through his notes. Hank sighed in relief. Darcy actually smiled. And Dick pounced.

"Back again with sheriff candidate Hank Worth. Let's get to know you as a person. You're from Mexico?"

Hank's jaw dropped. Dick leaned back in his chair with the smug look of someone who thought he'd just pulled a rabbit out of a hat.

"No. I'm from California. Where I was born and raised."

"So you're an American citizen?"

Hank's fist was aching to connect with something. He

answered in the affirmative. In the corner of his vision, Darcy flashed a hand signal that had to mean "keep going."

"My parents are also U.S. citizens," he said. "I spent my childhood in the Central Valley and came to Missouri for college." He tried to find words through the anger fogging his brain. "And, uh, I love it here."

"But your mother is Mexican," Dick said in a tone that clearly implied he'd caught Hank in a lie.

"My mother was born in Mexico. My grandparents immigrated—legally—when she was four years old. They are now all U.S. citizens."

"But have they assimilated?" Dick leaned closer to his microphone and consulted his notes. "When someone called, the phone was answered in Spanish. That's not really embracing the American way, is it?"

The only one who answered the phone in Spanish was—

"You called *mi abuela*? At her assisted-living facility? You're harassing a ninety-one-year-old woman? How dare you, you—"

The pounding he thought was in his temples finally penetrated fully into his consciousness, and he saw it was Darcy banging on the studio window. At the same time, he realized he was on his feet and leaning over the table toward an astonished Dick Battenberg. He slowly sank back into his seat, choking back the torrent of outrage that desperately wanted to take voice.

He calmly explained that his grandmother was quite elderly and frail and it was pretty darn unethical for someone to hound her with phone calls when she had nothing to do with the election. Battenberg then made some idiotic comment about how everybody loves their grandmothers and threw it to commercial.

Darcy burst into the room, followed by the producer, who was loudly insisting that yes, they do treat all candidates for local office this way. Darcy pushed the microphone away from Hank's face, motioned for him to take off the headphones, and turned toward Battenberg.

"We're done here. Nice that you use oppo research on my candidate, but not the other guy."

The producer tried on a look of exaggerated affront. "We asked him about his family, too."

Darcy glared. "Yeah, his four-generations-in-the-Ozarks family. But did you ask him why his wife divorced him? Or why he didn't want custody of his kid? Hmmm?"

Radio Dick had the decency to look sheepish. The producer just shrugged. Hank was pretty sure his head was going to explode if he didn't get out of there soon. Darcy sized him up and hustled him out without another word.

Once they were in her car, Hank let loose again. It had to have been the law-firm PI. No one else could have found his mother's mother in an assisted-living facility with unlisted phone numbers. And God knew what the guy said to her—he could have gotten her worried, he might have caused her to—

"Stop."

He did. He glanced over at her for the first time and saw that she looked as upset as he felt. He leaned his elbow against the car door and ran his hand along his forehead.

"Did I just blow everything?"

Darcy took off her designer glasses and pinched the bridge of her nose. "No . . . yes . . . I don't know. You totally flew off the handle, which was exactly what they wanted. And a sheriff who can't keep his temper is not good." She put her glasses back on. "And you'd been doing so well. That's probably why they pulled out the grandma card, though. They couldn't rile you with anything else."

They both stared out the windshield for a while. Hank fought the urge to dig out his cell phone and call his grandmother. Instead, he turned to his campaign manager.

"Tell me what to do. I'll do it. I'm the one who just screwed this up. If there's any way you can fix it . . ."

She nodded, the wheels behind those icy blue eyes turning rapidly. "The only big thing we've got left before the election is that animal-shelter event. You need to get your family and that dog ready . Wholesome, charming, well behaved. All of you. It'll be our last shot."

Hank cringed at the impossibility of a well-behaved Guapo but nodded anyway. "Absolutely."

She pulled out of the parking lot. "I'll drop you at your car. Then I'm going to go have a chat with a few people."

He walked into the Forsyth Easy Come & Go in desperate need of coffee. And a candy bar. Anything to give him enough energy to finish this day from hell. He filled a Super Easy–sized cup, grabbed a Snickers and a packaged Danish for good measure, and walked to the front.

"Heeeey, Sherf."

Gursey, a Come & Go purple polo shirt hanging off his gaunt frame, stood behind the counter. Hank could not have been more surprised if it was Johnny Cash himself manning the register.

He said hello. "You, um, you got a job, Gursey? That's . . . great. I'm really impressed. I hope that means I won't be seeing you inside again."

"No way, Sherf. I don't need to be stealing no more. Got me an income now." He smoothed the front of his shirt. "And it's purple." He broke into giggles. "Ain't that the thing?"

Hank handed over a ten-dollar bill and eyed the kid as he made change. Very slowly. While swaying slightly. Hank nodded his thanks and walked out into the pleasantly warm morning, pondering the state of Gursey's sobriety. Between that and juggling his snacks, he didn't see the man walking toward the store.

"Excuse me—oh, hi, Sheriff."

"Hey, Pete. Sorry about that"—Hank gestured back toward the store—"I was . . ."

Pete Wiggins groaned. He owned this and the three other Come & Go locations in the county.

"He gave you the wrong change, didn't he?"

"No, it's right, actually," Hank said. "But he wasn't looking altogether . . ."

"Sober. I know. But I test him. I tested him before I hired him, and I make him pee in a cup every damn morning. And he comes back clean." Pete shook his head. "I still don't know that I did the right thing, though, takin' him on."

"You that hard up for employees?"

Pete shrugged. "Sometimes yes, sometimes no. Turnover is brutal. If they're smart, they find a better job pretty quick. And if they're stupid, I end up having to fire them. So if I can get ones that aren't stupid, but maybe don't have a good enough history to get hired someplace else, it can work out good for both of us." He tapped his nose. "But that's why I drug test. Everybody. My pass rates have been really good lately. A lot better than normal. I was starting to think maybe the drug tide was startin' to turn. But then I get one like Gursey. Maybe acting stoned is just his normal sober state, too, and we all just never knew?"

Hank grinned. "Well, you keeping him here is a lot better for society than him coming back to me."

Pete laughed ruefully. "Lot better for society, maybe, but probably not so good for my business. I better go make sure he hasn't fallen asleep on the Lotto tickets."

CHAPTER

32

Hank wasn't even halfway through his iced raspberry Danish when Sheila burst into his office. He cringed.

"What? You don't even know what I'm going to say yet." She frowned at him.

"Oh. You weren't going to comment on my radio interview?"

Now the hands went on the hips. "You think I got time to sit around listening to the damn radio?"

"That was not what I was implying," he said, slapping his food down on his desk. "I screwed it up royally, and I expected you to call me on it."

Her hands fell to her sides. "Oh. Well . . . really? You did that bad?" She paused and then made a chopping motion with her hand. "I can't think about that now. I've got to keep thinking like I've got a job. Like I'll keep having a job."

The last words were said almost to herself. Hank looked at her and thought, for the thousandth time, how up a creek she'd be if Tucker became sheriff. More than he himself would be, really. He pushed away the Danish.

"So, what's up?"

She sank into one of the chairs across from Hank's desk and crossed her legs with an exaggerated nonchalance.

"I got the Rotten Doe preliminary DNA results."

"Really?" Door number one, or door number two? Please don't let it be door number three, the one that doesn't match either of our theories, he thought.

"It's Jackson Taylor. Or rather, it's someone with the same mother as our boy Lloyd." She gave a wry smile. "So I suppose it could be Boone, but I'm going to stick with it being the one that Lloyd hasn't seen in the longest while. Plus, Boone's the one who physically matches the guy they're tracking through the woods. "

"That means Ned Bunning goes back to a voluntarily missing adult," Hank said. "And lets us narrow our focus on that investigation, at least."

Sheila nodded. "So why was Jackson Taylor filled with buckshot?"

Hank shook his head in exasperation, just as Sam walked in lugging his omnipresent stack of files.

"So, it's Jackson? Awesome." He sank into the chair next to Sheila's as they both stared at him. "Oh, uh, you know what I mean. Awesome that we have an ID."

He smacked his stack. "And a lot better than I'm doing. I've put aside the ones that don't fit the time frame of roughly thirty to fifty years ago. Then I went through all the rest again. And this one just—well, listen to this."

He opened the top file, and Hank saw it was the one for the 1985 city of Branson case where the family had been suspected in their six-year-old son's disappearance. Sam unfolded a page of his handwritten notes and started reading.

He'd tried to contact the parents, whose last known address was up in the northern Missouri city of Kirksville, but found that the whole family was dead. He finally tracked down one very elderly aunt of the boy's mother who lived in Michigan. She was able to tell him how and when she'd heard about them all passing away—the father of a heart attack, the mother in a car accident, the sister by suicide, and Tommy from pneumonia complications.

He raised his head from his notes. From the puzzled looks on his bosses' faces, they weren't quite following.

"That's what she said," Sam continued. "But she's super old, so I double-checked." And according to the death certificates, both parents and the sister had died just how the aunt said. As had Thomas William Havich, age nine. Three years after he disappeared in Branson.

Hearing nothing, he looked up from his notes. Hank and Sheila were staring at him openmouthed. He pulled out a copy of Tommy's death certificate and slid it across Hank's desk.

"Not what we expected, obviously," Sam said. "So I called up there. Tommy was, according to his local medical records, a pretty sickly kid. Out of school a lot, tons of doctors' appointments, that kind of thing. And they just sent me a picture." He took out his phone and pulled up a photo of a gravestone. THOMAS WILLIAM HAVICH, JAN. 18, 1979–NOV. 2, 1988.

"They're going to need you to do some paperwork and officially ask for an exhumation to do a DNA test to make sure it's him, but they didn't see a problem with it, considering," Sam said. He carefully refolded his notes and then looked at his rapt audience with a satisfied gleam in his eye.

Once Hank and Sheila regained their powers of speech, they all spent the next fifteen minutes puzzling about where the hell little Tommy Havich had gone when he disappeared and what kind of people would not bother to let the police know that he'd been found. Or did it mean that someone else was in the Kirksville grave and Tommy was the one who'd been in that crevice in the woods all along?

It took a few moments for Sam and Sheila to realize that Hank had fallen silent. He was staring at that old water spot in the ceiling and drumming his fingers on the desk. The splotch went in and out of focus as he pondered. Death, government, poor record keeping, deep roots.

He whirled toward his desktop and started pounding on the keyboard. Sam started to speak and then hesitated. He turned to Sheila, who shrugged and shifted in her seat to get a better view of the computer screen. Hank clicked furiously from page to page, finding what he'd expected. Until he didn't.

He smacked the mouse to close the Internet browser and rose to his feet.

"I gotta go to Springfield."

They both stared at him.

"What?" Sheila almost yelled. "You got the marshals wanting a briefing, and this exhumation to authorize, and Ted's wife called, and . . ."

He knew that. And he knew he should stay. He was the boss, and all those tasks were what came with it. And he also knew that, in his heart, he was an investigator. This was his case and he wanted—needed—to do his own legwork. He looked at his staff with their what-the-hell expressions. And sat back down.

He took a deep breath and tore through his desk for a blank sheet of paper. He scrawled on it and handed it to Sam.

"It's not online. You've got to go up there and find it. Don't let them stonewall you."

Sam looked at the paper and then back at Hank, confused.

"Just go," Hank said. It killed him to say it, and it killed him to sit there and watch Sam hustle out the door. Then he turned to Sheila, who looked like she wanted to kill him, and not metaphorically.

"You think you can just go gallivanting off whenever a lightning bolt strikes?"

"I'm still here, aren't I?"

They glared at each other. Finally, Sheila sighed and started to look just the slightest bit sympathetic. "This job still fits you like a too-tight pair of shoes. You can walk in 'em, but it isn't pretty."

He gave her a weak grin. "I'm trying. I promise you, I'm trying."

She stood. "You're going to need to keep on trying, real hard, because now we get to go see the marshals."

"Go see them? I thought they were coming here."

"Oh, no. They've 'requested' we go out there. Something about sharing the misery."

Hank snorted. He wasn't sure who was more miserable at the moment, him or the guys in the woods.

It turned out to be the guys in the woods. The marshals were bug-bitten, sunburned, citified messes. Even the Branson PD Commando looked tired and sore. Hank handed out cold water and protein bars, and listened to their plan to penetrate the knob to the west that they were now ninety percent sure was Boone Taylor's hiding place. Hank hoped the immigrants had made themselves scarce.

Wayne Pondo was the only one who didn't look like he wanted to pack it in. He was resting easily off to the side, sitting on a log and doodling in the dirt with a stick. Hank left Sheila to hash out the group's radio communications and walked over. Wayne looked up from his drawing.

"Shouldn't you be out campaigning or something?"

"I was this morning. Didn't go too well."

Wayne shook his head. "That jackass Tucker can't win. It'd be back to croneyville in that department. Plus, he's an idiot."

Hank chuckled. "I appreciate that . . . I think. But you can't help—you don't even live in this county."

"Nope. I can't vote for you. I did put in a word with my ma, though. She lives down in Hollister."

"Now, I definitely appreciate that."

Hank sat down on the log and looked at the conservation agent's artwork. Wayne smoothed it away with a shrug. It was what he did when he was trying to think through something, he said. But he wasn't having any luck. Something was bothering the heck out of him, but he couldn't figure out what it was. Some particular in this whole business was off, but every time he came close to putting his finger on it, it flitted away.

Hank knew that feeling. They both stared at the smoothed ground for a minute. Then Wayne got up to join the group, which was arming itself.

"You look like you want to come," he said.

Hank smiled sadly. "I do. But I'm an administrator now, which means I don't get to *do* anything. I just get to talk about it."

One of the marshals hollered that they were leaving. Wayne stood and gave Hank a penetrating once-over.

"I don't know," Wayne drawled. "I got a feeling that you might figure out how to get around that."

He handed Hank the stick and walked over to the hunting party, slinging his rifle over his shoulder as he went. There'd be no camera today. The group of men moved off into the woods, leaving Hank, Sheila, and one young Branson PD radio operator the only ones in the clearing.

A half hour later, Hank's cell phone rang.

"It's those little purple flowers. And now they're all gone."

Hank was thoroughly confused as to why he should give a damn. "Were you planning to gather a bouquet, Wayne?"

"No, wiseass," Wayne crackled through the tenuous phone connection. It wasn't just the flowers. The plants. The whole plants were gone. Roots and all. He realized that what rankled him was he'd never seen purple ones before, only white. Goldenseal only came with white flowers. So what the hell was the purple stuff—some kind of damn subspecies maybe?—and why had someone come out to the middle of nowhere in the past couple of days and harvested it all? Wayne's irritation was clear even through the static.

Hank stopped in mid-step, his foot hanging in the air inches above the packed dirt. He brought it down slowly as everything sank in.

"Wayne, you have to find me a plant. A purple one. The whole plant. They can't all be gone."

"I'm telling you, I don't see a single damn one. And now I'm getting yelled at. I got to get back to it. We can talk about this later."

Hank barely heard him over the blood pounding in his ears. He whirled toward his cruiser. "No, Wayne. This is just as important. You have to get me a plant."

He ended the call and wrenched open the car door. Sheila stared over at him in surprise.

"I have to go back to Forsyth."

The look she gave him would have burned through the patrol car had it still been there. But Hank was gone, reversing in a cloud of dust as the pounding in his ears got louder and louder.

CHAPTER
33

He roared down Highway 160 through Forsyth, blew past the sheriff's department, and turned into the Easy Come & Go with a skid. He slammed the cruiser into park and stormed into the air-conditioned building. Gursey's greeting died on his lips as Hank reached across the counter and grabbed his shirt.

"What're you using, and where're you getting it?"

Gursey's eyes bugged and his feet scrabbled against the tile as Hank's grip threatened to drag him over the counter.

"I ain't on no drugs," he gasped. "He tests me."

"And what are you on so you can pass the test?"

The question took a split second longer to process than it should have. Gursey's eyes got even bigger and he groaned. "Now I'm going to get fired again."

Hank didn't give a rat's ass about Gursey at the moment. He walked around the counter, still holding the kid's shirt, and sat him down on the stool next to the cash register.

"Who are you buying it from, and for how much?"

Gursey scratched his patchy goatee. It was expensive, sho'

enough, but since he was able to be working, it was mostly doable. He had some money left from before his last stretch in jail, and he'd paid a hundred for a baggie of the powder, which was two or three doses. You mixed a teaspoon of it with water the night before you knew you'd be tested. And the effect lasted two or three days so, you know, that cut down on the expense-ness somewhat. And after he got paid here at his job, he'd have enough money left over for pot, his favorite cough medicine, and occasionally some oxy.

He nodded matter-of-factly at Hank and fell silent.

"Damn it, Gursey, why don't you just quit the drugs?"

Gursey looked at him like he was an idiot, which he was. He stared at the pockmarked tile floor for a moment and pondered the futility of it. Where, he asked slowly, did Gursey get it?

Gursey got it from his buddy Sven. And Sven had gotten it from Axel, who knew a guy up in Nixa whose cousin—

Hank held up his hand, and Gursey stuttered to a stop.

"Who is the supplier?"

"I don't know, man. Some dude."

He reached for Gursey's polo shirt again, and the kid started waving his arms as if a yellowjacket were about to land. "I swear, man, I don't know. I go to Svenie."

Hank counted to ten. Then he inquired as to Svenie's particulars. And Axel's. And the cousin's. He'd always hated this about drug investigations. They were all such good friends that they'd crash together for the night, and they knew how everybody liked their joints rolled or their heroin ingested—but ask for a last name, and no one knew a damn thing.

It took Gursey five long minutes to remember that Sven worked a bit up Highway 160 at the motor lodge. It took him no time at all to remember he had none of the powder left.

"I don't believe you," Hank growled.

His arms started windmilling again. "No, man, seriously. I'm suppose to meet up with Svenie tonight to get more. I couldn't get a lot last time. He said ever'body's low on it, man."

Which made sense, because if Hank was right, harvesting of the raw materials had only just started up again. That didn't mean he believed Gursey, though. And he wasn't going to until he had a chance to search his residence. And right now, he didn't have the time. He hollered for Pete Wiggins, who came running out the office in the back like the place had caught fire.

"Take him," Hank pointed, "and walk him down to the jail. Just go in the front and tell them I said to put him in his normal cell. I'll do the booking paperwork later. "

Gursey's shoulders slumped. Pete's shoulders did, too. "Can I at least get him out of my polo shirt, first, Sheriff? I reeeeally don't want a mug shot with Easy Come & Go in it."

Fair point. Hank nodded and turned to leave. He paused at the door.

"Hey, what's this stuff called? On the street?"

Gursey, one arm already out of his shirt, looked at him.

"Purple Pass." He hoisted that lopsided grin. "Some of us call it PP for short."

"Of course you do."

Two hours, one stoned Svenie, and three construction workers later, Hank was finally getting somewhere. One user led to another, until he got to the last man, a framer working on a new housing development in Hollister, who had been using Purple Pass for several months. He'd failed testing twice and had been about to be cut loose.

"And, dude, my boss ain't cool. He woulda told everyone from here to Springfield about it, and I couldn't a gotten hired anyplace," the man said, once Hank convinced him that talking discreetly by the water truck was a whole lot better than getting hauled off the jobsite in handcuffs.

So he and a few of the boys had gone to drown their sorrows. At a bar. Out in the woods. Where a man said he could solve the problem. And for fifty bucks, a one-dose baggie of the stuff was his. A discounted sample, as it were.

"It worked, oh, yeah. So I went back for more. He called it Purple Pass, and said he'd be obliged if I let my friends know."

And there you had it. It had spread like wildfire on the Kansas prairie, letting all sorts of stoned and high folks keep ringing up candy bars or hammering nails or driving delivery trucks down crowded roads. All the possibilities made Hank's head hurt.

And now, the guy named Ray said, he heard tell that office workers were catching on. Those assholes could afford to pay more, so that was driving the price even higher, which was awesome. Until . . .

"Until what?" Hank said slowly.

Ray shrugged. "Until the other source started up. They started flooding the market. People could get it for cheaper from them. Totally tanked my business. I talked to my guy, and he said he'd pass it on to the grower. Maybe think about lowering our prices."

"Who was this other source?"

"Some jerk-offs up in the north part of the county. I don't know names, but there were a couple of them goin' around, taking my business. Like a gang or a family or somethin'."

Hank started to feel a little giddy.

"And did you tell that to your distributor?"

He shrugged again. "Yeah."

"And then what'd your distributor do about it?"

"Nothin'. Cuz then it all stopped. There was no more of it, nowhere. From anybody."

"But now there is?" Hank said, remembering Gursey's scheduled rendezvous with Stoned Svenie.

Ray started to respond, but stopped, the rusty wheels in his head obviously trying to turn. "Uh . . . I don't know. What you're talking about. I ain't heard anything.

"So, if that's all . . . I better get back to it." Ray took a tentative step back toward the skeletal condos. The expression on Hank's face stopped him.

"Let's take a look in your truck, shall we?"

Ray was not cut out for the sterner realities—like police interrogation—of a true distribution business. His face fell and his shoulders slumped. He halfheartedly pointed toward an old GMC parked off by a stand of trees. Hank gave an "after you" wave, and they walked over. Ray climbed into the truck bed and unlocked the steel toolbox installed up against the back of the cab.

He pulled out two gallon-sized zip bags and gave them to Hank. One was full of smaller baggies, stuffed and ready for sale. The other held loose powder, maybe a pound's worth. Or should one measure ground-up Ozark herbs in kilos? He supposed so.

There were one hundred doses in the divided bag, Ray told him, again reluctantly. The loose stuff probably would amount to almost that many, but he hadn't had a chance to divvy that up yet. Buyers usually bought two baggies, at a hundred bucks a pop. If they looked like they could pay more, he charged them two hundred. But after the shortage, who knows, Ray said almost tearfully.

"They mighta bought three or four and paid twice as much," he sniffed.

"And how much of that goes back to your guy?" Hank asked.

"Ninety percent," he said. "I keep the rest."

That was a pretty high cut, Hank mused, turning the bags over in his hands. Had Ray ever thought about keeping more back for himself?

"Hell, no." Ray shook his head emphatically. "Those dudes out there—I don't know who the grower is, but he's gotta be out there somewhere. And you don't mess with them people. That's why I ain't telling you where I get it. You can't say I told you anything." He was practically shaking with fear."I didn't give up no names."

Hank longed to take him in, throw him in a cell for a bit, make him sweat. But on what charges? Carting around a bunch of pulverized plant root? It technically wasn't even something he had solid grounds to confiscate, except that it was material evidence in a homicide investigation.

But, as he walked away with his bags of Purple Pass, he knew where to go next. Ray hadn't dropped any names, but he'd dropped enough.

CHAPTER
34

He called and invited Sheila for a drink. That stopped her grumbling at his sudden departure from the manhunt command center. She met him on the side of the road just out of view of the Redbone with a caught-canary smile on her face.

"We can prove it's Kinney?"

"Almost," Hank said. "We're just one degree of separation away. This is where the construction worker got hooked up with the powder."

Her grin flattened into a puzzled line.

"Oh. There are some things I should tell you before we go in there," he said.

He briefed her on his line of inquiry, which put the smile back on her face and her department-issue shotgun in her hands.

"I'm going around the back. We think he's the only one in there, but . . ."

He did love the way her mind worked.

He crunched across the gravel parking lot and closed his eyes for a moment before opening the door and stepping into the dark bar. He stepped to the right until he had solid wall behind him, his hand on his gun.

Behind the bar, the barman turned around. He had a clipboard in his hands and looked to be taking inventory. He set it down and put his palms flat on his granddaddy's stretch of wood.

"You don't listen very well, do you?"

"Nope." Hank slid the bolt on the door closed, and only then walked into the room. "See, I got a problem. . . . Well, I got a bunch of problems, but only one of them pertains to why I'm here right now. Your bar has apparently been used as a distribution center for a substance that helps people break the law."

The bearded face was impassive.

"Who's supplying you with the stuff?"

Nothing.

Dust motes floated through the stale air. Hank took another step forward. The beard finally moved.

"Unless you got an actual crime to talk about, you need to leave my bar."

Another step closer.

"Oh, good. Then we will have a conversation. Because there is a crime. There's a Taylor brother shot dead and dumped in the woods. That's murder, which I think we can agree is against the law."

Willie straightened and took his hands off the bar. "You identified that body you found in the woods?"

Hank nodded.

"And that's who it is?"

He nodded again. The barman smoothed the papers on his clipboard as he thought about that. "Can't say as I'm sorry to hear it. The Taylors are a plague on this county."

The two men stared at each other for a while.

"What would he have been doing around here to make someone want him dead?"

"No idea."

"Really? I'll bet if you thought a bit, you could come up with something. Because, how the law works—if you participated in the action that led to the murder, you're on the hook, too."

The barman ran his hand along the varnished wood. The beard seemed to tremble a little, but he stayed silent. Hank walked forward until he was only a few feet from the bar. "You handed out some powder. Powder that, by itself, isn't even illegal. Do you really want to go down for murder? You tell me who's making the stuff and giving it to you, and you won't. You can keep polishing that hickory slab of yours for as many years as you want. Or you can go to prison."

Willie Boyd glared at him and then pivoted and headed for the back door. He pushed it open, and light flooded into the dim bar. The men's eyes adjusted to find a relaxed, perfectly coiffed deputy and her Remington twelve-gauge blocking the way out. Willie stopped short and let out a long, slow breath.

Say it, say it, say it, Hank thought. Say it, so I can go arrest the bastard.

It took four more minutes of warring with himself for Willie to crack. He turned to face Hank.

"It was Jasper. He came to me, said I probably had some customers who could use what he had. And that it would make us a fair amount of money. And that it wasn't illegal. He said he'd do it himself, except that he didn't come into contact with that many folk, now that he was retired and all."

"And how many people do you distribute to?"

There were about two dozen. Willie wrote down as much of their names as he knew. Ray was the second one on the list.

"And what's your cut?" Hank asked.

"Five percent of what I take in."

And with Ray and his ilk taking another ten, that left Jasper with a whopping eighty-five percent. He'd been taking in millions. Sheila shook her head in amazement.

"And how much have you personally made so far?"

"About eighty grand."

A pretty big payday for a guy who ran a backwoods watering hole.

Willie Boyd didn't know where Jasper got it, or how he made it. And yeah, the supply had dried up after that deputy got shot and all those cops started flooding into the woods. He hadn't connected the two until now. People had not been happy about it. They'd come in, demanding their usual weekly amount, saying their customers were up shit creek if they didn't get it. He'd passed that all on to Jasper. Just yesterday, he'd finally gotten a new supply. It was already gone. His distributors had practically been lined up out the door to get it.

"What about earlier? Were you getting undercut by anybody?"

The barman shrugged. He'd heard a few rumblings from his distributors, about other people starting to show up with their own supply of powder and selling it for cheaper.

"Did you mention this to Jasper?" Hank asked.

"I can't recall."

"Do I need to go over the whole accessory-to-murder thing again?" Hank said.

Sheila raised her shotgun just the slightest fraction of an inch. Willie closed his eyes. His beard seemed to have a lot more gray in it than it did ten minutes before.

"Yes. Yes, I told him. I didn't know who it was," Willie said. "I told him that, too."

"You mention any theories that any of your guys might have had? Any rumors they'd heard about who the other source was?"

Willie swallowed hard. His face had lost all color. Sheila took a step closer.

"Well?"

He shook his head.

"Does that mean you're not going to answer the question?" she said.

Willie looked at the shotgun in her hands and stayed silent. Now Hank moved closer.

"And what did Jasper say?"

A long pause. "He said he'd take care of 'em."

Hank let out a long breath and gave Sheila a nod. They walked out the back door, leaving a pale, woebegone man slumped against the wall. Hank didn't envy the hit his reputation would take among his patrons once they found out he'd said all that to the cops. Sheila, however, had a spring in her step as they walked back to their cars.

"Means, opportunity—and finally, motive." She did a little celebratory shuffle in the gravel.

Hank chuckled and waited while she stowed her shotgun in the cruiser. "We need to get Jasper fast, before he realizes we're on to him, and before he can sell any more of this Purple Pass stuff."

She patted at her hair. "And we need to get every cop we can find to come with us. I'll start working on that."

It was true, but Hank couldn't tell if it was also a criticism. He thought about Ted still in the hospital, and that now-familiar ache settled into his gut again. He looked at Sheila and nodded. He couldn't manage anything else.

Sheila called in favors from as far north as Springfield and rounded up a dozen officers from various jurisdictions that still had a few folks to spare after already loaning personnel for the Boone Taylor manhunt. Everyone was supposed to meet at the main office in Forsyth at 6:00 A.M. the next day in full tactical gear. Excellent. Hank and Sheila grinned at each other as they turned out their office light and headed for the parking lot. And then Hank's cell phone rang.

He answered it and slowed to a halt as he listened. Sheila

stopped as she saw the look on his face. He hung up and turned to her.

"We're not done yet. There are a few questions the Miles siblings need to answer."

They climbed into a cruiser, and Hank sped through the falling darkness down roads he had come to know too well in the past month. They pulled up to the farmhouse. Both the Audi SUV and battered truck were parked out front. Good. He rapped sharply on the door.

Before the footsteps inside reached the door, Sheila turned to him.

"Is this a notification, or an interrogation?"

"I'm not sure yet."

The door swung open. Donna Kolpeck gave a surprised smile and showed them into the living room. She hollered for her brother, who came in from the kitchen wiping barbecue sauce from his hands.

"This is nice of you, Sheriff," she said, "but we kind of figured that our slippery elms weren't too much of a priority right now, with the manhunt going on and all."

"That's not why we're here, ma'am," Hank said.

They sat on opposite ends of the stiff, high-backed sofa and stared at him questioningly. Sheila stood in the corner.

"We need to talk about Charlie."

They looked like he'd just asked them to solve a quadratic equation. *Why on earth would you want us to do that?*

"How did he die?"

Donna squinted in puzzlement. "He had cancer. I think we told you that."

Hank nodded. He just needed a few more details.

It had been cancer of the bones—that's what their parents had told them. He spent a lot of time up at the hospital in Springfield, and that was where he had died. He was seven. He had been cremated. The family had continued to celebrate his birthday every year, because it seemed to make their mother happy.

They both trailed off and stared at him some more. He leaned forward and rested his elbows on his knees.

"Well, you see, there's no death certificate. For Charlie. Not up in Springfield, not in this county, even. And there's no record at any hospital up there of a Charles Miles ever being treated. For anything. Especially cancer."

He watched them both very carefully. Vern stared at him blankly.

"What are you trying to say?" Donna said, her face flushed. "That Charlie isn't dead?"

"No," Hank said. "What I'm saying is that he didn't die the way everyone has always said. And that is of concern to us as law enforcement, because we have a dead child in the woods not far from here."

Donna went from a pink flush to an ashen pallor. Vern took a second longer to make the connection. Then his jaw dropped.

"You think that's Charlie, out in the woods?" He flung his arm up in the direction of Kinney's property. "You think that he, what, fell in that ravine and died?"

Hank saw the grim line of Sheila's lips out of the corner of his eye. They had never publicly released the cause of death, or that a bullet had been found with the skeleton.

"Our parents took him up to the hospital," Donna said. "They went back and forth for weeks—months. He didn't wander off into the woods . . ."

"Did you ever see him again—after your parents said they took him up to the hospital?" Hank asked.

There was a beat of silence, and then Donna drew in a deep, horrified breath. "No," she whispered.

Vern dropped his head into his hands. "They said it would be too painful for us. That they didn't want us to see Charlie like that."

Hank gave them a moment. Then he reached into the inside pocket of his windbreaker.

"We're going to need DNA samples from both of you. To determine if it is indeed Charlie that we found out there."

He held out two buccal swab kits. Vern wiped at the inside of his cheek without getting up from the couch. Donna, crying now, took her kit into the bathroom. Sheila went with her. Once they left the room, Vern leaned across toward Hank.

"What . . . what do you think happened? Why would my folks lie?" He looked like a little boy hoping someone would explain his bad dream.

Hank steeled himself. "Did they ever abuse you?"

"God, no." He sat back as if Hank had slapped him. "No way. They were old school, sure. Strict. But they never raised a hand except a switch when we done wrong. And even that was a tap, more like. Nothing that really hurt."

"What about sexual abuse?"

Now Vern was on his feet, swearing. "How dare you? My parents were God-fearing Christians. They would never . . . you bastard. You—"

Hank suggested, quite firmly, that he sit down again. These were routine questions in any case involving an unexplained child death, he said. They went round and round until Donna and Sheila came back from the bathroom. It was obvious the same conversation had taken place in there. Donna was sobbing. Sheila's face was carefully blank.

Hank asked a few more questions and then rose to his feet. They had no warrant, but it was worth a shot. "I'm going to need to take all of your guns."

Both siblings stiffened.

"Why?" Vern asked in a tone that said he'd already made up his mind to agree.

"You said they were all your daddy's," Hank said. "That means we need to take them in. You'll get them back."

Vern nodded and sagged down into the cushions. Donna slumped a little, too, against the arm of the sofa. They all watched silently as Sheila left the room and started emptying the foyer gun racks. She made six trips out to the squad car, then searched the rest of the house. There were no others. Hank promised to have them back to Vern as soon as possible. He couldn't promise the DNA results as quickly, but said he would let them know the minute he himself found out.

He and Sheila showed themselves out. They got in the cruiser and drove off down the driveway in a cloud of dust. They stopped just out of sight of the farmhouse.

"What'd you get?"

Sheila turned toward him. "A flat-out arsenal. Five shotguns, two Winchester 94 rifles, three Marlin rifles, two revolvers, and one semiautomatic Smith and Wesson. Half of 'em don't look like they work, though. Haven't been cleaned in years. And . . . his .22 isn't there."

"What? The one he always carts through the woods?"

"Yep. Not there. I even searched his truck while you all were waiting inside. Nothing."

"If he didn't know anything about how that skeleton got dead, he'd have no reason to hide that rifle," Hank said.

"Exactly."

Hank thought about that, rubbing the stubble that was starting to adorn his chin. Then a flash of something in the rearview mirror caught his eye. A dark figure was running from the direction of the house toward the woods. It appeared to be carrying a gun.

CHAPTER
35

Hank spun the cruiser around and raced back up the long driveway as Sheila unfastened the Remington 870 from its storage slot. They both leapt out of the car as a second figure, shorter and slimmer, ran across the grassy expanse and followed the first into the woods.

Hank broke into a run after them.

"Wait."

He froze. Sheila was back at the squad car. She dug in the trunk and then ran to him.

"This is the best one of the lot, and it's loaded." She handed him a Browning shotgun from Vern's confiscated collection. "That pinging sound"—she jerked her head back toward the house—"must be his motion-detector alarm."

Damn.

They moved forward quickly and then slowed when they reached the tree line. The day was fading, and they could see a bobbing flashlight up ahead. It was unclear whether it was Vern or Donna. They gained ground rapidly, following the light toward the creek and God knew what else.

They got close enough to see that it was Donna with the flashlight. She heard them and stopped. "I lost him," she whispered angrily.

Hank motioned for Sheila to fan out to the left. He took a few steps to the right, pantomiming that Donna was to stay next to him with her flashlight off. He wanted to send her back to the house, but at this point had no idea whether someone was now behind them. Or whether Vern would mistake her for an intruder and start shooting. Safer for her to stay close.

They all crept forward and had covered about a hundred yards when they heard the rack of a shotgun. Vern's voice carried through the still-warm air just as clearly.

"You're trespassing, you murderin' son of a bitch. Stand up."

Sheila immediately peeled off so she could circle around and approach Vern from the opposite direction. Hank pushed Donna up against the protection of a sizable oak and ordered her to stay put. Then he headed toward what he prayed wasn't the last battle of a border war.

He stopped at a last screen of trees and brush and saw Vern aiming his shotgun at Jasper Kinney, who still knelt on the ground. A bulging cloth sack and small shovel lay next to him. He held an uprooted plant in his hands.

"You stupid, ignorant bastard. You got no idea what you have," Kinney said. "This should still be Kinney land."

Vern took a step forward, so Hank did, too. He emerged from the cover of the trees aiming Vern's own gun at him. Both men froze.

"Put the gun down, Vern."

"Hell, no. He's trespassing."

"And I'm going to arrest him for that," Hank said. "So put down your gun."

Vern hadn't taken his eyes off Kinney. "You going to arrest him for murder, too?"

Kinney's eyes widened a millimeter, but he remained otherwise perfectly still. Hank moved forward, treading carefully.

"Why do you say that, Vern?"

"He killed my brother."

"What?" The surprise on Kinney's face was genuine. It was the most reaction Hank had ever seen from the man.

"How else," Vern said, his voice shaking, "do you explain Charlie being dead on his land? And it must be murder, if you're taking guns as evidence. So he shot my little brother to death."

"We don't even know for sure yet that it is Charlie," said Hank. "So you are not going to take the law into your own hands. Put. Down. The. Gun."

Vern finally looked over at Hank, and slowly lowered the gun. Hank had him lay it down and kneel with his hands on his head. Then he turned his gun on Kinney and told him to do the same. Creosote didn't move.

"Put down the Purple Pass, Jasper, and put your hands on your head."

A smirk tugged at the side of his mouth that normally held a cigarette. "Very good, newbie. You figure that out all by yourself?"

It was going to be such a pleasure to cuff this guy. Hank said it again and took a step forward. Kinney whipped around fast as a striking snake, lunging toward the far trees and, beyond them, the creek. He got six paces.

And then he met the stock of Sheila's own shotgun, right in the gut. He folded with a grunt, and Sheila kicked him the rest of the way over.

Hank watched as she cuffed his hands behind his back, thinking that was even more satisfying than doing it himself. She settled him flat on his stomach in the dirt and walked the short distance to Hank as she shook the feeling back into her right hand.

"That was like ramming into a concrete wall," she muttered. "I can't believe a guy that old is that solid."

Hank handed her his pair of handcuffs and she walked over to Vern Miles.

"What the hell? I didn't do anything. This is my land." The last words came as a shout. He started to get up but stopped at the icy look from Sheila. She cuffed him and patted him on the head.

"We've got a few more questions for you before we're done tonight," she said.

Vern swore under his breath. Kinney shifted in the dirt and tried to sit up until a prod from Sheila's shotgun made him reconsider. Hank looked at his two trussed-up landowners and sighed. They'd have to march them out of the woods—Kinney at gunpoint, the slippery bastard—and call for another squad car. No way he was putting them in the backseat of the cruiser together.

And then there was Donna. Great. He muttered an explanation in Sheila's ear and left her to stand guard as he went looking for the younger Miles sibling. He found her exactly where he'd left her, only now she looked worried enough to be close to getting sick.

"You going to be okay?" Hank asked.

"I just can't take this anymore. These stupid men and their stupid feuds. I just want to go back to my kids." She pushed off from the tree she was leaning against. "I just want to go. Please, Sheriff, can I just go home?"

Hank told her she could go back to the farmhouse, but she couldn't return to St. Louis quite yet. Her shoulders slumped, and she turned back the way they'd come. Hank watched her go, the bounce of her flashlight no longer urgent as it cut through the gathering darkness.

He returned to the men just as Sheila finished snapping photos of the herb-pilfering crime scene. They hauled Creosote to his feet and set out after Donna. Hank had Vern go first. With his hands cuffed in the front, he was able to walk fairly easily. Kinney, hands cuffed behind him, was less steady. Hank kept hold of his elbow as they made their way through the trees. Sheila brought up the rear with her shotgun at the ready and the sack of Purple Pass slung over her shoulder along with Vern's rusty old double-barreled Ithaca.

They walked in silence. Kinney hadn't said a word since getting felled by Sheila, which didn't surprise Hank in the least. Vern's silence, on the other hand, was quite out of character. They made it about four hundred yards before he reverted to form.

"I just don't understand here, Sheriff, why you got me cuffed. I'm on my own land, defending my own property."

Hank told him they would discuss it once they were back at the house. Beside him, Kinney's lip curled in contempt.

"A man's got a right to protect his property. You ought to know that, Sheriff, even if you are from the city." Vern stomped on and talked on, irritating Kinney more with every step. A comment about the sanctity of Miles land finally did it. The older man let out a hiss and took too long a stride forward.

Hank yanked back on Creosote's elbow, hard. He leaned in and whispered, "Maybe you'll get lucky and have a prison cell-mate who talks this much. You can spend the rest of your life listening to him."

Kinney pulled away as much as he could and reverted to his chemically preserved stoicism, but Hank could tell it took effort. Good. Maybe once they got him to the station, he'd be mad enough—and need a cigarette badly enough—that he'd start talking.

Vern had moved on from property rights and was now complaining about the tightness of his handcuffs. Hank would have seriously considered gagging him if he hadn't been annoying Creosote so much. They finally reached the clearing and approached the house, and Kinney seemed almost relieved when Hank shut him in the squad car. The night wasn't cooling off any, so Hank started the car and turned on the air-conditioning. He wasn't going to give Kinney any reason to claim poor treatment at the hands of the sheriff's department. He gave the man a cheery wave through the metal grating separating the front from the back and locked him inside.

Now that the more dangerous of their suspects was contained, Sheila lowered her shotgun and swung the sack off her shoulder. It dropped with a thud at her feet. Hank chuckled.

"You look like a backwoods—"

"If you say Santa Claus, I *will* hit you."

He bit back another laugh and turned toward Vern, who was now complaining about local zoning laws. He needed to put a stop to the torrent of words before Sheila decided to use the stock of her twelve-gauge for the second time that evening.

"C'mon," he said, grabbing Vern's arm. "We're going to go inside and have a conversation. Until I start it, you are going to stay quiet. Got it?"

Vern mumbled something in response and allowed Hank to lead him into the farmhouse. As they approached, the guy's motion-activated floodlights clicked on, shooting brightness throughout the whole area and causing both men to squint painfully as they walked up the porch steps. Sheila followed after stowing Vern's old shotgun with the rest of his armory in the cruiser's trunk. The front room was empty. Hank noticed that dust had started to collect on the smooth wood surfaces. The clock in the corner had wound down. The curtains remained wide open and the windows, turned opaque by the night, reflected the little group.

Vern bellowed for his sister. She came down the stairs at a mockingly slow pace, carrying a suitcase.

"I'm leaving."

"Not quite yet." Hank extended a hand toward the stiff sofa. "Sit."

She blinked back tears and complied, carefully setting her suitcase next to her. Sheila put Vern as far away as possible, in a wingback chair by the fireplace. Then she gave him a look that about melted the brick hearth.

"Where was the gun hidden? The one you took into the woods? You knew we wanted them all." Sheila leaned in.

He gulped. "The shed. Out back the house. With the shovels and such."

Sheila demanded to know why.

"Daddy always kept one out there." Vern shrugged haplessly. "He just did."

Hank stepped forward, and Sheila moved to the side to give him a clear sight line. He bored into Vern.

"What about the rifle? Where's the .22?"

Vern blinked at the change of subject. Then he rounded on Donna.

"Her . . ." he practically growled. "She destroyed it. She stole it, and she had it melted down. Just to spite me. My favorite gun."

CHAPTER

36

Hank stared at the older Miles, then slowly turned to the younger one.

There was only one explanation.

"Why would you do that, Donna?" he asked softly.

She knit her fingers together in her lap and took a deep breath.

"He was too attached to it. It was dangerous. You can't be taking a rifle everywhere you go like that. He was going to hurt somebody. He's so careless with things. It was . . . it was for the best."

She kept her gaze fastened on her brother and did not meet Hank's eyes. Hank took a step toward her. "But why would you choose that one? The one he's had forever? Why didn't you just ask him to put the gun away? Why didn't you ask him to put *all* the guns away?

"You didn't do that, did you?" Hank continued. "You only cared about the one."

"Yeah, why didn't you—" Vern stopped as he saw Hank's face. He looked to his right and saw the same expression on Sheila.

But neither of them were looking at him. Hank stepped over and sat down on the coffee table, inches from Donna's knees.

"What made that rifle so special, Donna?"

She shook her head. "Only that it was the one he carried around all the time."

"Ever since he was, what, twelve?" Hank said.

She nodded.

"And that would have made you nine, and Charlie would have been four, right?"

Another nod. Behind him, Vern was mercifully silent.

"So this gun was around when Charlie died." It was not a question. Neither was this. "You never expected him to be found."

The effort to keep from flinching made Donna's knuckles turn white. She managed it, though.

"That gun was never a threat," Hank said, "because Charlie was supposed to have died from cancer when he was seven. But then his skeleton turned up in the woods. And you couldn't be sure of exactly what else we'd found."

He leaned in.

"Why didn't you destroy that rifle months ago when Vern moved in here and started taking it everywhere? Why destroy it only now? Because the skeleton had just been discovered. And because you knew he had been killed by a .22."

A confused moan came from the wingback chair. Hank did not turn around.

Donna drew in several quick breaths.

"Our parents must have killed Charlie. Then they said he died of cancer. Ask anybody. They told everyone he died in the hospital in Springfield. They lied to us and to everyone—that's obvious."

"That makes them accessories. Not murderers," Hank said.

Donna unwound her fingers and smoothed her slacks. Then she looked Hank in the eye for the first time in the conversation. She was about to play her only card. And it was a good one.

"It would be impossible to find the gun that killed him. That was more than forty years ago."

And there it was. By destroying the rifle, she showed consciousness of guilt. But if they couldn't prove that Vern's rifle was the murder weapon, there was no link between its destruction and the skeleton, and their case would fall apart before it even got to court.

He felt more than saw Sheila move forward.

"Oh, no, honey. Not impossible at all," she said. "Because Vern was dangerous with it. Shot it off at the least provocation. Including right in front of me. So I have a bullet. In evidence. Properly logged and everything. And you do know what ballistics are, don't you, honey?"

My God. She was a genius. He had no idea she'd saved that. He fought back a gleeful grin and refrained from looking over at her, afraid that he would give in to the urge to go for a high-five. He kept his gaze pinned on Donna. The little color left in her face was draining slowly away as she stared up at Sheila. She reached up and tucked a blond tress behind her ear. Her hand was shaking. Hank leaned farther forward. Their knees were practically touching.

"Tell us."

She dropped her hand back into her lap, and her gaze wandered around the room. She had always been the baby, you see. And then Charlie had come along, unexpectedly. At least for her. It hadn't been a big deal at first. But as he got older, it turned into "the boys" and then her. Left out. She didn't get a gun when she turned twelve. She didn't get the camping trips or the hunting lessons like she did before Charlie got older and took her place. And he'd rub it in.

One day, she'd had enough. She decided to scare him. She said they were going for a walk. Vern was at school, so it was just the two of them. She took the rifle—after all, Daddy said to never go near the border without it. She was just going to point it at him, tell him that she was just as much a "Miles boy" as he was and he'd better start respecting her. He'd listened, all serious, but then started laughing. She wasn't a boy, he snickered. She told him that wasn't what she meant.

But he was already off, trotting away from her, laughing and singing. She swung the rifle up and fired. Just up in the air. Just to show him that she was as good as Vern. And he collapsed. He was playing with her, she thought at first, as she walked toward him. Then she saw his head. And she knew that there was no way he was alive. Not with that much blood, and with his limbs all crumpled underneath him like that.

She walked away and sat on a downed tree for a while. Then she tried to move him. But you wouldn't believe how heavy a seven-year-old could be. She only got about ten feet before the weight became too much. So she went home. And got her mother.

Mama had wanted to bury him proper, but Papa said no. They couldn't be visiting no grave, he said. It had to be done and gone. So he had walked out alone, and come back an hour later with dirt and blood smeared on his clothes. He said he'd buried him in a ravine across the creek , then put the rifle back in its slot on the gun rack. And they never spoke of it again.

Charlie got cancer, suddenly, and was up at the hospital in Springfield, they told everyone, including Vern. After a good six weeks, her parents judged that enough time had passed and announced his death. They held a memorial service at the elementary school.

"I sat at that and held your hand." The words came out cracked and brittle. Vern swayed in his chair. "I . . . you . . ." He trailed off and stared at his sister.

She turned her wandering gaze on him and her eyes hardened.

"It's all your fault." The words came out like knives, flying through the air with only one purpose. "You and your damn herbs. If you hadn't been selling them, you wouldn't have needed those illegal aliens. And if they weren't there, then that one wouldn't have gone and fallen into the hole. Everything would have been fine. No one would have ever known anything.

"You did this."

Vern swayed again. Hank was glad he was sitting down.

"I . . . this isn't happening. This . . . he was only seven," Vern stuttered.

"And I said it was an accident," she snapped. "And now you've ruined my life. And my kids' lives. Everybody's."

A reflexive look of apology flashed across his face. It took him a second, but he shook it off.

"Wait, are you kidding? Me? *I* didn't kill anybody. *I* didn't lie for forty years. *I* didn't use—"

He stopped and turned the color of the moon just visible out the side window.

"Oh, God. I carried around that rifle all over. My brother's murder weapon."

He doubled over and retched.

Donna pressed her lips in an angry line and looked away.

Sheila went over and silently laid her hand on Vern's shoulder. When he raised his head, she gently took off the handcuffs. She handed them to Hank, and he fastened them around the wrists of a twelve-year-old killer. At his gesture, she rose and walked toward the door without another glance.

Hank followed closely. He couldn't bear to look back at Vern, who had hunched over again and was rocking back and forth with his arms wrapped around his knees. Sheila was kneeling in front of him and asking who she could call to come and stay with him. There was no way they could leave him here by himself tonight.

He escorted Donna out of the front room and past the empty gun racks in the foyer. Her posture was still stiff with anger. He took the opportunity to rub his eyes, trying to rid himself of the headache that had come on in the past ten minutes.

Sure, there was consciousness of guilt with the destruction of the rifle, but there was no guilty conscience. Forty-plus years with that weighing on your soul, and when you finally confess, it comes out with only anger and blame. No sorrow at ending a young life, no regret at the effect on your surviving brother. He shook his head and reached forward for the doorknob.

And then from the driveway, he heard a thud. And a snarl that did not come from an animal. He shoved Donna back toward the front room and drew his Glock.

CHAPTER
37

Hank flattened against the wall and tried to see out the frosted glass of the little window set in the middle of the Miles front door. It was impossible. He barked Sheila's name and cracked open the door.

The narrow viewpoint didn't help any more than the frosted glass had. All in, he thought, and shoved it all the way open with his foot. He stayed behind the doorjamb and waited a beat. He heard Sheila ordering the Miles siblings onto the floor.

"At least one unknown subject. By the cruiser," she reported from her better vantage point by a front-room window.

She'd just said the word "cruiser" when a shot flew through the open doorway and embedded itself in Mama Miles's daffodil wallpaper. Another followed, shattering a front-room window, and then a third, followed by a more distant explosion of glass. Sheila swore, Donna shrieked, and Vern made no sound.

Hank dropped to the floor and peered around the doorframe. He couldn't see anything in the dark yard. Donna was now sobbing, and Sheila was on the radio calling for backup. He shifted back and away from the door and looked around the entryway.

A pile of shoes sat against the wall. He grabbed a heavy hiking boot and hefted it carefully. He needed to aim perfectly. He stood, spun into the open doorway, and threw. It arched through the muggy night air, sailing far wide and short of the squad car and heading exactly where it was supposed to. It flew directly in front of the motion-activated light on the right side of the house, and the bulb burst into its high-wattage glory. Hank made his move.

He broke into a crouching run, skirting to the left of the car. The shooter was caught in the brightly lit open, frantically kicking away at the driver's door, every inch of his ragged, filthy form clearly visible. He howled and threw his arm up to shield his eyes. Hank made it to the opposite side of the car and used it for cover as he moved into a better position. The man raised his handgun and aimed at the floodlight.

"Put it down, Boone."

Still blinded, the Taylor brother spun around toward Hank's voice and fired. But Hank had moved several feet to the right and the shot flew by harmlessly. The thudding Hank had heard before the first shot continued. Boone, yelling incoherently, reached through the shattered driver's window and opened the door. He must have shot out the glass, Hank thought. And the car's running.

Boone climbed in. And the thudding got louder. The back window on Hank's side of the car started to crack. Worn, steel-toed boots let loose one more kick, and the glass finally gave up. Kinney's legs shot through. He quickly pulled them back and flipped so he could wiggle out headfirst, just as Boone figured out how to put the car in gear. He hit the gas with Kinney half out the window, and the car leapt forward. Straight toward the house.

Sheila dove out of the way. The cruiser slammed into the porch and stopped. For a split second, it was completely silent. And then a thick support post toppled onto the car's roof and the light bar cracked. Loudly.

Boone started shouting again, a torrent of berserk babble

punctuated by every variation of the word "fuck" that Hank had ever heard. He couldn't find reverse gear. Sheila scrambled to her feet, her uniform and the Glock in her hand covered in dirt. Hank holstered his own gun and lunged for Kinney, who hung limply facedown from the back passenger window. He grabbed the old bastard's shirt and bent forward to pull his injured frame all the way out of the car.

Only Kinney wasn't hurt. He reared up and head-butted Hank directly in the face. Hank's vision exploded with pinpoints of light, and he suddenly felt hard-packed dirt underneath his cheek and thick wetness in his mouth. He heard Sheila shouting, but couldn't understand what she was saying. His hearing had gone all staticky.

He had to get to his feet. He was not going to be bested by a seventy-six-year-old herbal drug lord. He made it to his knees just as Sheila tore past him, shouting something and readying her Glock. He gave his head a neck-snapping shake and lurched to his feet.

His vision wasn't so hot, but he realized his hearing was just fine—it was the cruiser engine that wasn't. Boone had managed to get it into reverse, but the front wheels were stuck on the ruins of the front porch. The car was trying to respond, shuddering and whining every time he stomped on the gas.

Hank drew his gun and moved even with the front passenger window. He yelled for Boone to get out of the car, but the screaming berserker couldn't hear him. He was beyond what little reason he'd had in the first place. There appeared to be only one way to get his attention.

Hank aimed and fired. The nine-millimeter bullet cratered into the hard vinyl upholstery of the backseat, the equivalent of a sonic boom in such close quarters. Boone froze and then slowly took his hands off the steering wheel and shakily put them on top of his head. Hank moved so that he again had a clear line of sight toward Boone and was about to order him out of the car when the porch finally stopped resisting.

Another support beam started to topple, taking with it most of the railing and some of the skirting. That was enough. The car leapt backward, free of its lumber restraints. The post lying on the roof slammed down onto the hood and then the ground. Hank jumped out of the way and watched as his cruiser sped rear-first into the yard carrying an astonished Boone, hands still on his head. Apparently he hadn't realized his foot was still on the gas. Hank hadn't, either.

They both recovered their senses at the same time. Hank raised his gun. He had to stop the car before the only thing visible to shoot at was the trunk full of Vern Miles's personal armory. Boone slapped his hands onto the wheel and yanked it sharply to his left, trying to turn the car around.

But the porch had done a number on the front axle and the wheel wells. The car wouldn't turn more than a fraction of what Taylor needed. It lurched off at a modest diagonal across the yard. Boone slammed on the brakes and threw it into drive as Hank sprinted toward him. Boone was now yanking the wheel to the right, toward the road, but the steering wasn't responding. The best the car would do was go straight. Hank changed course with it, struggling to catch up. His vision was still blurry, and now the horizon was tilting in an alarmingly vertical way.

The wounded cruiser managed another forty feet before the left front wheel well crumpled enough to stop the tire. The car skittered to a stop, or at least Hank thought it did. He wasn't trusting his eyes at this point. He blinked rapidly and went around to the left, his Glock raised.

Boone saw him coming and started to scramble over the middle console and toward the passenger door. Hank sighed. He'd really had enough of this. He aimed for the back driver's-side window and pulled the trigger. The light bar on the roof exploded instead.

Fine.

He fumbled for the door handle, finally found it, and ripped open the door. Boone had stopped halfway over the middle section, his ass in the air. Hank grabbed his belt and hauled him out of the car. He shoved the penultimate Taylor onto the dirt, ground a boot into his back, and reached for his handcuffs. Which were currently on Donna Kolpeck.

He shoved his weapon back in his holster and yanked Boone's belt out of his pants. The dirtbag let out a yelp and started wiggling. Hank cinched Boone's wrists as tightly as possible behind his back and then considered his prisoner's legs. He really only had one option if he didn't want the scumbucket walking away, which he most assuredly did not. Keeping his hiking boot on Boone's spine, he stripped off his own belt and bound the scuzzball's ankles.

He stood up and leaned against the car until the dizziness subsided, then grabbed a flashlight from the cruiser and pushed off toward the woods. He had to find Sheila.

CHAPTER
38

He stood just inside the tree line and listened. It was the only hope he had. It was too dark to see anything. He thought he heard a twig snap and was slowly shifting in that direction when something poked him in the back. Something cold and metal.

"Don't move," Sheila hissed in his ear. "You're gonna spook him."

She moved even with him, her service weapon raised and steady in a two-handed grip. He silently unholstered his own Glock and waited for her direction. She motioned him to the left, away from the twig sound. She went right, angling deeper into the trees. Another twig cracked and then a slight, rattling breath came from a set of creosote-soaked lungs. He started to carefully circle around in that direction.

They closed in. Hank could feel him, throwing off loathing and disgust like heat off a kerosene camp stove. His fingers tightened around his gun and he took a slow step. A quick shuffle in the dirt cut through the humid air and Sheila let out a yell. Hank lunged deeper into the trees just as blue and red lights sliced through the trees and a dozen cars skidded to a stop in the Mileses' front yard.

A flash of blue denim darted along the edge of Hank's sight and disappeared. The old bastard had seized the moment and bolted. Hank broke into a run, crashing through the brush after him. The pounding in his head got worse and he prayed his balance wouldn't start playing Tilt-A-Whirl again. He sprinted on, but he wasn't going to be fast enough.

Another flash caught the corner of his eye. It turned into Sheila, who cut across in front of him and launched herself into the air. She timed it perfectly, felling Kinney as he ran out from the cover of a tree. They hit the ground together in an explosion of breath and shower of dirt.

Hank got there seconds later and trained his gun on Kinney. Sheila slowly got to her feet and wiped dirt off her cheek. Back by the house, car doors slammed and people started yelling. Kinney lay inert. Sheila prodded him with the toe of her boot. He stayed facedown in the Ozark loam. She gave him a shove with her foot to roll him over. That generated a groan—his hands were still cuffed behind his back.

"I know you ain't broken," she snapped as she reached down. She grabbed the front of his shirt and hauled him to his feet.

He leaned forward and growled in her face. And Sheila Turley, professional hard-ass and world's greatest peace officer, just smiled. Hank grinned. Then he stepped directly in front of the murdering bastard.

"I recommend that you not disrespect this deputy any further. Who knows what she'll have to do to you next?" He smiled and gently nudged the barrel of his Glock into Kinney's gut, right where Sheila had shotgun-butted him earlier. "She's going to lead you out of here, and you're going to behave. And I'm going to be right behind you with my gun, just in case."

They walked out of the trees and into chaos. Squad cars and un-marked federal vehicles littered the front lawn. All of them had their lights going. Paramedics were trying to figure out how to get past the pulverized porch and into the house. Members of the search team patrolled the perimeter. And Sam was circling Hank's totaled cruiser in disbelief. He was the first to see the trio emerge from the woods.

"Chief," he yelled, darting toward them. "Where have you been? What's going on? We got Sheila's call about the same time the guys in the woods tracked Boone Taylor this way. But . . ."

He broke off as the dirt-spackled Kinney spat at his feet. Sheila yanked him away and packed him into the backseat of a squad car, then made Bill Ramsdell come over and stand guard.

Marshal Number One caught sight of Hank and came bearing down like a cannonball.

"Where the hell is my fugitive?" he yelled. "This . . ." His arms stabbed the air furiously as he surveyed the scene. "This cock-up you've done. If you lost me my fugitive, I'll—"

Hank sighed. Presumably, Boone Taylor was no longer lying next to the battered cruiser. He held up his hand to stop the torrent of words from the marshal. Then he walked—slowly, because his head was still having problems keeping the horizon straight—over to the car. Sam and the marshal trailed after him. Hank reached the spot where he had left the most wanted man in the state of Missouri and started to laugh. He bent down and peered under the car.

"Hey, there, Boone. Comfy?"

A whimper came from between the wheels. The marshal elbowed Hank aside to find the belted Taylor wedged between the torn-up lawn and the torn-up undercarriage. The idiot had rolled underneath and gotten stuck.

The fed pivoted back toward Hank, who gave him a slap on the back as he rose to his feet.

"There you go, Marshal. He's all yours.

"Oh, and when you get him out of there, I'm going to want my belt back."

CHAPTER
39

He had to explain Purple Pass to the marshals—twice—and then again to a sleepy DEA special agent, who was not happy that there might be another controlled substance added to his list of responsibilities.

He had Bill Ramsdell and Doug Gabler catalog the contents of one burlap sack—which turned out to be eighty-two plant roots and eleven ounces of dirt—and place it into evidence. And he'd made sure that Vern's pastor was out at the Miles place to care for the man whose life and home were irrevocably broken.

He and Sheila booked all three—Donna Kolpeck, Jasper Kinney, and Boone Taylor—into the jail and then gave each a chance to talk. Donna had nothing left to say. Kinney refused to even come out of his cell. And Boone, even after being pumped full of fluids and given a protein-packed meal, was still incoherent after a week fending for himself in the wild and then accidentally stumbling right onto the Miles property as he fled the advancing marshals.

So Hank sent him back to his cell and tried another one. Leroy Taylor, his spider tattoo crawling out of the neck of his jail scrubs, merely blinked when told of Jackson's murder. He was just as responsive when asked about the powder.

So now it was down to Lloyd. Sam brought him into the interview room and locked him into the ankle cuff. Then he leaned against the wall as Hank took the remaining chair.

"I want to talk about Purple Pass."

Lloyd's eyes went from bleary to alert instantly. But he insisted he had no idea what Hank was talking about.

"We've got your money. From under the trailer. All of it."

Lloyd swore.

"You need to tell me how you came to know about the stuff and where you got it from."

"Why?" Lloyd spat. "I don't need to tell you nothin'."

Sam straightened and took a step forward so he loomed over the much slighter Taylor. Lloyd shrank away from the look on his face.

"You don't have to," Hank continued. "But I do think you need to. See, your brother Jackson is the one who was murdered out in the woods. We've positively identified him. Somebody shotgunned him at close range."

Lloyd snapped back like he'd been hit. Sam pressed closer.

"It seems to us like the kind of money you all had would be enough to kill somebody over," Hank continued. "What do you think?"

Lloyd moaned and slumped forward over the table.

"And finding Jackson's killer would be a lot easier if we knew about your operation."

He quite purposefully didn't bring up Jasper Kinney. He knew the video of this interview would be picked apart by defense attorneys, and he didn't want to be accused of planting accusations in Lloyd's limited brain.

Several minutes passed as Lloyd, again remarkably similar to a possum, stared at the table. Finally, Sam cleared his throat—loudly. Lloyd flinched and mopped his runny nose on his shirt.

"It had to be that old bastard. The mean one that owns all that property." More sniffling.

"Why do you think it was him?"

"Because he's the one we was stealin' from."

A smile spread slowly across Sam's face. And the pain in Hank's head suddenly eased. He kept his expression neutral and motioned for the possum to continue.

All four brothers had been stealing tree bark and other plant junk for more than a year. The brothers would follow the growers home after they dropped off their deliveries to Lloyd. It was so easy. Nobody paid any attention that far out in the middle of nowhere. And then one day, Jackson and Boone had seen that old guy in the woods. Pulling up these little purple flowers by the roots. And nobody'd bother doin' that if it weren't worth some money, right?

So they'd started stealing that plant, too. Just kept it in sacks, until Jackson figured out that it was like that ginseng or goldenseal stuff, where the valuable part was the root all ground up into powder. And a powder was gettin' sold all over the place, making it so you could pass a drug test even when you were using. People were payin' hundreds for it.

And there you had it. Sheila came in with a six-pack photo lineup and Lloyd picked Kinney out immediately. Hank almost thanked him. Instead, he let Sam ask about Ned Bunning, who Lloyd said owed money for a delivery of Purple Pass but hadn't been home when Lloyd showed up to collect. Sam's satisfied smile was a great thing to see. Hank thanked him again for his hard work, then sent both his deputies home. He spent a half hour making sure no one was going to show up soon for the 6:00 A.M. raid that was no longer necessary, and then placed two very difficult phone calls to Patty Alton and Calvin Holm. He ended his conversation with Calvin blinking away tears and trudged out to his car just as dawn broke over the eastern hills.

He pulled into the driveway just as Dunc and Guapo came back from their walk. They were both breathing heavily.

"Trying to wear him out," Dunc panted. "I figure we got a better shot at him behaving himself if he's all tired and—wait, you're just getting home?"

Hank nodded, got out of the car, and limped toward the house, mumbling something about a nap.

"Don't sleep too long," Dunc called after him. "We got the animal-shelter thing at noon."

The only response was the slam of the front door.

He didn't feel any better five hours later when Maggie gently shook him awake. He groaned and rolled over.

"You have to get up, babe. We've got to go to the shelter fund-raiser." More groaning. She lay down next to him. He threw an arm over her and closed his eyes.

"Come on." She kissed him and rolled out from under his arm. "It's the last one. Your last campaign event. Then it'll all be over, one way or the other."

He sighed and sat up. She ran her fingers through his hair and gave him a kiss. "I love you."

He kissed her back. "I love you, too." He heaved himself out of bed and headed for the shower. "Oh. We got 'em. All of them. The two murderers and Ted's shooter."

He shut the door to the bathroom, leaving his wife staring after him, her mouth hanging open.

He wasn't sure what he was more worried about—small talk with strangers, his untrainable dog, the two-year-old who'd be missing his regular nap time, or the business mogul willing to spend any amount to defeat him. "You should probably smile." Dunc eyed him as they stood in the parking lot. "You look like you're going to throw up or something. And that swollen lip isn't helping."

Hank glared at him. "I told you—"

"Yeah, that you got beat up by a seventy-six-year-old. I remember." He shot Hank a rascally smirk and turned to get Guapo out of the minivan.

Hank tried a smile, but it felt awkward and probably looked even worse. Then Maggie grabbed his hand and gave him a look that melted his worries and settled his stomach all at the same time. He might be able to do this. He certainly didn't have a choice, he thought as he watched Darcy double-time it across the parking lot. She gave them all a once-over, nodded her approval, and herded them into the facility.

Guapo entered like a conquering hero. His swayback was remarkably straight, his good ear perked up, and his stubby legs started high-stepping on the hard linoleum. He wasn't even pulling on the leash. They all paused for a picture by the *Daily What's-It* photographer, and Hank gave thanks it happened when they were all fresh and pretty, instead of melting down at the end of the day. Darcy gave him a wink as she thanked the photographer. She'd obviously thought the same thing. The woman really was a marvel.

They mingled their way through the crowded hall, which had Henry Gallagher's name plastered on every available surface. Kids cuddled kittens and puppies, and there was already a line at the adoption paperwork table.

Dunc grabbed him and pulled him over to a tall, trim man in a Branson Valley High School polo shirt. A local celebrity.

"Tom, meet my son-in-law. He'd appreciate your vote on Tuesday. Hank, this is Tom Barstow, the football coach."

They chatted briefly about the upcoming season, and then Barstow turned to Dunc.

"We all sure do miss Marian. The school hasn't been the same. She was the best principal we'd ever had."

Duncan nodded briskly, which Hank knew meant that he couldn't speak without tearing up. Hank quickly thanked the coach and steered Dunc into a quiet corner. He knew better than to say anything, so he gave the old man a pat on the shoulder and left him alone with Guapo.

He made his way outside onto the grassy dog play area, which today had picnic tables, umbrellas, even a lemonade stand. And a group of people bunched together around a computer tablet. As one, they all turned to look at him and then went back to the iPad. Several snickered.

Great.

A mane of gray curls detached itself from the back of the group and casually meandered toward him. Lovinia turned before she reached him and went back into the hall. Hank let a family with two new calico kittens pass in front of him and then followed her.

"They've got pictures," she said as soon as he caught up to her. "Of a smashed-up squad car. What happened?"

And there was the department leak again. Hank sighed. "What are they saying?"

Lovinia rolled her eyes. "That you destroyed a police car during a wild-goose chase last night. That you don't know what you're doing."

That was it? He laughed. "That's no big deal. It won't hold. I made the arrests. Two murderers in custody, plus the Taylor brother who shot Ted Pimental."

Lovinia gawked at him. She hadn't heard anything about it. Hank shrugged. No one had, he said. He'd decided taking a nap was a higher priority than writing a press release. Lovinia rolled her eyes again, this time at him.

"You've got a lot to learn about this politician thing," she said, and walked off, shaking her head.

He turned around to find Darcy bearing down on him with

Guapo in tow. She handed him the leash and a scolding. The dog wasn't doing him any good if people didn't see him with it. Now get back to socializing.

Hank looked down at the mutt, who had lost his regal bearing and was back to his usual slovenly, scent-driven self. He let Guapo lead him back outside as the dog tracked a smell onto the grass and started to roll in it. Hank used the moment to take another look at the group around the iPad, which had grown even larger. The only thing garnering as much attention was—damn it—Gerald Tucker. He'd commandeered the cutest puppies and was holding court in the shade of a giant hickory in the middle of the yard.

The jerk didn't even own a dog, and Hank would bet money he had no intention of adopting one today. He was wondering how he could point that out to people when a cell phone was shoved in his face.

"You . . . you destroyed county property. You ruined a police car. Do you have any idea how expensive those things are?"

Edrick Fizzel snatched the phone away and scrolled through more pictures of the poor cruiser.

"I'm sure you'll let me know how much it costs," Hank said with a smile he didn't feel.

Fizzel jerked his attention from the phone to Hank, his prickly hair quivering. His finger waved way too close to Hank's nose.

"You are going down, Worth. You destroy property, and you can't solve your cases. Hell, you couldn't solve a jaywalking, let alone a murder."

Maybe he should have written that press release. He started to speak, but Fizzel wasn't done. He moved even closer.

"And this doesn't relate to our previous . . . discussion. That wasn't about your election. There's no deal for that. I'm coming after you."

Fizzel was exactly right. They had no deal for that. He batted away the commissioner's hand.

"Go for it, Edrick." The man would look like an idiot when the arrests did become public. Which was a happy by-product of his delay in releasing the information, Hank thought as he walked away.

He spent the next half hour parading Guapo around the facility, drawing a mixture of admiring and pitying looks. But no matter what they thought, everyone wanted to ask about him. So Hank had more conversations than he would have thought possible. Darcy, hovering in the background, was ecstatic. And Guapo, through some miraculous intervention, kept control of his behavior and his bladder.

He moved from the lawn to the hall and back, where he saw Gallagher working the lemonade stand, complete with crisp straw hat and noblesse oblige smile. He averted his eyes before he got sick at the sight, and his gaze fell on Tucker, who was talking to the kid from the newspaper.

Jadhur asked a question, and Tucker turned purple. Jadhur, standing in front of him with his notepad at the ready, began to back away. Tucker's mouth opened and closed but Hank was pretty sure he hadn't said anything. Then his opponent spun around and disappeared into the administration offices at the back of the facility. Well.

Jadhur scribbled madly in his notebook and then spotted Hank near the hall. He hurdled several adoptable puppies on his dash across the lawn.

"Can I help you with something, Jadhur?"

"Oh, yeah. You sure can, Sheriff. I was just talking to Mr. Tucker, and it occurs to me that you might not know, either." His pen and pad assumed the ready position. "Are you aware that former sheriff Darrell Gibbons has endorsed you?"

Hank stared at him. And then burst out laughing. He laughed

so long, Guapo started pawing at him. He finally was able to gasp an apology and catch his breath.

"No . . ." he told the clearly nonplussed Jadhur, "I was not aware of that. When did you hear about it?"

Jadhur had gotten an emailed press release that morning, about nine. He'd called to confirm and spoken to Gibbons himself. "He said that after careful consideration, he'd decided that keeping you at the helm would be best for Branson County, and he was happy to endorse you for election."

"Do you know if he sent that press release to anyone else? And if so, when?"

Jadhur shrugged. "If he did, it was this morning. I know nobody knew anything about it before then."

Hank thanked him and excused himself to take Guapo off to the sandy side yard to pee. That was where Dunc found him. In a low voice, Hank told him the "good" news.

"Well, in one way, that's great. It means you're going to win the election. I told you Gibbons has never backed a loser."

"Yeah, but why is he finally confident that I'll win? Because he knows. He knows I've made arrests in both murder cases. He knows Taylor is in custody. That's got to be it."

Dunc pondered that. "And you haven't made any of that public yet, have you?"

Hank shook his head.

"You've known you had a mole, though."

Hank shook his head again and started thinking out loud.

"It's not the same one. The person who leaked that"—he pointed toward the people passing around the iPad photos of the wrecked car—"wants to embarrass me and help Tucker. The one who leaked the arrests isn't out to hurt me . . . necessarily. But they are out to protect Darrell."

Dunc let out a low whistle. "That could be bad—in the long run. That man is the serpent in the apple tree."

Hank nodded, gave him Guapo's leash, and started to walk back to Jadhur, who was waiting with more questions, probably about a certain pulverized squad car. He'd been oddly relieved to see the photos. It meant that he knew who was in Tucker's camp and had been feeding him information. Only one person had been present at both the discovery of Charlie Miles's skeleton and the processing of the wrecked car.

He really liked Bill Ramsdell. But now he couldn't trust him. He'd have to think about the best duty to assign him. Or maybe he'd just leave him be and not let on that he'd figured it out.

He reached Jadhur, who was trying to access something on his phone.

"Don't bother," Hank said. "I've seen the photos. And yes, the car was wrecked during a pursuit last night. But that pursuit resulted in the arrest of Boone Taylor, the fugitive wanted for the shooting of Deputy Pimental."

Jadhur almost dropped his phone. He stuttered for a second and then started scribbling madly. Where? How? Who was involved?

As Hank answered his questions, people started to drift over. By the time he'd explained Boone's capture, a decent crowd had gathered around them. Someone in the back raised a hand. Surprised, Hank pointed.

"What about the other Taylor brother? Weren't there two of them on the loose?"

Excellent.

"Actually, no. We"—he paused, hearing Darcy's voice in his head telling him to take personal credit—"me . . . my department and I have determined that the other Taylor brother, Jackson, is the man found deceased in the woods two weeks ago. And we made an arrest in that case last night as well."

A murmur went through the crowd. More and more people

started to gather. Jadhur was having to fight for his spot at the front. People were jostling him, pressing forward, thrilled at the unexpected opportunity to get close to a police investigation. Gallagher was left with a dozen cups of lemonade and no line. Hank fought back a smile.

Emboldened by that first audience query, other people started calling out questions. Jadhur sighed in resignation and moved off to the side. Hank started to speak and then stopped. How was he going to explain a drug war involving a never-before-known herb that technically wasn't even illegal, a long-running family feud, and a cancer death that was really fratricide?

"I am not at liberty to say too much today," he began. "But I can tell you that the murder of Jackson Taylor was prompted by a . . . business dispute. We have arrested the owner of the land where Taylor's body was found. He will be charged with murder on Monday."

He could tell by their shocked gasps which people were from that part of the county and knew who he meant. The formidable, fearsome Kinney had finally been brought low. He didn't think he'd ever felt such a surge of professional satisfaction. He continued.

"I'm also pleased to announce that we have arrested the person responsible for the death of the child whose skeleton was also found in those woods." He stopped, not for effect, but because he suddenly realized how many kids were listening. How many families could hear him. People who were there to choose a pet, not hear about the murder of a seven-year-old at the hands of his sister. "More information about that case will be available next week. I'll be here for a while if anyone wants to talk about the sheriff's department. Right now, why doesn't everyone go and get some lemonade?"

Gallagher had just abandoned his drink stand and stomped off toward the administration building. He jerked around at a little boy's shout and gawked at the stampede of kids headed his way. He stared over their heads at Hank, who saw the loathing on Gallagher's face and gave up the fight with his smile. He added a casual wave and turned toward the folks waiting to shake his hand.

CHAPTER
40

As the returns came in, Hank finally allowed himself a beer. He had just won an election.

The Springfield news station had just called it for "appointed, and now elected, Sheriff Hank Worth." He'd beaten Gerald Tucker fifty-two to forty-eight percent, give or take.

Supporters at the Branson Country Eatery were high-fiving one another and cheering. There weren't a whole lot of people but it was a respectable turnout that included many of the campaign's volunteers. Lovinia gave him a hearty handshake, and said she had brand-new batteries for her police scanner and was all ready for his first full term in office. Dan Larkson asked about Lloyd Taylor's potential prison term and walked away smiling at the high number Hank gave him. Darcy, both giddy and tipsy, gave him a big hug and then proceeded to take a marker and start drawing a cowboy hat on the picture of him adorning a campaign poster.

He decided he did not need to see how that came out and headed through the scatter of tables. His elderly neighbor stopped him.

"Hello, Mrs. Crawford," he said. "How are—"

"Is Duncan here? I thought that he would be . . ." She turned in a circle, eyeing every corner of the restaurant. "I just put 'Ring of Fire' on the jukebox."

Hank explained that Dunc had stayed home with the kids. She scowled. "That's the second person who shoulda been somewhere today and wasn't."

Hank, halfway through his beer, decided to humor her. "How's that, ma'am?"

She put her hands on her sizable hips. "Well, I stopped by church this morning. To see Father Tony. He always appreciates my advice on the weekly church bulletin, you see. And he wasn't there. Teresa—she's the church secretary—told me that he had borrowed some parishioner's van and was taking a road trip to Chicago. Can you imagine? Who does that?"

She stomped off toward the bar, shaking her head in bewilderment. Hank stared down into his beer and fought back a smile. He wondered if the priest had packed sandwiches for the ride.

He made his way to a quiet corner and scanned the room. Campaign volunteers, a few of Maggie's colleagues from the hospital, a couple of Kiwanis friends of Duncan's. And no deputies. Not a single one. He wasn't surprised, he supposed. In a way, it was good to know. The county might have voted him the new boss, but that didn't mean the department necessarily agreed. The days of watching his back weren't over.

At least he had Sheila and Sam. Ah, Sammy. Now there was one person he was glad didn't come. He hadn't talked to the kid since they'd finished processing the crime scene at the Miles property early Saturday. He was still a mess—a volcanic mix of anguish, guilt, and rage that Hank didn't know how to fix. So he'd ordered Sam to take a week off. That had been met with heated protests that stopped only when Hank threatened to call his mother. He hoped the time would allow the Pup to start healing.

It was going to be a slow process, though, just like for Ted—who was now in stable condition but wouldn't be fully healed for God knew how long.

He gave himself a mental shake and moved to rejoin the party. He needed to act like the happy winner. Smile, nod, shake hands. Repeat.

He was doing pretty well and was thinking about getting another beer when there was a stir by the entrance. He turned away from the window to see Darrell Gibbons glad-handing his way into the restaurant. He did not move forward to greet him.

Darrell took a good ten minutes to mosey over to Hank. He was wearing his usual bolo tie and had dressed it up with a Western-cut sport coat. Hank did not appreciate the gesture. Or the slap on the back. Gibbons did it twice, turned to point and nod at someone by the bar, and then finally looked Hank full in the face.

"Congratulations, Worth. You have prevailed. I'm glad my endorsement helped you out."

He stood there with a patient smile. Hank desperately wanted to give him what he deserved, and it wasn't a thank-you. He pasted Gibbons's tolerant look on his own face.

"And I'm fully confident, Darrell, that you will support me, in public and behind the scenes, as I serve my term."

Gibbons's face didn't move a muscle, but a glint flashed in his eyes, as if he'd just taken up a challenge. Well then, game on, you bolo-tied bastard.

Hank stepped away and turned toward a group of people in the middle of the dining room. He accepted a few more congratulations and then slipped out the back door into the quiet rear parking lot and called Sheila.

"Yes?"

He heard a snippet of the same Springfield news show in the background before it went silent. She said yes again.

He cleared his throat.

"I just wanted to tell you that now that I have the authority, I want to make you my permanent chief deputy. If you'll take the job."

Silence. Then what he thought might have been a sniffle. Or not.

"All right," she said. "I accept. I will see you at work in the morning."

He agreed and said good night. And he was positive— almost—that the sound he heard as he hung up was a sigh of relief.

He put the phone in his pocket and turned back toward the restaurant. Maggie stood there against the wall. She smiled.

"I wondered where you'd gone. Little peace and quiet?"

He nodded and pulled her into his arms.

"Thank you, babe. For everything." He kissed her.

She pulled back and looked at him with that twinkle that made his knees weak.

"I'm proud of you, honey. I know this wasn't easy for you, but you did it." She ran her hand through his hair. "You need another haircut."

"No way," he said, nuzzling her neck. "I won. I don't have to get another haircut for four more years."

She burst out laughing, kissed him hard, and led him back inside, where his constituents awaited.

ACKNOWLEDGMENTS

There are many people who helped bring this book to life. My agent, Jim McCarthy, and my editor, Elizabeth Lacks, continue to provide wonderful advice and feedback, and Shailyn Tavella is a true help with publicity. David Rotstein's second Hank Worth cover design is as beautiful as his first. Once again, I was lucky to have the keen critiques of Kristi Belcamino, Bridget Gray, and Paige Kneeland, as well as the continued support and counsel of Claudia and Mike Brown. I relied on the expertise of Zachary Heyde, Tommy Gray, Brian Hall, and Kathleen Ryan, whose generously shared knowledge of several different subjects helped me enormously.

I also want to thank my family and friends for their enthusiastic support and willingness to drive long distances to get to book signings. I appreciate it more than you know.

To my husband and children, you bring joy to everything I do. Thank you.